Cowgirl Strong

Jenny Hammerle

***

For my grandmothers,

Frances Decoteau and Cynthia Chesser,

who helped mold me into the woman I am today.

***

So faith, hope, love remain,

these three;

but the greatest of these is love.

1 Corinthians, 13:13

Chapter One

The bells on the front door of the shop rang as another customer entered the Western store. It had been four weeks since Rachael and Travis had bumped into Amber and her mother- Rachael had thought of nothing else since.

Scenes from a slumber party last year replayed through her mind over and over again. Rachael remembered all of her friends, their opinions about relationships, and the conversation that followed. For the most part, the conversation had been fun, lighthearted, and casual. That was until one shocking revelation made by Amber. Rachael still remembers feeling unsure about Amber's announcement. She advised her to speak to her parents.

Today, seated behind the register, labeling the newest earrings to arrive at the store, Rachael remembered all the things she could have said. Should have said. And now... wished she'd said. Travis could try to convince her it wasn't her fault.

But wasn't some of the responsibility mine? My responsibility to warn her? My responsibility to protect her?

"Excuse me, miss. Could you help me please?" An elderly woman with a sweet face stood on the other side of the counter from Rachael. "I'm shopping for a gift for my granddaughter. She's around your age- and I think you might be better at selecting something she might like."

Rachael snapped herself out of her own thoughts, and stepped from around the counter to assist her. "I'd love to help you. Did you have anything particular in mind?"

"Nothing specific, but I was considering a nice top with some matching earrings or a bracelet. She's very feminine in her tastes."

"Sounds like something I could help you with." Rachael walked over to the ladies section of the small store, and eyed the various t-shirts and dress shirts. If the girl was around her age, a fitted t-shirt would be something she would wear a lot more often than a Western, dress shirt. Rachael browsed the rack and found one in a pale purple with a large cross on the front and angel's wings. The large script read 'Forever Cowgirl.'

Rachael loved this t-shirt when it first came in-stock two weeks earlier. If she'd had the money, she would've already bought it for herself, but since she hadn't she would need to settle for the enjoyment of picking it out for others. Maybe this lady's granddaughter would like the shirt as much as Rachael did.

"What's your granddaughter's name?"

"Misty."

Rachael's head whirled around. She reconsidered the cross and angel's wings adorning the front of the shirt.

Could it be the same person! I hope not! If so, then this is definitely not the right shirt for her.

"Misty- you say? I know a Misty that dances with me at school." Rachael tried sounding nonchalant, hoping her face wouldn't betray the deep feelings of animosity she had for this particular Misty.

"Oh, my word! It must be my granddaughter. She goes to school at East Manatee High School." The woman's face conveyed her love for this child.

Could we be talking about the same girl?

Rachael pondered that thought for a moment.

Everyone has a grandmother who loves them dearly- regardless of their shortcomings, flaws, and personality defects. Didn't they?

"Wow. What are the chances?" Rachael muttered but added a sweet, unconvincing smile.

"I love the shirt, dear. I think it's perfect and seeing as you already know her, I'm sure you'd agree!"

"Most definitely."

Most definitely not! Angel's wings...a cross!

Is it a sin to lie to a dear, old Granny? What else can I say?

No, on second thought, I think it's a horrible choice for her. She is definitely no angel. I can't imagine her in my shirt!

Rachael scanned the store for something more appropriate for Misty. Something that would suit her perfectly. A few racks over she spied it. It was a pink t-shirt that said in bold letters across the front 'The Cowgirl Way.'

Hmm. If only that 'W' were an 'L'- then it would be perfect.

Be nice Rachael...her conscience warned.

Rachael decided selecting an alternate shirt was out of the question and scanned the sizes for the fitted t-shirt...*her shirt*. She considered her own recent, newfound curviness. She knew it would need to be a medium, at least. She'd tried it on herself, it was snug around her small rib cage but allowed for her bust line up top. Rachael hated that she and Misty were similarly built now.

She pulled a medium hanger from the rack and held it in her hand examining it more closely.

"This should fit her nicely." She announced, yet found the words were not easy to say, nearly choking her where they stuck in her throat.

Rachael continued the torturous shopping experience of selecting matching earrings for Misty. She thought about asking what the special occasion was, but decided it was better not to ask. Her mother had always taught her if you really didn't care, or were simply asking for the wrong reasons- you shouldn't ask at all.

Rachael walked over to the display case and looked in it.

"There's a wide assortment of earrings here. Do you see anything you like, or think she might like?"

"Oh, honey, I'm really out of my element here. Is there anything that jumps out at you?"

Rachael knew what the answer to this question should be. There was a pair of beautiful silver feathers that hung from simple wires. The silver feathers were long and tapered. They would hang to her jawline and be easily visible, even when her hair was down.

Rachael hated the thought of Misty wearing her earrings. The ones Rachael had picked out just for herself.

Rachael scanned the case for other options. That's when she saw them.

Those are the ones...

To the far right of the case there was a hideous pair of large dangling cowgirl hats. The earrings themselves could double as small soup bowls. They were gaudy, ostentatious, and hideous-when Rachael thought of these earrings, she thought of Misty, but knew in her heart she just couldn't do it.

She sighed. "The long ones that are shaped like feathers are my favorites, but there are several other equally beautiful options in the case." Rachael suggested hopefully.

"No, you're right. They're the first ones I noticed when we walked over here. I'll take them and the matching necklace and bracelet, too."

Rachael's heart hit the floor. She'd loved the earrings, but it was the matching feather pendant necklace and bracelet which had been her favorites. The set was one which could be worn with jeans and a simple top- or a nice dress for that matter. The necklace was long, maybe twenty-six inches in length, made of a simple braided silver rope. The feather pendant exactly matched the feathers on the earrings. Now they would be Misty's.

Rachael unlocked the case and pulled the set out. She carefully walked over to the counter and set them on top.

"If you'll excuse me, I need to go to the back and get some gift boxes for you."

Rachael walked to the back and selected three small jewelry boxes for the earrings, necklace, and bracelet. She located a shirt box, as well. After grabbing some tissue she returned to the register.

"Do you gift wrap?" Misty's grandmother smiled sweetly.

"Of course we do, but I only have one paper to choose from." Rachael motioned to the roll of wrapping paper on the long counter behind her, where a large spool of paper hung, decorated with cowboy boots of every type.

"It's perfect."

Rachael finished up the purchase in near silence. After it was totaled and paid for, she began the painful process of wrapping Misty's gifts with care. When she finished, she eyed the array of bows she had in a large box on the back counter. There were bows in every color and size. She opted for a beautiful teal bow and matching ribbon that perfectly picked up the teal tones in the wrapping paper. She placed the wrapped boxes in bags and turned to hand it to Misty's grandmother, forcing a grin.

"Will there be anything else?"

"No. Thank you for your help today! I couldn't have done it without you- and to think you know my lovely granddaughter! I can't wait to tell her how much you helped me."

"Anytime." Rachael heard herself offering, but hoped and prayed this wouldn't be a regular occurrence. "I hope she likes them."

"She will, dear."

Rachael walked over and reopened the jewelry case, in need of something to do with her hands. The belt buckles were dusty and would require some polishing. Rachael grabbed a polishing cloth made for silver jewelry and feverishly set to work cleaning each one.

Why does Misty bother me so much?

Rachael let the thought roll around in her head a little. The bells on the door tolled again. It was busy for a Tuesday afternoon in July. Rachael lifted her head and greeted the customer who had just walked into the store, not making eye contact.

"Good afternoon. Welcome to Linda's Ranch Wear." Rachael turned and nearly dropped her polishing cloth when she saw Amber standing at the door.

"Hi, Rachael." Amber hesitated. "I hope it's okay I stopped by."

"It's more than okay. It's fantastic!" Rachael went over and gave Amber a huge hug. A look of relief washed over Amber's face.

"I wanted to stop in and say hi. I couldn't leave things the way they were the other day. I'm sorry I ran from you and Travis. I saw you guys- but I wasn't ready to face anybody just yet." Amber fiddled with the strap on her purse. "I'm sorry for lying to you at the beach that day as well. My mother had asked me not to speak about it to anyone. I wanted to tell you the truth then, but I couldn't."

"There's no need to explain anything, Amber. A true friend doesn't need to ask questions. I'm here for you. That's that."

"I'm so glad to hear it. At least I've got one friend left." A single tear fell down Amber's cheek.

"I'm sure you have more friends than you realize."

"I'm not so sure anymore. I ran into Alex and her mother in the grocery store. Alex was kind to me, but I could tell her mother wasn't at all happy about my current condition- she barely allowed us to talk. That's the reason my mother pulled me out of EMHS and sent me to Christian school. She explained the situation and I was able to complete the semester at home. I can return in the fall after the baby comes. I'm due next month."

Rachael stood taking it all in. She set the polishing cloth down on the counter. Amber was going to be a mom and in a very short amount of time. She would be having a baby!

What about Clay? Does he know? Rachael wanted to ask, but couldn't bring herself to pry.

"What are you having?"

"A little boy." Amber announced.

"You must be very excited." Rachael smiled.

Something in Amber's body language changed, and Rachael could see there was something else she wanted to share.

"No, Rachael. I'm not. I'm giving the baby up for adoption."

Rachael wasn't sure how to respond. She stepped toward Amber, nearly tripping over her own boots, and said the first thing that came to mind.

"I'm sure this hasn't been an easy decision."

"No, it hasn't. My parents feel it's for the best. I'm too young to be a mom- to really be a mom."

Rachael thought of Shannah and her mother. Her mother had given birth to her at fifteen. The stresses of being a young mother had been too much for her. She'd left Shannah with her father, only to resurface from time to time.

Rachael felt like a fish out of water in this conversation. Amber seemed to have a way of doing that to her. She didn't have the life experience necessary to offer the help Amber needed. Maybe Amber hadn't come in search of help- maybe all that was needed of Rachael was to listen.

"What about you? How do you feel about the adoption?"

"I'm okay with it now. As okay as I am going to be with it. Getting pregnant and having a baby at seventeen wasn't what I had planned."

"No, I realize that. I wanted to apologize for not giving you better advice last year when you told me you were considering a more intimate relationship with Clay. I should have been sterner."

Amber smiled and laughed, though her amusement was fleeting.

"I don't know that it would've helped. I had made my mind up. I chose to do what I did and now I can't undo it. Not that I would. A baby is a blessing and mine will make someone very happy."

"You have a great outlook on things. Have the adoptive parents already been chosen?"

"Yes. We found them through our church."

"That's great news." Rachael searched her mind for something more to say, but was at a loss for words.

"I better get going. Don't be a stranger," she grinned. "Maybe we could do lunch next week."

"I'd love to."

Rachael resumed her dusting and polishing duties. Amber had looked so happy and sad at the same time. She was making a family's dream come true, but would she be ending her own dream in the process?

Rachael heard of many young mothers who gave their children up for adoption and knew it was a viable option. A good option. But was it the right option for Amber? It was times like these Rachael wished her father were out of prison and here, face-to-face, with her. This conversation was one of the most difficult ones Rachael had ever encountered. Part of her wanted to cry, part of her wanted to rejoice in Amber's mature decision- which couldn't have been an easy one, and finally ... a part of her was angry.

Angry this had happened to Amber. Angry that any young girl should have to face such a decision. Where was Clay's responsibility in all of this? Rachael was angry the burden was only Amber's to carry. Rachael was angry Alex's mother had made Amber feel unwelcome. Mostly- Rachael was angry her friend's life would be forever changed over one decision. A decision she wouldn't be able to take back or undo. One word, and one word alone, returned to her mind over and over again.

Unfair...

Why is life so unfair?

Chapter Two

Shannah was gone for the summer- as usual. She popped into Rachael's mind early the next morning while Rachael was feeding Taffy and ole' lonesome George.

Shannah unknowingly had become Rachael's sounding board and voice of reason over the past two years. Rachael credited Shannah with helping her to see the error of her ways where Travis had been concerned, and subsequently guiding her to fix their broken relationship. Now, faced with Amber's current situation, Rachael wished to speak with either Shannah or her father- but neither were around.

"What are you doing?" Rachael heard the familiar voice from behind her.

Rachael glanced at the pitchfork and rake leaning against the wall beside her. She was lying carelessly on a bale of hay topped with a saddle pad, her legs and feet extending to the concrete floor of the barn. Rachael hadn't even realized she lay down. She was mentally exhausted from going over and over the Amber situation in her head last night. She realized she hadn't rested well. She must look pretty bad.

She jumped up and righted her disheveled hair as best she could. "Just resting."

A quick glance at Travis revealed he was in his best jeans paired with a Western shirt with the sleeves cuffed exposing his tanned forearms. His hair was spiked and he had on his favorite boots.

"You look nice! What's the occasion?" Rachael took in her own appearance- boxer shorts, loose t-shirt, and boots. Wild, out-of-control curly blonde hair. It was quite the look, even for her.

"Your birthday." He smiled quizzically

"Holy crap! I forgot today was my birthday."

"I thought I'd take you to breakfast and shopping, unless of course you'd rather lay around her all day in your current state of mopey-ness."

"I wasn't moping!"

"That was certainly moping. I know moping and all of the various other moods of Rachael- and that girl, was moping."

"Okay. So you're right. I was moping."

Travis pulled her to her feet. He smelled so good, like pine trees and aftershave. He gave her a sweet kiss, took her by the hand, and led her to the back porch.

"I'll make you a cup of coffee. Pull yourself together, and then you can tell me what brought on this most recent bout of the mopes." Travis stood in the kitchen looking *oh so hot,* pouring her a cup of coffee. He turned and glanced over his shoulder. "It's not PMS is it?"

"Travis!" Rachael stomped off.

"I'm just saying. Michael warned me- and after several months of dating you- well let's just say I'm keeping track. You're a moody one and I need to be prepared to do battle with your twin every four weeks if I want to survive."

Rachael could hear him laughing in the kitchen as she made her way into the bathroom. She tamed her hair as best she could with water. She stared at the Medusa-like mass crowning her head. It was obviously a hat day! She donned a baseball cap of Michael's she found in the hallway for the Bucs, then slipped on a pair of jean shorts and shirt. Some lip gloss and flip flops, she was ready to go. She trudged back down the hallway where Michael and Travis were sitting in the kitchen. Michael looked up and just laughed.

"Definitely that time."

"Yep. She's wearing the jean shorts, cap, flip flops, and a scowl. Get back boys." Aunt Margaret chimed in.

"Are there no secrets in this house?" Rachael frowned.

"No secrets." Travis winked. "So, about this birthday. Let's get going."

He stood and pushed his barstool back in. Rachael's mother appeared from her bedroom down the hall.

"I'm ready." She called out and grabbed her purse off of the table in the foyer.

"We're all heading out for a birthday outing at seven o'clock on a Wednesday morning?"

"Sure are." Michael smiled.

"Okay."

When Travis mentioned shopping, she never imagined it would involve the entire family.

Everyone went outside where Travis' mother's SUV was parked. Rachael had only ridden in it a few times before. Usually only on occasions when there were so many of them that they needed all of the extra seats it afforded them. Travis was driving, so Rachael took shotgun up front with him. Everyone else piled in as well.

"Where are we heading?"

"It's a surprise." He squeezed her hand, where he held it on the middle console.

Rachael and her family rode listening to music. She nibbled on the toast and sipped the coffee Travis had made her. They got onto I-75 and headed north. Then after an hour or so they began taking a series of exits and turns toward their destination, all the while her mother giving Travis driving directions from the backseat. Suddenly it dawned on Rachael where they must be going.

Her father's minimum security Federal Prison Camp was located somewhere outside of Tampa. She'd never visited it before, but knew it must be where they were headed. He'd been in prison for a little over a year. Her mother had gone to visit him on weekends and holidays during scheduled visiting hours, but she and Michael had never been permitted to go. Rachael knew that if that was where they were going, this must have been a special visit. Her mother and father must have made all of the plans way in advance. Rachael wasn't sure of all of the details of visitation, but she knew that specific forms must have been submitted.

A few more turns and they were there. Tears stung Rachael's eyes. Rachael wasn't sure what she'd been expecting, but this was not it.

It was a prison. Plain and simple. Her father had been convicted of a white collar crime and had received two years in this facility. Rachael took a deep breath and calmed her emotions. This would be her first chance to see her father in over a year. She wouldn't allow sadness to creep into this special day and ruin it.

"Kids, it's not as bad as it looks. Your father is doing great and he's very excited about today's visit." Her mother gripped their shoulders.

"I'm excited, too." Rachael announced, wiping away any trace of tears. "Michael? Are you ready?"

"Sure am. I've known for a week. I can't wait."

"Some things you should know before we go in." Their mother quickly supplied them with a list of prison do's and don'ts. Among them were these simple rules: "Make eye contact. Leave all personal belongings in the vehicle. No jewelry- leave it here. No speaking about your father's crime or questions about anyone else's crimes or convictions either." Then she turned to Rachael. "You need a longer pair of shorts. Nothing above the knee can be worn, so I grabbed you another pair right before we left the house."

Everyone exited the vehicle giving Rachael an opportunity to pull on the pants her mother had brought her. She climbed out of the SUV announcing "All set. Let's do this."

Travis took her hand as she looped her other arm freely over her brother's shoulders. They all walked into the prison yard where they had to go through a double security gate. Next they arrived at a sign-in desk, where they each had to present photo id. Rachael's mother led the way through this extensive process, having repeated it several times over the past year.

They all went through an area that contained a metal detector. After passing this area, they proceeded to the visitation area where they were instructed to have a seat at a table. A few minutes later, her father was led in.

Rachael was surprised that he looked much better than he'd looked the last time she'd seen him before his trial. He looked relieved and rested. Maybe this experience hadn't been as bad as she'd anticipated. Maybe he'd been more worried about the possibilities and the actual reality of prison was not as bad. Whatever the reason, Rachael herself was relieved- immensely. Her mother walked over and gave her father a hug and a kiss. Everyone else followed this pattern, with the exception of Travis who shook her father's hand.

Her father sat down at the table with them.

Michael immediately launched into a story about baseball and how he'd hit his first homerun last season. Everyone shared in his excitement. Their mother talked about her job- that while it was unfulfilling for her- it paid the bills. Aunt Margaret commiserated with her about that part. Rachael shared her story about how she got her Mustang and how it had belonged to JJ's mother. After a while, everyone sang Happy Birthday to Rachael and it was nearing time to go.

Travis, her mother, Aunt Margaret, and Michael all stood to excuse themselves. Rachael knew the visit would only last two hours and that the time for her to leave would be approaching. Her father stood and hugged each of them closely, kissing everyone on the cheek- even Travis whom he told to take care of his "Baby Girl".

"Why don't you take a few extra minutes, Rachael?" Her mother prodded.

"Thanks, Mom."

Rachael sat across from her father. She wanted to talk to him about Amber, she knew she had to.

"Dad, do you remember that friend I told you about at the slumber party last year? The one who found herself in a bad situation?"

"Yes, I do."

"Well, it was true. She was, or is rather, in a bad situation."

"I feared that was the case when her parents transferred her to another school. How is she?"

Rachael shrugged her shoulders, "I ran into her. On the outside she seems okay, but she has made the decision to go with adoption."

16

"Not an easy decision."

"No."

"And you're fearful it's a decision she will regret?"

"Yes."

"And you want to know what I think?"

"Like always."

"I think life is never easy. We all make decisions we regret." He smiled knowingly. "It's her decision though. No one can make that decision for her. Be supportive. Be a good friend. That's all you can do."

"You're right, Dad. I miss you so much."

"I miss you too, Baby Girl. Only one year to go. I'll be home soon." He paused. "How about you?" He lowered his voice. "No changes in that department."

"No! Of course not!"

"Just as I thought, but try not to take the Cool Dad's Fashions too far, honey." He said glancing at her outfit of loose t-shirt, baggy pants, and flip flops.

"This wasn't planned. I'd have dressed up if I had realized where we were going. This is what you'd call PMS Wear."

"Glad to hear it. How is everything else?"

"Misty's grandmother came into the store to pick out something for her and ended up buying the shirt I had picked out for myself."

"So?"

"It bothered me. A lot."

"I can understand."

"Yes, but the really bad part was the fact that I started wanting to pick other things out for her. Things that would've been insulting or unkind."

"At least you realized that it was wrong and didn't do it."

"Yes."

"And now you have something to work on- moving past your jealously and dislike of Misty."

"I didn't even realize that it still bothered me- the fact she and Travis have shared something intimate." Rachael smirked, remembering back to their break-up. While they hadn't actually slept together, he and Misty had come very close to it. It still hurt.

"Well, it shouldn't. It was before your time. Only you can fix what you're feeling. It's no one's responsibility but your own. The realization that you're imperfect hurts."

Rachael stood and walked over to embrace her father. He kissed her forehead.

"Take care. I love you."

"Love you, too, Dad."

"And Rachael," he called stopping her. "Happy Birthday. Have an extra slice of birthday cake for me."

"Thanks. Will do."

As Rachael made the long walk out, alone, she thought about her father and mother. Their strength and courage. Her mother had made this same journey many times before. Each time leaving her father all over again. Each time saying goodbye. She had renewed respect for her mother and her commitment to their family. She was a woman of immeasurable character.

The rest of her family waited for her in the public reception area. Rachael was glad to see them, but also wanted to go and hide for a moment or two of quiet solitude. Her mother came over to hug her, as did her aunt. Travis and Michael stood talking quietly, but Rachael didn't miss the look in Travis' eyes searching hers-quietly asking if she was okay. She walked over and took his hand squeezing it. They all walked out and headed for home.

Once home, Aunt Margaret and her mother set to work to prepare a birthday feast. Michael disappeared to his game lounge with Levi, Travis' cousin, who appeared at their door.

Rachael and Travis went to the barn and climbed the stairs to the hayloft letting their legs dangle from the open doors.

"You okay?"

"I am. Surprisingly, I feel better. Seeing him in person and knowing he's okay. I'm at peace with it. Two years is a long time, but it'll be over before we know it."

"Yes, it will." His eyes sparkled in the bright Florida sun, setting low in west. "So what had you so down this morning?"

"Amber. She came into the store yesterday."

"How is she?"

"Okay, I guess. She's giving the baby up for adoption."

"I heard. After we bumped into her and her mother last month...I called Clay. He knew of course, and is supportive of whatever she wants to do."

"He's okay with her giving the baby up for adoption?"

"Yes. He thinks he's too young to be a parent, too."

"Wow."

"Is something else bothering you?"

"You're very good at reading me, Travis."

"Getting better at it every day." He winked.

Rachael smacked his leg, leaving her hand on his thigh.

"Misty's grandmother came into the store yesterday to pick her out a shirt and earrings."

Travis raised his eyebrows. "Go on."

"I helped her pick out a few nice things."

"Uh, huh." He smiled.

"No really. I picked out the shirt and earrings that I had chosen for myself."

"That was nice of you."

"No, not really. I was really angry about her getting them and even contemplated selling her grandmother some hideous earrings instead- and a few other *choice* garments." Rachael confessed.

"But you didn't, in the end you did the right thing."

"Yeah. I guess so. I'm still not happy about it though."

Rachael felt as if she'd gone to confession- twice. *First to Dad, now to Travis. Who next? The mailman?* But all the confessing in the world wouldn't make her feel better. Dad was right. She needed to fix it herself, but wasn't sure how to.

"That's okay. You're human, Rach. Do you want to open your present?" Travis pulled a small box out of his shirt pocket.

"That's not what I think it is- is it?"

"Nope. It's not an engagement ring. You have me on a seven year plan- remember? I'm pacing myself."

Rachael opened the box. Inside there was a long white gold chain with a heart-shaped ruby pendent.

Travis took the box from her and put the necklace around her neck, gently lifting her hair to fasten it at the back.

"You have my heart. You always have." He kissed her sweetly. Their tender moment ended when they heard Maysie hollering from the top of the stairwell.

"Come on you two lovebirds. We're all holding dinner for the guest of honor here. Besides- if I can't get any kisses, you two can't have any either."

"Great." Travis mumbled.

"She does have a point, Travis. If she can't kiss Tristan- we shouldn't be allowed to kiss either."

"Holy hell. Someone shoot me now." Travis jested.

"I think that's a great idea, Rachael!" Maysie squealed. "We're all going to make a no kissing, no holding hands pact for the entire year."

"That would make both our Dad's happy." Rachael surmised.

"Yes- and one guy really grouchy." Travis warned. "Not gonna happen, Maysie. If you'd choose a guy your own age you could date as well."

"I don't want a boy my own age." Maysie retorted. "I want Tristan."

"Come on you two. Dinner is getting cold." Rachael intervened.

Tristan and Maysie were still not allowed to officially begin dating- not until after she graduated high school this year and turned nineteen. He was older, more mature, and after what happened last year- Maysie was fortunate her parents allowed her to still see him at all. They'd set a few simple rules and Maysie was following them. *So far...so good.*

At the table everyone said grace. Her birthday dinner was a grand affair. Mashed potatoes, fried cubed steak, gravy, and yellow corn on the cob. Corn bread, still warm from the oven, with honey butter set Rachael's mouth to watering. Large mason jars filled with sweet tea accompanied every place setting. Rachael glanced around the table- all the smiling faces. Everyone was happy, even Rachael.

"What a lovely heart pendant." Her mother took notice of the ruby pendant. Rachael touched it where it hung around her neck.

"It was smooth of Travis to give Rachael his heart." Michael nodded his head toward Travis. "Levi and I've been taking mental notes from the 'dating master'."

"The dating master?" Rachael eyed Travis.

"That was before you, baby. Now there's only one girl I want to date."

"Add that line to the list." Levi instructed Michael.

"I will."

"You're not helping here guys." Travis glared at them both.

"What list?" Rachael asked. Travis had a look of *shut up, you morons* on his face.

"Our Travis Baxter: How to Date Hot Chicks' List." Michael appeared very proud of himself.

"Travis is a legend around here." Levi interjected.

"A legend, huh?"

"Yep. Before all the girls you know about there were at least ten others."

"Really."

"Yep. The list goes on and on." Maysie chimed in.

"Hmm."

"Okay you two. I'm going to whip both your butts in a bit if you don't zip it." Travis threatened as he stood up, walked over, and gave them both a noogie.

After dinner was over and birthday cake served, Rachael said her goodbyes to both Maysie and Travis outside. Fortunately for them, Maysie had driven over in her own car. After Maysie drove out of the driveway, Travis turned and held Rachael close.

"There really weren't all that many, baby."

"I'm not bothered by you being a super dater. I've dated fifteen guys myself. It's not really that big of a deal."

"Fifteen!" Travis' eyes opened wide and his voice rose a notch.

"Yep. It's just a number, Travis. It doesn't mean a thing."

A sideways glance proved to Rachael she'd really gotten to him this time. She could almost hear his thoughts. She knew if he asked her questions about it, he would be opening himself up to a whole slew of questions from her- so he kept quiet.

"Fifteen?"

She smiled, "Yes, but I only kissed ten of them- or was it eleven. I can't remember."

"No wonder you're such a great kisser. It's all that practice." He sounded hurt. "I've no room to judge though."

She considered letting this little charade play through a little bit longer, but the concern she saw on his face was more than she could bear. Besides, she'd never been a liar and since it wasn't April Fool's Day, she didn't see how her little hoax could be left as it was.

"I'm just playing with you. I haven't kissed eleven guys!" She giggled.

"Not funny, Rachael."

"So who's the mopey one now?" She pulled him close and kissed him. "One. I've kissed one cowboy. Just one."

Technically she told the truth. She'd never kissed any other cowboys, and of course he knew about her kissing Colten- but why did she feel he needed to know anyhow? As she learned at dinner- he could practically be considered a kissing bandit to hear her brother and Levi tell it!

He held her close.

"I'm a more jealous guy than I knew. Thanks for taking the teasing at the dinner table so well tonight. I don't think I could've handled it the same way if I were in your shoes."

"Thank you for going with me to see my father. I don't know many guys that would've wanted to step foot in a prison."

"It wasn't fun- that's for sure, but I was glad to share it with you."

Chapter Three

Rachael and her heifer, Taffy, progressed beyond the typical round pen exercise routine to a more dog-like relationship. Taffy now weighed over eight hundred pounds and enjoyed long walks down the driveway with Rachael on her lead rope. Sometimes Rachael would bring along a good book to read while Taffy enjoyed munching on the grass and wild flowers that dotted Aunt Margaret's vast front yard. Rachael noticed a change in the weather, the sky began to cloud up and the breeze began to blow.

"Come on, Taffy. We better head to the barn."

Moments later, it began to pour. Rachael and Taffy made it into the barn and to her stall just in time to get drenched. Ole' lonesome George had already ventured in on his own and glanced at them as if to ask, "What took you two so long?"

Lightning zigzagged across the sky. Rachael waited out the storm for another ten minutes, but when there was no sign of improvement she decided to make a run for it. Once inside, Rachael dried off in her bathroom and changed into dry clothes. She could hear Michael's television on and knew he was probably playing video games with Levi, as usual.

Aunt Margaret and her mother were at work at the beach resort, and wouldn't be home until much later. Rachael heard her cell phone ring and went to answer it.

A very upset Maysie was on the other end.

"Slow down, Maysie, and start over again. What's wrong?"

Maysie drew a quick breath. "It's Gabe. I just heard from Alex that Gabe was at the beach today with another girl."

"Okay, so don't freak out." Rachael soothed.

"Don't freak out? We know the girl couldn't have been Shannah. She is still in South Carolina! So, if it's not Shannah, then who was it?"

"I don't know, but it could have been anyone. His cousin, a good friend. Anyone."

"Kissing cousins? Literally." Maysie spat.

"That changes everything- and you are sure? Alex is sure of what she saw?"

"She said so. They were holding hands! Kissing in the water! She said they were quite natural about it. But that was until they spotted Alex and Fred. I guess they made a bee line for the snack bar in order to flee. Alex said that Gabe looked terribly uncomfortable."

"Well, he should be- the cheater!" Rachael yelled.

"Exactly! What are we going to do?"

"I'm not sure. Shannah isn't due back until next week. We certainly can't go calling her in South Carolina with this type of news. She'd be devastated!"

"Definitely. I can't believe that after almost two years of dating he's spotted hooking up with some skank at the beach."

Maysie must've been angry, very angry. In the past two years, Rachael had never heard her refer to anyone by that name- or to even speak ill about anyone for that matter.

"Maybe she already knows." Rachael suggested.

"Don't you think she would've called us if she did?"

"Not necessarily. She's pretty private about those types of things."

"You're right. I think we need to drive over there."

"To his house?" Rachael sighed.

"Yes, to his house. I'd like to give him a piece of my mind." Maysie offered.

"Bad idea. Besides- what if they're broken up? Then what? We'd look like a couple of crazies!"

"Shannah will be back next week, and when she is…we'll sit her down and tell her."

"Okay." Rachael was anything but 'okay' with it all.

"I wonder if Travis knows." Maysie murmured.

"Of course not! He would've told me if he knew."

"Maybe not. Guys stick together. Maybe he didn't want to out his best friend."

"No. There's no way he knows." Rachael defended her boyfriend.

She heard the rumble of his diesel truck outside, amid the cracking lighting and drumming rain.

"I'll ask him. He just pulled up outside. I'll call you in a bit. Don't do anything stupid."

"Who me? Never, but I've been brainstorming a little."

"Maysie- sit tight." Rachael set the phone down.

She jumped off her bed and ran to the front door. She'd opened it even before Travis had the opportunity to knock or ring the doorbell. Travis had a strange, hard to describe look, on his face.

Rachael frowned, "So you've heard."

"Yep, I've heard all about Gabe and Heather at the beach. I guess they've been hanging out for a couple of weeks."

"And?"

"I think it's a crappy thing to do to Shannah. She is away for the summer and he didn't want to break up with her over the phone."

"So he starts dating someone else while she's gone? He doesn't even wait until she gets home?"

"He said he never expected to like Heather. He knows her from his Tae Kwon Do class. They were sparring a lot near the end of the school year...and I guess things became..."

"Became what?"

"Somewhat physical." Travis smirked.

"Somewhat physical? Define *somewhat physical*."

"You know what I mean."

"What a pig!"

"I don't know that I'd go that far. They were only dating. It's not like they were married or anything, Rachael."

"Oh. And that's what you'd say if I went out and met some other guy, things progressed, and we became *somewhat physical*?"

"Of course not. This isn't about us. It's about them."

25

"But we are only dating- yes? And we're not married- right?"

"Yes, but don't misrepresent what I said. I don't know the inner workings of their relationship." Travis spouted. "Maybe things between them were different or changed somehow."

"Obviously! She wouldn't do 'it' with him last year and he has probably gone off and found someone else that would!" Rachael yelled. "Someone who'd get *somewhat physical,* as you described it!"

"Don't kill the messenger, Rach. As soon as I heard, I came straight over here to tell you."

"But you sound like you're defending him." Rachael crossed her arms across her chest and cocked her right eyebrow.

"No. Definitely not defending him- I'm merely pleading the fifth. He's my friend."

"And she's mine. She's going to be heartbroken and I'm heartbroken for her." Rachael walked over to the sofa and plopped down.

She thought back to the 'it conversation' from the slumber party last year- it seemed to haunt her now. *First Amber, now this.* And then there was the later conversation she and Shannah had shared. Shannah's mother and her teen pregnancy was no secret among any of the girls- and for that reason alone, Shannah had deep convictions against premarital sex, and anything else that went along with it. She didn't want to end up in the same situation as her mother. Rachael thought that Gabe respected that- understood it. Gabe obviously needed something more, and Shannah had been unwilling to give it.

Travis sat down next to her and took her hands.

"Baby, try not to worry. You don't even know how she'll react. You may be borrowing trouble. He has every intention of going over and breaking up with her in person when she gets home."

"So she can be blindsided by it? I don't think so."

"So you think it's a better idea to call her and tell her over the phone? I think that's an awful idea."

"If he were halfway decent, he would've done so himself, or had the decency to wait until she returned home."

"Maybe you're right."

"Maybe I am right!" She stood and gestured toward the door. "You better leave, Travis Baxter!"

"So now you're kicking me out?"

"I am. I'm kicking you out! Go over and console Gabe in his moment of need! Maybe there's some sort of cheaters' counseling you can help him with."

Travis laughed.

"This isn't funny, Travis."

"No it's not- but I like it when you get really feisty with me." He winked.

"See yourself out." Rachael stomped down the hall.

After a few minutes, she felt rather childish. When ten minutes had passed and she still hadn't heard Travis' truck leave, she opened her door and slunk back up the hall. He was in the kitchen fixing himself a sandwich.

She exhaled sharply, "Go right ahead and help yourself."

"This isn't for me- it's for you. Since we are past the twin's evil appearance, I figured you must be hungry, so I fixed you a sandwich."

"Food doesn't fix everything."

"If you're a guy it does."

"I'm not hungry."

"Okay, I'll eat it. So back to our conversation before you threw a temper tantrum and disappeared down the hall."

"Be careful, Travis, I'm not my usual chipper self."

"So I've noticed. Let me start again. I think what Gabe did was wrong and unkind, but he's my friend and it's not my place to judge. That's it- plain and simple." He took a huge bite of the sandwich.

"I respect that, but I feel very differently. If a friend of mine were to do something like this- I'd march over there and set her straight. I'd tell her that she'd disappointed me."

"That's you- not me. I believe he will see the error of his ways soon enough. Shannah is a great girl. He traded that in for a *good time*. He'll regret it. Eventually. Not now, but once the newness of the *other* wears off."

"The *other*?"

"I don't have details, so don't ask me. Do you want to go to the movies tonight?"

"No. I have plans with your sister."

"I've been put on the back burner for my sister?"

"Yes. Besides- don't you have some good ole boy two-timing cheater friend that would like to hang out with you?"

"So you *are* still annoyed with me? I haven't really done anything wrong."

"Except for the fact that you still want to hang out with the cheater."

"I'm not going to stop being his friend- if that's what you mean. He has made a mistake, but I'm still his friend."

"If you lay with dogs, Travis, you're bound to pick up fleas."

"Okay, I'm leaving this time. I need to seek cover until this storm blows over a bit."

For the first time, Rachael just watched him leave, making no effort to walk him to the door. A few hours later the rain had subsided and it was getting dark. Aunt Margaret and her mother brought Chinese food home for dinner. They brought a carload of groceries, too.

When Rachael heard the horn honking, she called for Michael and the two of them ran out to carry everything inside. The smell of Chinese food from the dining room was tempting, but Rachael still had very little appetite. The dinner table was unusually quiet until Michael broke the silence.

"Heard about Shannah and Gabe. Not cool."

Rachael blew out a ragged breath. "Even a fourteen-year-old gets it." Rachael stopped herself, realizing she'd actually said that last thought aloud.

"What was that, honey?" Aunt Margaret questioned.

"Gabe is dating someone new. Shannah doesn't know because she's still out of town. I'm annoyed at Travis because he's still friends with Gabe. Guys suck. That's all."

"Not all guys suck." Her mom protested.

"Yeah. Come on. Cut him some slack." Michael interjected. "They've known each other forever. He's not gonna just write him off."

"I think he should. Once a cheater- always a cheater."

"You're only in high school. This isn't an indicator about the rest of his relationships, or his future ability to commit, or anything, Rachael." Aunt Margaret pointed out.

"So everyone is siding with the cheater." Rachael stood up. "May I be excused?"

"Yes, dear."

Rachael slipped into her jammies and climbed into bed.
*

A while later, there was a light tap on her window.

Rachael sat up in bed and glanced at her clock. Three o'clock.

Who would be coming by at three o'clock in the morning? Travis.

Rachael strode over to the window and opened the blinds with a harsh pull of the cord. She was surprised to see Maysie and Shannah!

Rachael tiptoed down the hall to the front door and opened it.

Shannah's eyes were puffy from what looked like hours of crying. Rachael threw her arms around her.

"What are you doing home? I thought you had another week to go?" Rachael whispered.

"Grab your shoes and come on. There'll be time to explain in the car."

"In the car?" Rachael squeaked.

"Shh." Maysie chastised her for making too much noise.

All three girls went and climbed into Maysie's convertible. They drove out of the driveway, the top down, hair flying wildly in the night breeze.

"What are we doing?" Rachael looked at Shannah and Maysie, both wearing short pajama shorts and fitted tank tops. Their hair standing on end. Had they just gotten out of bed?

"We are on a mission- a little Redneck Retribution." Shannah explained. "My father had made arrangements for me to come back early this summer. My mom has some business trip next week. The timing couldn't have been any better. When I hadn't heard from the butthead in over three weeks, I was smart enough to know that something was up. Little did I know it was his…"

"Shannah!" Maysie cut her off midsentence, sounding horrified.

"Sorry, Maysie!" Shannah apologized. "So anyhow, I texted Maysie when I got home tonight and went to her house where she explained all."

"He has no idea you're here in town?"

"None. So after everyone went to sleep we hatched this plan."

"I can't wait to hear this." Rachael knew if it was one of Shannah's ideas of Redneck Retribution, she may need to be the level-headed one tonight.

"She can get pretty creative when she's fired-up like this!" Maysie smiled.

"Maysie and I decided the shoe polish we had left over from writing on our car windows for the band competition last year might be a nice touch."

"Sure, as long as it won't cause any permanent damage." Rachael questioned.

"None. Just to his over-inflated ego." Shannah surmised. "Unless of course we get it on the paint job as well." A naughty sparkle flashed in her eyes.

"Let's just stick to the original plan, windows only. Anything else is off limits." Maysie interjected.

Rachael reached into the plastic bag on the seat beside her. She pulled out two bottles of white shoe polish.

"There are only two."

"Maysie is driving the get-a-way car. You and I'll take care of the writing. Only the windows." Shannah winked conspiratorially at Rachael.

"Got it."

They slowly pulled into Gabe's neighborhood. There weren't any neighbors outside or up and about at this time of the morning.

"I'll drop you, circle the block, and come back by. You'll only have a minute or two."

"We'll get it done." Shannah narrowed her eyes, while Rachael's heart drummed widely in her ears.

Maysie slowed her car as Shannah and Rachael jumped out of the back over the doors- so as not to make any noise. They ran up to Gabe's car and began writing on the windows. When they were finished one set of windows read 'Cheaters Never Prosper', while the other said 'Hope She Was Worth It'. Shannah managed to scribble 'Cheater' across both the front and back windshields in extra-large script, as well. A neighbor's dog barked loudly.

Maysie pulled back up just in time for both girls to jump in over the side of the car and into the backseat.

Things had gone incredibly well and all three were feeling rather proud of themselves until flashing blue lights in the rearview mirror caught their attention ten miles up the road.

"Great." Maysie muttered, as she pulled over. They were almost home. She glanced at her watch. It was nearing 4:30 in the morning.

Shannah opened the glove box and handed Maysie the title, registration, and insurance information.

"I've been pulled over before." She smiled over at Rachael and Maysie. "Just cry. It really does work every time."

Maysie looked like she was about to cry and for real- no faking necessary.

A young, rather robust deputy walked up to the side of the car.

"Good morning, ladies. What brings you girls out at this hour?"

Rachael looked at the three of them. They must be a sight- all wearing PJ's, hair wild from blowing in the wind, and to top it all off, Maysie was wearing pig slippers!

Maysie appeared to have stage-fright, she uttered not a word. Rachael decided she should serve as the spokesperson. She still held the shoe polish in her hand, even if she hadn't been- her fingers were covered in white polish.

Always tell the truth. She remembered her mother's words and decided that was her only option.

"Yes, sir, I can explain. Shannah's stupid boyfriend cheated on her and planned to dump her when she got back in town. So we were a little upset and decided to pay his vehicle a visit. I shoe polished his windows with descriptive words like *cheater* and such. Now we're on our way back home."

"Have you ladies been drinking?" The officer used his flashlight to shine around the car.

"No sir." All three answered in unison.

"Can you ladies step out of the car?"

"Yes, sir."

Rachael, Maysie, and Shannah piled out of the car.

"Do you mind if I search your car?"

"No, sir." Maysie answered.

The officer shined his flashlight all around the vehicle.

"And you say that you only shoe polished the windows- not the paint."

"Only the windows." Rachael nodded.

Maysie was shaking, she was so nervous.

"Okay- then get on home, Miss Baxter."

The deputy handed Maysie back her paperwork. Rachael, Maysie, and Shannah climbed back into the car, buckled their seatbelts, and pulled cautiously out onto the road.

"How did he know your name?" Rachael asked Maysie.

"From the license and registration." Shannah answered.

"And the fact that I recognized him, too." Maysie spoke in a hushed whisper.

"You knew him?" Shannah sounded nervous.

"He's from around here. He knows my dad." Maysie admitted. "Like I said, I recognized him, and that typically goes both ways. If I recognized him- he would've recognized me also."

"Great! We'll all be shoveling crap in the barn tomorrow." Rachael sighed.

"Probably, but it was sooo worth it!" Shannah teased.

"For sure." Maysie added.

Chapter Four

Rachael crawled back into bed around five o'clock and slept soundly until there was a light knock at her door. Her mom walked in and handed her a cup of coffee

"So," she paused. "I got a call from Mrs. Baxter."

Rachael sipped her coffee, careful not to look up over the rim of her cup. After a minute or more she realized her mother was waiting on her to say something.

"Really? What about?"

"Oh, just a little something to do with Gabe's vehicle and some graffiti painted on the windows."

"Oh, no, what could he have done to deserve something like that?" Rachael feigned ignorance.

Her mother laughed. "I was thinking the same thing, poor guy."

"It didn't do any damage, did it? This graffiti stuff." Rachael feigned worry.

"Nope- no damage, but he called Travis this morning and was out there scrubbing his car windows like a madman. I guess it really ticked him off."

"Poor Gabe. I feel for him. I really do." Rachael pouted her lips trying to appear sad.

"I thought so, my little angel. I knew you had nothing to do with this." Rachael's mother stood and they shared a knowing smile.

So Mom understands after all...

"Oh and Rachael, honey, scrub your nails. There is still polish on them." She walked out and closed the door behind her. Rachael could hear her laughing all the way to the kitchen.

Rachael climbed out of bed and set to work feeding animals and cleaning stalls. She didn't hear from Travis all day and surmised by dinnertime he was not happy with her. Rachael wouldn't give in and call or text him. He was the guy- that was his job.

*

Two days passed and still nothing. Now he was really beginning to make Rachael angry. By the third morning, she decided she would march right over there and set him straight.

She climbed in through the still broken window of her Mustang, and drove over to the Baxter Ranch. Maysie was out in the round pen riding Pretty Girl.

Rachael parked her car and climbed out through the window. She walked over to the round pen. Maysie galloped over to her.

"You can't stay to visit. I'm grounded."

"Grounded?"

"Yep. The officer friend of my dad's called and ratted us out. So I'm grounded."

"Bummer. My mom knows but she didn't ground me."

"That's because your parents are cooler than mine."

"Where's Travis?"

"He's grounded, too."

"Why is Travis grounded?"

"For arguing with me over the whole Gabe thing. Dad said that blood is blood and he shouldn't be fighting with me over it. I'm grounded for two weeks- for driving the get-a-way car and all. He's grounded for one week for fighting with his sweet, little, innocent baby sister."

Rachael knew by Maysie's comments that Travis must be standing behind her. She turned to hear him saying, "Hardly. We're twins. I'm ten minutes older than you- not ten years. Hey Rach- so I guess you've heard. We're grounded."

"Just found out. I guess I should be going. I don't want either of you to get into trouble. Can I hug you?"

"Make it fast."

Rachael went over and hugged Travis.

"Sorry you're grounded."

"Sorry for defending Gabe."

"Hi, Rachael." Mr. Baxter bellered from the barn. "If you'd like to be grounded too, there's always room for one more. Come on out here and grab a shovel. I could use some help with these stalls. Maysie, you and Travis, too."

Four hours later, the three of them were still working tediously in the barn. They heard a horse trailer coming down the driveway. Maysie lifted her head in the direction of the doorway where Tristan's truck and trailer pulled into view.

Maysie shrieked, "Great. And I look awful. Just plain awful."

"Don't worry about it. He'll like you dirt and all." Rachael offered.

"Not stank and all." Travis grinned.

"More working, less caterwauling." Mr. Baxter barked as he went outside to greet Tristan.

The rattling of the metal gates on the horse trailer made everyone stop and take notice. Tristan led a new filly into the barn. She was a buckskin and appeared to be a little over a year old. She was walking nicely on her lead rope and didn't seem to be bothered by all of the activity in the barn going on around her.

"She's gorgeous, Tristan. What's her name?" Maysie greeted.

"I've been calling her Prissy, short for Priscilla."

"How old is she?"

"Eighteen months."

"She's a baby." Maysie cooed.

"Here we go, again." Travis chided.

Rachael and Maysie set their shovels aside and walked over to pat the filly. They both rubbed her neck and shoulders.

"She's so tiny- for a baby horse." Rachael amended. Prissy wasn't exactly tiny, but she was a baby still.

"She's too small to ride, but she needs lots of ground work. I thought the girls would enjoy working with her."

"Could we?" Maysie squealed. "I've never had a filly before."

"Okay, girls." Mr. Baxter directed. "Lead her down to the end stall and make sure she has fresh water, hay, and feed." He paused, "And by the way, y'all consider yourselves un-grounded. Now go get washed up for dinner. I'm heading up to the house."

Rachael wasn't quite sure what had just happened. First they were grounded, now they weren't. As if reading her thoughts Travis explained. "Dad always doles out quite the punishment at first- then sometimes he has a change of heart and paroles us early."

"Good."

Rachael and Travis put away the shovels and walked out behind the barn to empty the wheelbarrow in the back pasture, leaving Tristan and Maysie alone in the barn.

"What do you think about the filly?" Rachael glanced sideways at Travis.

"I think it's a gift for my sister."

"I think you're right."

"My dad must've known though because he didn't seem surprised."

"Yep- and so the courtship begins." Rachael beamed.

"Hmmm."

"You have to try to stop seeing her as a sister and more as the woman she's becoming. She will be eighteen in two weeks, Travis."

"Yes, I know."

After dumping the wheelbarrow and pushing it back to the barn in silence, Rachael started speaking in a very loud voice when they neared the doors. "I sure am glad you aren't grounded anymore!" She was nearly yelling.

Travis shot her a look.

"What?" She smiled.

"You know what. You were firing a warning shot. Letting them know that we were coming back in."

"Who me? No, I was just talking."

"You can't lie to me, girl."

Travis smacked Rachael on the butt. To their surprise Tristan and Maysie had already made their way back up to the house. Travis flipped on the barn lights before heading up to the house, stopping long enough to kiss Rachael softly. They strolled hand-in-hand into the house.

Inside they were greeted by the smell of baby back ribs, coleslaw, garlic toast, and baked beans. Rachael texted her mother to let her know she would be staying for dinner and to find out what time she needed her home. Her mother was fine with it and told her not to rush.

Dinner was a beautiful, elegant affair. Mrs. Baxter had set the table with real linen napkins, china, and everything. After dinner Travis and Rachael went for an evening swim while Maysie and Tristan visited on the back porch. Mr. and Mrs. Baxter had retired to the family room for a little TV time.

"So, I've been thinking, I'd like to have a back-to-school party and invite all of our friends." Rachael announced.

"Sounds like a great idea."

"Amber, too."

"I'm not so sure about that." Travis disagreed.

"Why not? She's still our friend."

"Yes, but she is pregnant. You don't think that your mom and mine will have a problem with us hanging out with a pregnant chick?"

"No. Why would they? It's not like her pregnancy is going to rub off on us or anything."

"Good point. We can always ask and see." He offered.

"Why would we ask? She's pregnant- not a felon."

"Yes, Rachael- she's pregnant. I've got the definite feeling that moms, plural, as in yours, mine, and other people's moms- will see it as us condoning teenage pregnancy."

"You're wrong. If anything they'll encourage us to embrace Amber. You'll see."

"Okay, if you say so."

"I do say so."

"I just don't want you to be disappointed."

"I won't be because you're wrong- in this case. Everyone will surprise you and receive Amber with open arms, hearts, and minds."

"So let's discuss what I want for my birthday." He winked.

"I bet I can guess."

"If you think you can, be my guest."

"A new compound bow."

"Would be nice, but no."

"A new stereo system for your truck."

"Would love it, but you can't afford it on your pay."

"Don't tell me that you have been hanging around Gabe- and want to renegotiate our purity agreement."

"Be serious." He frowned.

"You never know, the thought may have crossed your mind."

"All the time, but no, I'm not wanting 'it' for my birthday if that's what you're asking. I was thinking more along the lines of his and hers fishing poles."

"Thank goodness. Had me scared there for a moment."

"You scared? I'm the religious one, remember? Let's get out of this pool and go babysit Maysie and Tristan."

Travis hauled Rachael out of the pool behind him.

"Renegotiate our purity pledge…not a bad idea. Maybe in a year or two."

"Not happening, Travis."

"It was worth a try." He joked.

Inside Rachael heard laughter coming from the kitchen table. Mrs. Baxter was dishing up warm apple pie and ice cream. Rachael sat down still wrapped in a towel and wearing one of Maysie's one piece swimsuits.

Tristan sat talking about Maysie's new filly.

"Her sire and the mare were both not that tall. She won't be taller than fifteen hands. I think she would be perfect for cutting, especially for a woman."

"She is so gentle and sweet. I think she'll be easy to train." Maysie advised.

"We shall see." Tristan raised his eyebrows.

"I think you two will have your hands full. Maybe even too full to go out in the middle of the night shoe polishing vehicles." Mr. Baxter grinned.

"I don't know about that. Don't mess with us country girls. We may seem all sweet and kind, but underneath it all, we're pretty tough." Maysie warned.

"You're preaching to the choir here, Maysie. Your mom has whipped my butt into shape for twenty years." Mr. Baxter teased.

Mrs. Baxter giggled, "And you've enjoyed every minute of it, too."

"That I have, my dear, that I have. Maysie and Travis, why don't you tidy the kitchen?"

"I'll help." Tristan stood and started to clear the table.

"Figured you would. Goodnight, Tristan. Rachael it was good seeing you. Lock the door before you come up to bed, Travis."

Mr. and Mrs. Baxter turned and exited the kitchen. Rachael went into the downstairs bathroom to change out of the borrowed swimsuit and put on her dirty work clothes, and boy did they smell. Maysie had gotten cleaned up just before dinner. Rachael hadn't had anything clean to put on. Climbing back into the smelly clothes after swimming was very unappealing.

If Travis noticed her stench he didn't let on. He walked her outside, down the steps, and kissed her goodnight.

"I'll call you tomorrow before you go into work."

"That reminds me, I was mad at you."

"For what now?"

"For not calling me for two days."

"I was grounded, remember?"

"Still could've texted."

"Not without a phone you can't."

"Didn't realize you lost that, too. Sorry, I just missed you."

"I'm just glad you didn't vandalize my truck or anything."

"Not this time, but watch out."

Chapter Five

Work dragged by, one hour at a time. Rachael had
unpacked and priced the little bit of new merchandise that had
arrived earlier this afternoon. Next, she dusted every display table
in the store. She knelt on the floor in front of the boots, making
sure that they were paired correctly by size and style. It was
amazing how mixed-up they could become in just two days. She
stood to walk back toward the front of the store when she heard the
bells chiming.

A girl walked in, carrying a store bag, probably needing to
exchange or return something. Rachael looked at her, realizing she
looked vaguely familiar but not recognizing her. Her hair was drab
and lackluster- and her overall appearance could have been
described as gaunt. Her cheek bones were high, but her face was
thin- too thin. Her exposed arms were bony and appeared to lack
all muscle tone. The skinny jeans she wore did nothing to conceal
her hipbones and her flat butt. This girl looked sick!

Rachael immediately felt for her and walked over behind
the register.

"Welcome to the Western Store. How may I help you?"

"Hi, Rachael."

Do I know this girl?

She removed her sunglasses- this super thin stranger
seemed to know her. Rachael's heart hit the ground…*Misty*…

But this wasn't the super beautiful, curvy in all the right
places Misty that Rachael remembered. This Misty was frail and
appeared as if a strong wind could blow her over.

"Hi, Misty."

Misty sauntered, or staggered rather, up to the counter.

"I believe you helped my grandmother pick this shirt for me. I love it- but it's way too big for me. I think I need an extra small."

"Let me grab the correct size." Rachael wandered over to the rack and selected an extra small. She brought it back over and scanned the first shirt as a return. Then she rang up the next one as a new purchase.

Misty made no attempt at small talk. Her eyes were deep set and had a sunken appearance. Her skin had lost its youthful appeal and she had a few sores on her face and arms.

What is wrong with her?

Rachael thought about asking, but knew she wouldn't be asking for the right reasons. Yet, something deep inside her told her Misty was in trouble. Something was wrong. She seemed very anxious and fidgety. Kind of strung out.

"Will there be anything else?"

"No. Enjoy my boyfriend." She smirked and turned to go.

"Whatever."

It took all of Rachael's self-control not to sail over the counter and knock Misty's frail, meager butt to the ground. She had a few words saved up for Misty, but couldn't bring herself to say them. Misty had never been nice. She'd never even been what Rachael had thought of as a decent person. For the two years that Rachael had known her, she'd been mean, snotty, slutty, and an all-around not good girl. Rachael realized that she hated Misty. Truly hated her to the core of her being.

However, no matter how much she despised Misty, she felt sorry for her.

Whatever was wrong with Misty it had to be serious. She must've lost nearly thirty pounds and she didn't have thirty pounds to lose in the first place. Rachael would've guessed that the skinny jeans were a size zero or maybe even smaller. Misty was tall. Weighing less than one hundred pounds was too thin for a girl her height.

Rachael's anger and hatred of Misty transformed itself into pity for her. Had her break-up with Travis left her more emotionally scarred than Rachael had known? *Had she truly loved him?* Was that in some way tied to her current state of uber thinness?

The last few hours of Rachael's shift dragged by, and she was relieved once again when she could pull out her vacuum, lock the doors, and cash out for the day. She put the deposit together for Tracey who would be opening first thing in the morning and locked it up in the safe for the night. She exited via the backdoor where her car was parked outside. Travis lazily leaned against her door. After her run-in with Misty, she was in no mood to talk to Travis about it.

He always made a habit of waiting for her after her shift. He didn't like the idea of her exiting a backdoor in a poorly lit alley behind a row of stores. He'd voiced his concern over this part of her job to her on many occasions and it seemed tonight would be no different.

As if sensing her upset, he walked over to her and hugged her. "What's wrong?"

"I had a little run-in with Misty tonight."

"Sounds interesting. Did y'all get into it or something?"

"Just a little. I wanted to beat her up or at least curse her out over her telling me to 'enjoy her boyfriend', but that aside, no."

Travis was laughing.

"It really isn't funny."

"Not the part about you *enjoying her boyfriend*, but the part about you beating her up. Now, that's funny. I never pegged you for the fighting type. You've been spending too much time with Shannah."

"Laugh if you will, but the only thing that kept me from doing it was her frail, super skinny, half-starved appearance."

"What?" Travis stopped abruptly, his hand on her shoulder.

"She looked bad, Travis, like warmed over. That bad. Emaciated."

"That's not good- at all."

"No and even though I've never liked her, I'm not going to pretend that I ever did or will, I'd never wish that on anyone. Not even her."

"That's because you're a good person."

"She even had some sores on her face and arms. She looked downright sick. Do you think it could be anorexia?"

"Not with the sores. I think it's meth."

"Meth?" Rachael exclaimed.

"As in, crystal meth, Rachael."

Rachael had heard of crystal meth. She knew it was a drug. She knew it was addictive. She knew that it was a real problem for kids, especially in rural Florida. Once she'd read an article referring to a few Florida towns as the crystal meth capitals of the United States. But that was all she knew.

If Misty was on meth it was even worse than Rachael had initially thought.

"I have to tell my parents. Maybe they can call hers. They've known each other for a long time."

Rachael was fine with Travis' parents calling Misty's parents and all, but she didn't want him rushing to Misty's rescue or anything else. She trusted him, but she in no way thought it was his duty to help Misty.

"That sounds like a good idea. Maybe I can call Honey and see if she knows anything."

"Great idea."

Rachael hugged him and climbed into her own car. When she made the turn into her own driveway, Travis sailed right on past merely honking his 'goodnight'. Rachael had a sinking feeling in the pit of her stomach. He'd never done that before. He'd always followed her home and kissed her goodnight before driving away. Tonight he hadn't taken the time. He must've been going home to tell his parents the news about Misty. *Does he still have feelings for her?*

Rachael stormed into the house. She was annoyed but wasn't even sure why. She stomped into the kitchen and warmed the plate her mother had left on the counter for her. She ate like a ravaged animal, barely tasting the lasagna. She rinsed her plate and put it in the dishwasher. She walked down the hall and to her bedroom. Opening her laptop, she decided it would be a good time to catch up on some email.

There was a new one from Ellery in West Palm. They hadn't spoken in a while and she was glad to have something to occupy her thoughts.

Hi Rach,

How are things going? So much to fill you in on. I've decided to apply to UF. There is an amazing pharmaceutical program there. TJ has no idea what he wants to study yet, but he is applying too. We have a four year plan- college, then marriage, and eventually kids and life. We've got it all planned out!

Brittany is still not overly friendly with me. It will never be the way it was before I started dating TJ- and she stabbed you in the back by dating Colten. I don't trust her and she doesn't trust me. I guess some friendships aren't meant to last forever. It hurts, even now after all this time. I kept hoping it would get easier, but it hasn't. I don't hate her or even dislike her, I just don't trust her. My mom says that trust, once it's lost, is hard to get back. She's right.

I miss you so much girl! There are days when I come running home wanting to share something with you- in person- and I am still bummed when the realization hits that you are not moving back. I just wanted you to know that you are on my mind and that I love you. Take care of yourself and don't be a stranger.

Hugs & Kisses,
Ellery

Rachael heard Travis' truck pull up outside.
Well it's about time.

Rachael glanced at the clock. It had only been twenty minutes. He must have driven home to tell his parents and then come right back. Rachael couldn't believe the feeling of relief that washed over her. He hadn't gone on home for the night, without saying goodbye. *Without kissing me...* Her bedroom door opened and there he was.

"Your brother let me in." He raked his hand through his hair. "Can I come in?"

"Sure."

He sat down on the edge of the bed.

"I only went home to tell my parents about Misty."

"I kind of figured that out."

"I felt like if I told them tonight, my mom could call ASAP. It's only ten o'clock."

"I think her parents probably know there's something wrong with her. Her appearance says it all."

"Sounds like it. Rachael," He patted the bed next to him. "Come sit with me."

Rachael did as he asked.

"I don't want you to get the wrong idea here. I'm concerned for her, the way you'd be if you heard something horrible had happened to Colten. But please don't mistake my concern for Misty for deeper feelings. I don't love her anymore and that is that. I just wouldn't want any harm to come to her or anyone else for that matter."

"Okay."

"You're upset with me."

"Not upset. I think I'm more upset with myself. I was actually jealous you might want to rush over and check on her. Be her rescuer or something."

"That's not my place. She has parents and friends."

"And you're not bothered by my insane jealously where you're concerned."

"It's understandable. She does try to provoke you every chance she gets."

"Thanks for coming back to say goodnight." Rachael squeezed his hand.

"Who said anything about saying goodnight? Come lay down with me."

"That's probably not a good idea, Travis."

"Nope, it's fine. I asked my parents and your aunt on my way down the hall. Besides we have a chaperone."

"Hello there." Michael waved from the doorway, sleeping bag in hand. He walked in and laid it down on the floor. "No smooching now. I'll be listening."

"You're too much." Rachael glared at her brother.

"You've had a rough couple of days. I wanted to hold you a little bit. I'm not staying the night. Just a few hours." He cuddled up behind her and held her snuggly.

"And you told your parents this?"

"That I was coming over to hold you?" He asked.

"Yes."

"Of course. My mother thought it was so sweet- as long as there was a chaperone."

"When will we progress past the point of needing a chaperone?"

"When you stop pressuring me to change our purity pledge." He teased.

"Travis! You knew I was joking about that! You didn't tell your parents that did you!"

"Sure did, you Vixen trying to lead me astray!"

"You didn't!"

"Of course not. But I did want to talk to you about something."

"Sounds serious."

"Next week, when I'm eighteen, we won't need a chaperone anymore. My parents trust us fully."

"About time."

"So you're ready for that."

"Yep. I trust us, fully."

"I *am* down here! Remember?" Michael protested from his pallet on the floor.

"How could we forget?" Rachael threw her pillow at him.

"No nookie talk with me in the room."

"We're not discussing nookie." Rachael hollered in Michael's direction.

Travis elbowed her in the side.

"Let's talk about the kids we'll have someday. And baby names." Rachael giggled.

"Baby Michael. Or Susan. I've always liked the name Susan." Travis added.

"I may vomit here!" Michael yelled and made vomiting sounds from where he covered his head with a pillow.

After that Rachael drifted off to sleep. Travis left sometime in the night. He'd covered Rachael with her quilt and carried Michael to his bedroom.

*

When Rachael awoke he'd even left her a sweet note on the bedside table.

"Good morning. If you're not busy today, my mom said she needs your help with something. <3 T"

What could she need my help with?

Rachael dressed and did her chores. She really had no idea what it could be, but she got in her car and drove over to the Baxter's house anyhow.

"Mornin', Rachael." Mr. Baxter greeted her as he started his truck and climbed in. "Travis is in the kitchen. Don't hold him up too long. Daylight's a wastin', and we've got work to do."

"No, sir. I won't."

Rachael walked into the kitchen where Travis finished the last of his ham biscuit.

"Got the note."

"Have fun. I'm going to build fence." He leaned and kissed her on the cheek. "Don't worry. Knowing you, I'm sure it's not what you think it is."

"I hope not." She admitted.

Out in the barn, earlier that same morning while feeding the animals, and then on the drive over, Rachael ran through her head over and over again the various topics that Mrs. Baxter might need her help with. Rachael knew she and Travis were getting more serious in their relationship. She could only imagine the endless possibilities Mrs. Baxter wanted to discuss with her. Her lack of regular church attendance, for one. She was sure that would eventually be at the top of the conversation list. Mrs. Baxter waltzed into the kitchen and fixed herself a cup of tea.

"So Travis gave you the message about helping me plan his birthday party."

"His birthday party?" Rachael breathed easily for the first time that morning. "He sure did." *A little white lie...*

That goober! Paybacks are hell Travis Baxter...

"I thought with them being twins and all, it's important that they each have something different. Something each of them would enjoy that celebrates their individuality. It's his eighteenth birthday and I want it to be special. Maysie wants a beach day complete with cookout and friends. Travis hasn't gotten specific, but together there must be something we can come up with." She sipped her tea. "And a renegotiation of his purity pledge is out of the question." She smiled.

Rachael could feel her face burning from her hairline to her collar.

He didn't...

"No need to be embarrassed. It was his idea. He asked weeks ago. He figured it was worth a try, but of course his father said no. All guys try."

"Weeks ago?" And Rachael had thought it had been her idea and a joke. Little did she know- he'd seriously asked his parents...weeks ago.

"Yes, about four weeks ago. Not only did I tell him that I wasn't going for it, but I knew you wouldn't either."

"Definitely not. What is it with guys and the physical side of the relationship? It's more important to them than it should be. I don't get it. First Gabe, and now, Travis." Rachael pulled a chair out, slunk down into it, and put her hands on her forehead. Maybe Travis hadn't been pressuring her...up until now...but was it coming? This certainly wasn't a conversation she'd planned on having with his mother on a Saturday morning in August. A church talk would've been nothing compared to this.

"It's important to all young men, and men in general for that matter, wait until you're married. That being said it's up to the woman to set the pace for all things physical in a relationship. My mother taught me that."

"I'll remember that. I think I'm going to kick his butt."

"Oh honey, he's just a man, a young man but still a man. I shouldn't have mentioned it, but I thought I should in case he brought it up."

"Well he hasn't." Rachael spat, a little more tension in her voice than she'd wanted. "Thanks for the warning."

When I brought it up the other day, I had no idea how accurate I was! What are we going to do when we don't have a chaperone? Am I going to be constantly telling him no? What gives?

"I just don't get it. He knows about Amber and how that ended up. Why would he even want to go there?"

"I think that's a question you need to ask him. I think he's thinking about something different than what you're thinking."

"Oh. Good."

Are we really having this conversation? So what? I'm thinking sex and he's thinking all the stuff leading up to it?

"He wants to marry you, Rachael, and most young couples find themselves asking the same question. If we're getting married anyway, why wait for everything? What does it matter? It's just a matter of time, right?"

Rachael nodded her head seeing his mother's point.

"But then as a parent or a girlfriend you can make another valid point. You're not married until you're married. Intimacy is a gift from God that is meant to be shared with your life partner and no one else."

"You're right." Rachael felt mortified.

I could just die. I'm going to kill you, Travis Baxter! Kill you!

Maysie walked into the kitchen and pulled out a chair.

"What are you two talking about so intensely?"

Rachael gave her *the don't ask* look.

"Oh! Is it the true love waits conversation? It looks like it's your lucky day, Rachael!" Maysie beamed.

Shannah sprang down the stairs and breezed in to the kitchen. Rachael didn't even realize she was there!

"Seriously? Are you all in on this?" Rachael sounded perplexed.

"No. Not really." Shannah poured herself a cup of coffee. "Discussing your sex life, or lack thereof, holds no interest for me at 8:30 on a Saturday." Shannah sat down. She winked over the rim of her mug, "Although- I've got to admit this is classic. A no 'it' talk with your two best friends and future mother-in-law. It doesn't get much better than that."

"Joke all you want ladies, but this is serious business."

"You don't have to warn me." Maysie grinned widely. "I've had the pleasure of this chat, Mama, at least three times."

"Me, too. When your mom gets pregnant at fifteen this is all you ever hear about!"

"At least I'm not alone." Rachael muttered unenthusiastically.

"If it makes you feel any better- I called your mom and spoke with her about it before talking to you. I didn't know if it would bother her if I brought it up."

"Fantastic. I'm glad she was okay with it- really. Thank you for talking to me, but Travis has been a true gentleman. He has never pressured me or even asked about anything like this." Rachael felt the need to defend him here. She didn't want him getting a bad rap. If he'd asked his parents, maybe he'd expected them to keep it between them. Wouldn't he see his mother speaking with her as a sort of betrayal? Rachael couldn't be sure.

"We didn't think he had. I was just warning you woman to woman. So let's get back to the birthday party planning."

Rachael sighed. If she didn't love Travis she would've run from this house! "I don't know if I can."

"Oh, Rachael. If all goes according to plan, you'll be my daughter-in-law someday. We will discuss all sorts of things- this is only the tip of the iceberg…so to speak."

Mrs. Baxter gave Rachael a much needed hug and left the room.

"You okay?" Maysie slid her chair closer to Rachael's.

"I think so. Travis hadn't prepared me for this little chat."

"He probably didn't know this little chat was coming."

"I think you handled it well. My parents are very upfront."

"I'll say." Shannah blurted. "Y'all aren't those crazies that have 'it' through a sheet and all when you get married are you?"

"Of course not, Shannah! We're Christian. I have no idea what religion you're referencing." Maysie defended her faith.

"I'm glad you don't have another brother, because I wouldn't want to be on the receiving end of that talk." Shannah confided.

"It really wasn't that bad. I appreciate it in a way. Travis stayed over for a few hours last night." At their shocked expressions, Rachael added, "And nothing happened! Absolutely nothing. No pressure. Nothing. Nada. Zip. Zilch. That is why this conversation caught me so off-guard."

"What are you going to do?"

"Nothing. I'm not going to bring it up unless he does. He's done nothing wrong here. He's never pressured me. So, I'm aware he's had these thoughts, that's all. I knew he'd felt *this way* since last year, but acting on it…a desire to do so…is totally new."

Rachael mulled this over a bit. No wonder he was still so uneasy about not having a chaperone after all this time. Maybe he needed to prove to himself that he could uphold his side of the purity pledge.

"I think it's time to unleash a new covert operation here." Shannah pursed her lips. "I think it should be called Operation Avoid Nookie with Travis Baxter."

All the girls started laughing.

Mrs. Baxter came back into the room.

"Let's party plan! I think some sort of paint balling party would be perfect."

"Great idea." Maysie squealed. She kicked Rachael underneath the table.

"Definitely, a paint ball party!"

"Maybe Gabe will come and I can shoot him where it hurts!" Shannah sounded excited by this prospect.

"Yes! We can all shoot Gabe!" Maysie cheered.

They talked on and on about the party, the guest list, and all of the details. School would start in a week and the party would be held the last Saturday of summer break. Rachael knew it would be a huge success. She suggested they invite Amber, but everyone felt that paintballing wouldn't be appropriate or safe for an expectant mother. After hearing their thoughts on the subject, Rachael had to agree.

Instead Rachael, Maysie, and Shannah opted to plan a second party suitable for Amber. An all-girls, back-to-school slumber party with most of their friends from the dance team. Even Mrs. Baxter showed her support of Amber and said she thought it was a fantastic idea.

*

A few short days later, girls began arriving for the slumber party at Rachael's house. It had been a long time since they had seen each other. Rachael hadn't finished the dance season the year before due to her embarrassing escapades which resulted in her being suspended from the team, but she planned on trying out again as soon as the school year started.

Their previous dance captain, Trisha, had graduated last year and as seniors there was a good chance that one of the girls at her slumber party tonight would be selected as captain by the band director. Rachael felt nervous about the upcoming try-outs and hoped she would make the team again. The other dancers had tried out at the end of the season, but Rachael hadn't been eligible to try-out at that time. Yet she hoped she would get one of two coveted spots, left vacant by Amber and another friend who had moved away.

Rachael considered the slumber party invitation list. She'd gone out on a limb and even invited Honey. She decided she needed to reach out to her regarding Misty and hoped that together they would all be able to help her.

Around eight o'clock sixteen girls had arrived. That was most of the squad minus Honey, Misty, Selena, and Alex. While Rachael wasn't shocked that Honey and Misty had chosen not to come, and Selena was out of town, the real shocker was Alex. Alex and Rachael were very close friends. Alex had even sent an RSVP text saying she would be there, yet here it was eight o'clock and she hadn't arrived. Rachael disappeared down the hall to her bedroom and checked her voicemail. Nothing. Just then, a text came in. It was from Alex.

'Not going to make. So sorry. Tell everyone I said hi!'

Back in the living room, Maysie led a line dancing session. Even Amber, at nearly nine months pregnant, was up and joining in the fun. The evening continued with an American Idol style karaoke contest with judges and everything. Rachael had gone down to Michael's room to recruit both he and Levi to serve as the judges. Her Aunt Margaret was the third. Rachael armed each of them with dry erase boards and markers. The real highlight of the night was when her own mother got up and sang Sir Mix-a-Lots *Baby Got Back*! Rachael had never known her mother to be a fan of rap or hip hop- and there she was rapping! She knew every word!

Rachael and her friends laughed so hard they nearly fell over. Michael, Levi and Aunt Margaret named Amber and Jody the winners for their duet of the theme song from the movie *Titanic.* Everyone crashed around three o'clock in the morning. Dawn came quickly and so did a few of the parents.

Rachael was surprised when the doorbell chimed before eight. It was Lisa's mother. She was there to pick up Lisa, Marcey, and Tina. Rachael thought it strange she would be coming this early to pick the girls up, but assumed they must have something important to do. Then as the doorbell chimed again, this time nearing nine o'clock, Rachael opened the door to Jen's mother. She looked very agitated.

"You have some nerve, Rachael Harte. I should've expected as much from you with your own father being in prison."

The lady swept past Rachael and called for Jen to grab her bags and meet her outside. Rachael was at a loss for words, as both Jen and Gina rushed past her with their sleeping bags and overnight bags in hand.

"Bye, Rachael. Thanks! It was fun." Jen whispered.

"Thanks for coming." Rachael called to her turned back and shut the door. She knew immediately what this was all about. *Amber.*

Was I wrong to invite Amber? She was pregnant, but that didn't mean she'd changed. She was still the same sweet person she'd always been. Rachael fought back tears and the hateful attack Jen's mother had made against her, her own father, and family. Rachael walked into the kitchen and got out orange juice and donuts for the remaining guests. Savannah, Caitlin, Jody,

Maysie, and Shannah attempted small talk to distract Amber from what just transpired, but to no avail. They'd all witnessed the scene at the door.

"Thanks guys for this wonderful display of friendship. I had fun. I truly did. My mother texted me and will be here in a few minutes." Amber was on the verge of tears.

Rachael hugged her friend, "I'm sorry."

Amber wiped away the tears trickling down her face. "Don't be. I'm not. This was one of the nicest things anyone has done for me. Thank you for being true friends and including me in your sleepover."

All of the girls went over, one by one, hugging Amber and wishing her well. Her mother arrived. Everyone helped her carry her things outside and load them in her car. She drove away.

"When is she due?" Caitlin asked.

"A few weeks." Maysie answered.

"I don't know about you guys, but I'm pissed." Shannah spat. "I can't believe how Jen's mom behaved toward Rachael."

"It's one thing not to want your daughter here, but it's something entirely different to attack another girl."

"She should've just picked her daughter up and taken her home."

"I guess I should've told all of the parents on the invite about Amber's pregnancy." Rachael muttered.

"No, it's each girl's responsibility to share that with their parents. Then, if their parents wouldn't allow them to come, then so be it." Jody advised.

"Jody's right. I told my mom. She didn't have a problem with it." Savannah added.

"I disagree." Shannah hissed. "Why should anyone have to take out an ad? I think it's ridiculous! Maybe everybody could have mentioned it to their mom, but either way there is no excusing her behavior."

"What's done, is done." Maysie surmised. "Let's go back inside and finish breakfast."

Most of the remaining girls were seniors, as well, and had driven themselves to the party. Everyone finished breakfast, packed up, and went home. Rachael, Maysie, and Shannah sat discussing the morning's events a few hours later on the back porch.

"I just don't understand. Jen's mom is supposedly this super Christian member of our church. We preach forgiveness…and that babies are a blessing…and all that other stuff. Then she shows up here and attacks poor Rachael." Maysie scowled.

"She didn't behave like a super Christian this morning. She behaved like a super jerk." Shannah verified.

"Don't worry about it guys. I knew along the way there would be those people who wouldn't approve of me based on my family and my father being in prison. It didn't come as a surprise." Rachael smiled tightly.

But no matter how much Rachael tried to reassure them, she knew deep down it had hurt her. *Am I going to be judged by the mistakes of my father and wrongly accused?* What she'd done in having Amber over had come from the heart, from some place good. For it to be turned into something ugly was upsetting.

       *

She spent the afternoon lying in the loft listening to music. She heard boots clomping up the steps, shuffling across the wood floor of the loft. Without even opening her eyes she knew it was him.

Travis lay down beside her in the hay.

"Want to talk about it?"

"Nope. You were right."

"Not entirely. I was wrong about the fact that most of the girls' parents didn't have a problem with it. Only a handful of the parents did."

"Yes, five to be exact."

"Are you okay?"

"Yes." Rachael knew she was lying, and that if she opened her eyes and actually made eye contact he would know the truth.

"My mom called Jen's mom and gave her an earful." He rolled onto his side.

"She did?"

"Yes, she did. She told her she was wrong and had behaved wrongly toward a young lady who deserved her kindness. There was a whole lot of scripture quoting in there, too."

"It was nice of her to defend Amber that way."

"It wasn't Amber she was defending, Rachael. It was you."

Shocked, Rachael couldn't speak. She hadn't told her own mother yet about what had happened because she'd been at work this morning and still was. Here was Travis' mother defending her.

After the conversation the other day Rachael knew just how serious she'd been when she mentioned their future together. Rachael had become much more to his family than just his girlfriend, she was family.

Rachael rolled over to face him, lying on her side. He reached his hand out and cupped her cheek.

"You did the right thing. Aside from a few crazy women, I heard the party was a total and complete success."

"It was. Amber is due in a few weeks. Then she will begin the difficult step of continuing her life and moving forward from this. I plan on being there by her side, every step of the way."

"I wouldn't want it any other way."

Rachael and Travis lay in the loft until dinnertime chatting about his birthday party that would take place in a few days- and the reward placed on Gabe's head. She, Maysie, and Shannah agreed that any girl that could take him out would receive a gift certificate for a pedicure. While he didn't laugh, she knew him well enough to know that Travis thought it was hilarious.

Chapter Six

The day of Travis' birthday party arrived. Anybody and everybody had been invited, with the exception of Misty. Travis' very own mother had sent the invitations, and for reasons of her own she thought it would be inappropriate for her to attend.

Rachael, Maysie, and Shannah went shopping the night before and purchased camo pants and matching tank tops. They wrote on them with a pink glitter, gel pen Team High Caliber in the spirit of paintballing. When they pulled into the parking lot and parked it didn't take them long to see that most everyone had come.

Most of the dance team and cheerleaders were present, as were the football players. Shannah locked eyes with Gabe- and there by his side was Heather.

"She's taller than I thought she'd be." Shannah noticed aloud.

"And blonder, too." Rachael added.

"She's not that tall, but she certainly is blonde. Perhaps Miss Clairol box number 101 if I had to guess." Maysie countered.

"Not compared to you she's not that tall, but not all of us are amazon women with strikingly long legs. And the hair- you're right. She's not a natural blonde. I should've brought a date. One who was hot, with big muscles." Shannah snarled.

"To a paintball birthday party?" Rachael smirked. "Come on, Shannah. You could outshoot her any day."

"True. Maybe I'll take her out while I'm at it." Shannah's eyes narrowed at Clay and Travis standing near Gabe and Heather. "What are they doing fraternizing with the enemy?"

Rachael had to laugh at her use of the word fraternizing. So Shannah… to pull out the big vocab word.

"My brother's not the enemy and neither is Clay. They're friends with Gabe, and while even they think he has seriously messed up, they've been friends for a long time."

"Whatever-but goldilocks over there is mine. No one take her out but me. Got it?"

"Got it." Maysie glanced at Rachael, arching a brow. "But keep it fair. Only shooting in the safe zones. Don't take her eye out or anything."

"She'll have goggles." Shannah countered.

"Am I going to have to hogtie you?" Maysie asked.

"Maybe, but not yet." Shannah grinned.

Shannah walked toward the equipment shed to get suited up. Her purposeful strides and quickened steps conveyed her mood.

"Something tells me we're in for a long day."

"Don't you know it! I've never seen her this mad." Maysie thought about it. "Never."

Rachael started to follow Shannah across the parking lot, Maysie in tow, and paused a third of the way to the shed.

"You go on. I'm going to go say hi to Travis."

She turned to see Travis coming across the parking lot toward her.

"Hey." He greeted sheepishly. He appeared anxious, like he was in trouble or something.

"I'm not mad at you for standing with Gabe." She admitted.

"I know but I didn't expect you to have to walk over there and say hi to him and his new girlfriend either." He glanced around behind her, scanning the parking lot.

"What's up? Are you looking for someone?"

He nodded his head.

"Who?"

"Rach, I've got to tell you something. Heather said Misty plans on stopping by."

"She wasn't invited."

"No she wasn't, but you know Misty. That's never seemed to matter in the past."

"Well, that figures."

"What?"

"That she and Heather would be friends. Birds of a feather and all that. I guess the same could be said of mean girls."

He sighed, "I don't want her here either, but what do you expect me to do?"

"Throw her out."

"I can't do that. Then I'd be no better than the women who so harshly judged you recently."

"Do what you want, Travis. I've gotta go."

Rachael turned and walked toward the shed. In seconds he caught up to her placing his hands on her upper arms, gently stopping her.

"Rachael, please don't be angry with me."

"If the situation were reversed and Colten showed up at my birthday party- you'd expect me to tell him to leave. It's not appropriate. She's no longer your girlfriend. She's not nice and she's a druggy."

"We don't know that last part, so we shouldn't spread it around."

"And now you're protecting her? Unbelievable." Rachael shoved past Travis continuing toward the shed.

She saw a sleek sports car pull into the lot. The doors opened, both Honey and Misty climbed out.

Travis caught up to her once more. She heard his footsteps behind her. She didn't stop walking, and merely tossed over her shoulder, "And now you'll get the chance to tell Misty because there she is." Rachael smirked in Misty's general direction. "Or should I ask her to leave?"

Rachael turned and strode toward the shed to join Maysie and Shannah inside. Their mouths looked pursed, jaws clenched tightly. Shannah's lips were moving in a flurry of words that couldn't be considered polite or delicate.

"Rachael? Where are you going?" Travis called.

"I trust you to handle it. I'm going to join my team."

Rachael selected everything she needed. She pulled on the pants and long-sleeved shirt. She watched as Travis made his way over to Misty and Honey. He was courteous in typical Travis fashion, but they couldn't hear what he was saying.

"They look like ghosts of their former selves." Maysie said.

"Yah. All frail and stuff." Shannah commented. "Weak. I like the odds, ladies."

Rachael placed a calming hand on Shannah's shoulder.

"Nope. I'm tired of dealing with her. Showing up at his house and stuff. Then there's what she said to me at the store. He needs to make it clear to her he's moved on. I'm above getting in some fight with her over him. If he hasn't made it clear he should. Then, if after that, she's rude with me, well that will be a different story." Rachael picked up her paintball gun and lowered her goggles.

Maysie and Shannah followed suit. All three of them stood liked armed guards at the entrance to the paintball field. They continued to watch Travis' conversation with Misty from afar.

"Whatever he's saying- it's getting heated." Shannah observed.

"Maybe I should go over." Maysie offered.

"No, ladies- give him a chance." Rachael ordered.

Misty was screaming at the top of her lungs about Travis' choice of white trash over her. Shannah made a movement to cross the parking lot. Rachael stopped her with her hand.

"No. I'll go."

Just then they heard Travis tell Misty to *go home.*

"You and I are over and will never be again." He yelled, "I'm in love with Rachael Harte and I will marry her." His finger was a mere centimeter from her nose, his expression conveyed fury. "And if you ever so much as step foot on any of our places- I'll have you arrested."

He stepped around Misty and opened her car door. Honey came over and grabbed Misty, pushing her inside the car. Travis whirled and stomped toward where Rachael stood, mouth gaping. He reached her in five long strides.

"How was that?" He barked.

"Good job." Rachael wasn't sure what else to say, but words weren't needed. He was kissing her in a way that conveyed he meant every word of what he'd just said to Misty. "And if pretty boy ever shows up again I'll expect the same. Now that we're clear on that- let's go have a party." He winked and tugged her along with him to join his friends.

Everyone was divided into groups of six. Rachael didn't know about anyone else, but she was roasting in the paintball gear. Travis and several of the guys only had on t-shirts and pants.

"Where's your hotter-than-hades gear?"

"We don't need protection- we're that good." He attested.

Rachael just rolled her eyes at him.

"Oh, and try not to kill Gabe." He teased.

He ran off toward his group, which of course included Gabe. Rachael looked around and saw Heather seated safely in the stands outside of the fenced-in field.

"Too bad." Shannah waved to her.

"Stop it!" Maysie squealed.

Rachael grabbed them both by the arms and headed for a blind she'd spied off in a far corner. Along the way, they received a lot of fire but managed to avoid getting hit by ducking behind obstacles along their path.

The girls found themselves squatting behind a climbing wall, occasionally firing around the sides and top, still an overwhelming twenty yards from the blind.

"What are we doing?" Maysie yelled.

"We're trying to make it to that blind in the corner." Rachael pointed it out to the others.

"We'll never make it. The guys are closing in on our location and I think they're down to two teams. With the other teams numbering six players each we are seriously outnumbered." Shannah observed.

"Okay, I've got an idea." Rachael offered. "You and Maysie make a run for it. I'll play decoy."

"Just get in the blind and wait for them to close in. I like it." Shannah said. "Then, I can pick them off one at a time."

"Go." Rachael jumped up and stepped out into the open, firing upon the guys on the other side of the hill. They shot her numerous times and she fell to the ground, holding her ankle.

Travis rushed over and his team halted fire.

"You okay?"

"I think I might have twisted my ankle." Rachael lay there in exaggerated agony, holding her ankle, and wincing in pain.

While Travis tended to Rachael and her ankle, three guys on his team got shot and were out of the game. It was now down to Clay, Travis, and Gabe. Rachael glanced over her shoulder at the girls who'd disappeared from sight into the blind.

"I think I'll be all right now." She jumped to her feet not even attempting a limp.

"Something tells me you were never injured in the first place." Gabe narrowed his eyes at her.

"It's probably just the adrenaline and all that, I'm sure it'll be killing me later." Rachael shrugged her shoulders and walked away. She could hear the exchange between Gabe and Travis where they hid on the opposite side of the climbing wall the girls had used as shelter only moments earlier.

"You gonna let her get away with that, man?" Gabe asked Travis.

"It was a smart tactical maneuver if you ask me. We're the idiots that fell for it."

While Rachael had been eliminated from the competition, she saw no reason why she couldn't still be out there. She worked her way around to the blind where she went in to sit with Shannah and Maysie.

"Are you okay?" Maysie asked alarmed.

"I'm fine."

"She was faking it goober." Shannah added dryly.

"We're cheaters!" Maysie exclaimed. "And cheaters never win."

"No really- my ankle got twisted on the way down. It's a little sore, nothing else."

"That makes me feel better." Maysie admitted. "I'm glad you're actually hurt."

"That our friend is actually injured?" Shannah held her finger to her lips. "They're coming, I can smell Gabe's cologne. Eau de stink."

Maysie looked out the cutout and spied Clay running toward the blind. She shot him in the upper thigh, paint splattering on his leg. He fell to the ground and lay there playing dead. A shot sailed in through the back slit in the blind and hit Shannah square in the back.

"Crap!"

"Take him out, Maysie!"

Maysie whirled around and planted a paint ball square in her brother's chest.

"Killed by my own sister! On my birthday!"

"It's my birthday, too. We're twins remember?"

There was silence from outside. No breathing or movement from anywhere.

"Where's Gabe?" Rachael whispered.

Shannah looked out the back, while Maysie looked out the right, and Rachael the left.

"I don't know. I can't smell him anymore." Shannah's eyes narrowed. "It's all up to you now, Maysie. Don't let us down."

"Oh I won't." Maysie gripped the stock of her paint ball gun. All of the girls listened in silence. After more than half an hour they began to lose patience and decided they may have to evacuate the blind.

"We could sit in here all day and Gabe may never attack us. I think he's waiting for us to come out." Shannah whispered.

Just then, the blind collapsed on the girls. Everyone screamed in the darkness fighting to get free. Rachael found a hole and pushed through it. Gabe let out a roar and pelted her with paintballs.

"I'm already dead, you jerk!"

In all the commotion Gabe hadn't seen Maysie sneak out the back of the blind just before it collapsed. She was right behind him.

"But I'm not!" Maysie opened fire shooting him in his butt more than five times. Gabe fell to the ground in faked agony, holding his own backside.

"Okay, Maysie. You got me! You win!"

"One more for good measure, just to make sure." Maysie splattered a final paint ball across his backside and turned to see who else pursued her. No one appeared to challenge her and Maysie was the self-declared winner.

"Let's go celebrate our victory." She announced.

Rachael jumped up and walked right over Gabe, narrowly missing stepping on his body. Shannah followed the same route, narrowly bypassing his outstretched hand.

"Please Shannah, be cool. Can't we at least be friends?"

"A real friend would've had the guts to break up with me face to face. No thank you."

Chapter Seven

Rachael sat cross-legged on the floor of Taffy's stall late one afternoon.

"Hold still, Taffy." She griped aloud.

Taffy lowered her nose to sniff the nail polish Rachael brushed on her left hoof. She sneezed blowing a little snot and spit on Rachael's hand.

"Gross!" Rachael brushed the slime off her forearm.

Taffy stamped her hoof in protest sending sawdust and wood chips scattering. There was a fine dusting now stuck in her polish. Rachael exhaled and blew her bangs out of her eyes.

"What are you doing, now?" Shannah stood at the stall gate, arms resting on top, wearing a smirk.

"Painting Taffy's nails. What does it look like?"

"They're hooves, not nails." Shannah laughed. "So are you going to the dance tryout next week?"

"I am. I hope they'll take me after the stunt I pulled last year."

"That was mostly Melinda's fault."

"Not really. I played my part in it as well. She never forced me to skip practice."

"True. Speaking of Melinda, she just moved away. Justin joined the military and they eloped."

"Eloped! Talk about crazy." Rachael jumped to her feet trying to absorb what she just heard. "Eloped?"

"I guess she got her GED this summer. Just like that, she's gone."

The sound of an unfamiliar truck pulling up the driveway caught both of their attention. Travis was working branding last year's heifers with Mr. Baxter today on the ranch, so Rachael knew it couldn't have been him. She stood brushing the sawdust from her jammy pants and butt. She unlatched the stall door and patted Taffy once more before leaving her for the evening.

"Aren't you going to turn her out?"

"No. It looks like rain."

The girls walked back up to the house and around the side. In the front yard JJ's Honcho sat idling in the driveway. It'd been a while since Rachael had last seen him. He cut the engine and climbed out. His face looked bleak and Rachael couldn't imagine what could've brought him over in such a state.

He was wearing jeans and boots. They were caked in mud and what looked like crap, cow crap. He usually wore shorts, no shirt, and no shoes. Rachael knew attired like this, and as filthy as he was, there was only one place he could've come from.

The cowpens on Baxter Ranch.

"Hello, Miss Rachael." He took off his hat and held it in his hands. "I wish I could say this was a social visit, but it ain't."

"What's wrong? Is Travis okay?"

"He's fine but whilst we wus in the pens this mornin' he got hurt."

Rachael's heart ached and panic filled her mind, sending it reeling. "What kind of hurt?"

"He was manning the head catch and a cow swung her head grazin' his side. You know how it can be taggin' and dewormin', Miss Rachael. It's dangerous work. Think he needs a few stitches is all. He's up at the hospital now."

Rachael realized that even after her summer working on the ranch and part of last school year as well, she had no idea what JJ was talking about. She'd spent most of her time building fences, both board and barbed wire. She'd also become an expert in all things related to barn cleaning. She'd even spent time in the saddle working cattle, but she'd never set foot in the cowpens. *What is a head catch?*

"Let me get changed, JJ."

"I've come to give you a ride. Mrs. Baxter and Maysie are already on their way to the hospital."

"I'll only be a minute."

Rachael ran inside and slipped on a pair of jeans, shirt, and grabbed a hair tie. She washed her face and hands. She grabbed her perfume and sprayed her neck and dabbed some at both wrists. A quick tooth brushing and swish of mouthwash would have to suffice.

A light rap on the doorjamb, she glanced and saw Michael. She spit into the sink.

"Come on. Travis is at the hospital. He got hurt and we're going to see him."

"What kind of hurt?"

"Something about a cow cutting his side."

"He got gored!"

"Not gored. Really, Michael? I hope not."

"Sorry, Rachael- I'm just shocked."

"Grab your shoes and meet me outside."

Rachael sprinted up the hall and back out the front door. It had taken her less than five minutes, but felt like an eternity. Shannah must've gone home in light of the situation, her jeep was already gone from the front yard. Michael closed the front door and jumped in JJ's truck beside her, careful not to spill the spit can on the front seat.

"Pass me that ther' can, Michael." JJ took the can and dumped it outside on the ground, tossing the empty can in the back of the truck bed. While normally that might have made Rachael squeamish, she was far too concerned about Travis to concern herself with a pile of spit in her driveway.

Things raced through her mind. In the two years she'd known Travis, she'd never heard of anyone getting seriously injured on the Baxter Ranch. Sure, she'd heard the ranch hands grumble about getting tagged, also known as getting kicked, while legging calves…or nicking their fingers marking calves' ears and all, but no substantial injuries. She herself had been bucked off of Creamsicle, and as a result suffered a concussion. Then there was the time she got the blister and a nasty splinter building fence. Of course, to Travis, those were very minor injuries, almost laughable with the exception of the concussion, which really seemed to worry him.

But this. Getting gored by a cow, this was something entirely different. Maybe she could convince him to take a desk job when they finished college. As soon as the idea formed in her head, she realized just how ridiculous it sounded. He'd never consider such a thing. He was a cowboy, through and through. A cowboy and a cattleman. The suggestion of him doing anything else was ridiculous.

JJ reached over and patted her hand.

"He's gonna be just fine, Miss Rachael. You'll see. He's had worse."

"Worse?"

"Well there was the time he got bucked off when he was five. The girth strap came loose after hours of riding. He wus young at the time. No one thought to retighten it. His saddle came loose and that horse went to buckin'. Launched him." JJ laughed.

Rachael couldn't see where this story was funny at all.

"He landed in a pile of saw palmettoes and hit a palmetto root with the weight of his body on his right arm. It broke."

Rachael looked horrified. "Broke his arm getting bucked off at five years old?"

"This is a working ranch. Ain't no preschool."

"His parents made him work cows at five years old? Was this on a pony?"

"No." JJ smiled. "Full sized horse. And there was no makin' him do anything. You couldn't leave that boy behind. Horses are to Travis like toy trucks or bikes are to other boys. He was something. I suspect y'all have one just like him. A whole lot physical and a little bit crazy."

Rachael wanted to protest.

Absolutely not. Not my son!

But she knew in her heart JJ was probably right. The apple didn't fall far from the tree was as true now as it was then. She was beginning to wonder if she'd be able to handle being married to a cowboy- and all that went with it. She didn't want to worry all the

69

time, but she didn't want to be married to a wimp either. She loved Travis, cowboy side of him and all.

She bit her bottom lip the remaining twenty or so miles to town, until the hospital came into view. She saw Travis' mothers SUV parked outside alongside his father's truck. JJ pulled up to the emergency entrance where Rachael and Michael jumped out. He drove off to go park.

Rachael was inside in less than three long strides. She scanned the lobby and waiting areas. There was no sign of the Baxters. At the information desk there was a retired nurse wearing a volunteer badge and nametag. It read Helen. Rachael's face must have communicated the dread she felt because the round faced, gray haired older woman merely handed her a visitor's pass.

"He said you'd be coming." She handed Michael one as well. "Take the hallway to your right. He's in the room waiting for the doctor. I'll buzz you back."

Rachael and Michael approached the double doors and waited until they heard the click of the door. It opened automatically, then closed behind them. She could hear his father's loud booming voice all the way out here and knew they must be nearby.

He was laughing, as was Mrs. Baxter, no doubt telling some insane story. Rachael followed the laughter and popped her head in. Travis lay on the bed, his head back and eyes closed.

"Try not to make me laugh. These ribs hurt like hell."

Mr. and Mrs. Baxter turned to greet Rachael, but she merely smiled their way. Her only concern right now was Travis. His eyes opened and the hazel flecks in his vivid green eyes met hers.

"Hey, you." He grinned.

She rushed over to his side. He was covered in a sheet up to his chest. A small smattering of black hair covered his amazing chest where it sat exposed at the sheet hemline.

"Hi, Michael. How are you?"

"Rethinking having accepted that job on the ranch during the weekends. How are you?"

Travis chuckled.

"Don't go and do that. Levi needs help with fence. I've gotta train you guys for while I'm off at college next year. Accidents like this don't happen all the time, and some we actually are able to laugh at down the road."

"I guess so." Michael didn't look convinced.

JJ appeared in the opened door.

"Well, I've seen yur alive. I'm going to ride back out to the ranch and put the horses away. Need anything else?"

"If you could water the cow dogs and feed them I'd appreciate it." Mr. Baxter advised him.

"Wanna ride with me?" JJ asked Michael.

"Can I?" He asked Rachael.

"Sure, Mom will be home from work around five o'clock. Make sure you text or call her if you're going to be later."

"Always do." Michael gave her a thumbs up, and disappeared with JJ down the hall.

"Where's Maysie?" Rachael asked.

"She and Tristan went to go finish working cows. Can't leave them standing in the pens overnight. They'll get stressed. It's one of the hottest Augusts on record." Mr. Baxter spoke like these were all things Rachael already knew. "Come on." He held his hand out to his wife. "Let's go get some food. Hungry Travis?"

"Starved."

Left alone, Rachael went over and kissed Travis' cheek. He reached up and held her jaw.

"It's not bad. I've had worse."

"So I've heard." Her voice was tight.

"Take a look. It'll make you feel better."

Rachael went to lift the sheet close to his waistline. He grabbed her wrist, stopping her.

"Don't pull that thing too low. You'll get an eyeful."

She glanced over at the chair in the corner where his crap covered jeans and shirt were draped. His boots and socks set just beneath it on the floor. She didn't see any undergarments- of any kind.

She put her hands on her hips and frowned. "Are you telling me you're naked under there?"

"I don't wear underwear, Rachael."

"What? Never?"

"Hate the things."

"And so now you're in here without ... drawers?"

For lack of a better word she used drawers. She'd never used that word in her entire life, but she felt odd saying underwear. Maybe she'd start using the word boxers instead. It was less personal, even she wore boxers. Just then a very attractive blonde haired nurse poked her head in to the room.

"In a few minutes I'll be taking you down for x-rays, Mr. Baxter." She chirped and then walked away.

"Thank you, Ma'am." He responded.

"I think not." Rachael scowled. "You're not going anywhere butt naked! Especially with some young, pretty nurse."

"Don't be ridiculous Rachael. She's a trained professional. She sees naked people all the time."

"Oh and so if I were laying around naked in a hospital bed wearing no pants, and some hottie walked in to take me for x-rays, you'd be okay with that?"

"Good point, but I never wear boxers or tightywhities ... nada. I wasn't exactly planning this injury. My mother just gave me the same speech, Rachael." He closed his eyes.

"I'm not happy."

She lifted the sheet, careful not to lower it too much, and saw the harsh line where the cow's horn had cut him. It was already stitched up, but was about five inches in length.

"See, it's nothing."

"It's not exactly nothing." Tears filled her eyes.

"It'll heal. We'll do some x-rays to check for broken ribs and then they'll send me on my way. You can play nurse." He smacked her backside.

"This is no time to joke, Travis. You're hurt and I hate it." She wiped a stray tear that ran down her cheek.

The nurse appeared at the door again with a wheelchair. She carried a hospital gown, one of the pale blue ones that had ties up the back.

"Please help him into this. I'll be back in two minutes." At Rachael's gaping stare she winked. "Or I could do it for you if you'd like to step outside."

She had a syrupy voice and Rachael immediately disliked her.

"Nope. I've got it." Rachael took the offered gown from her outstretched hand.

Travis chuckled from the bed.

"You'll have to help him sit up. Tie it in the back." The nurse instructed.

"Thanks."

She walked over and closed the door. They were alone once again.

"I can do it myself." Travis winced as he attempted to sit up.

"Be quiet. I'll just close my eyes."

"Why are you angry with me?"

"From now on, you have to wear underpants, of some sort."

"I don't think I've got anything she hasn't seen before."

Rachael decided to drop it for now, but the conversation was far from over. *What was he thinking?*

She walked over and helped him to sit up by using the automatic bed to lift his weight into a more upright position. While holding the sheet firmly in place he slowly swung his legs around to dangle just off the bed. He grasped the edge of the bed, teeth gritted, but never made a noise.

Rachael opened the gown and had Travis put his arms in it. Afterwards it was draped covering his lap to his upper thighs.

"Can you stand up?"

"My legs aren't broke if that's what you're asking."

"Ha. Ha." Rachael wasn't amused.

He gently shifted to the edge of the bed and stood up slowly.

"If they'd let us leave now, I could walk out of here."

"Not like this you couldn't."

"Hold the back of that gown closed." Rachael ordered.

She picked the sheet up from his feet where it'd fallen to the floor and folded it neatly placing it back on the foot of the bed.

"Could you hurry it up back there? I'm catching a chill." He teased.

Rachael rolled her eyes at him and started tying the top string near his shoulders. While his jeans and shirt were filthy, he still smelled of cologne, and a morning shower. She placed a light kiss on his bare shoulder above where the neckline exposed his skin.

"I wouldn't do that if I were you." He warned.

"That was a *I hope you feel better soon* peck. Nothing more."

"Too bad for me."

Rachael quickly tied the strings at the middle of his back. He let go of the back of the gown and she quickly turned away, catching a peek of his very nicely shaped butt.

He sat back down on the edge of the bed to steady himself. "Please grab the wheelchair."

His face looked pained and she could see he wasn't well. She thought he flashed her on purpose, but quickly realized something else was wrong. She quickly procured the wheelchair and brought it over to him. She ran to the door and called for the nurse who happened to be waiting just outside.

"I need your help to get him in the wheelchair."

She nodded and came into the room. After he was situated in the chair and the foot rests were placed under his feet, the nurse covered his lap and legs with a warmed hospital blanket. Travis closed his eyes.

"I'll wheel him down to radiology. We shouldn't be more than fifteen minutes or so."

"Okay." Rachael looked at him. He didn't look well. "Have you given him anything for pain?"

"Mary, the RN, did just before you came in. It should be kicking in shortly." At Rachael's concerned stare she added "He lost quite a bit of blood and once the meds kick in he'll be very sleepy."

Rachael kissed his cheek and could see what the blonde said was correct. He looked like he could pass out any moment. She wheeled him down the hall and through another set of double doors. They were gone.

Rachael went back in, spying the shirt on the chair. She looked at it from a distance. The nurse had said he'd lost quite a bit of blood. From where Rachael stood the side of the shirt facing up just looked dirty, muddied. She walked over and picked it up, opening it and holding it up to examine it more closely. The side facing down on the jeans was covered in blood.

Travis' blood.

It had a tear in it which could more accurately have been described as an actual hole. The cow had hooked him and then apparently raked her horn up, or down as the case may be, his side. His ribs were obviously bruised and maybe even broken. Rachael was hitting freak-out mode and instantly felt badly for giving him a hard time about the lack of boxers.

"It's not as bad as it looks." Mrs. Baxter said from the doorway. She handed Rachael a coffee. "Accidents like these are a common occurrence on a ranch, but they're seldom serious."

"I'll be honest- it's freaking me out."

"I was more bothered by the lack of underwear. The first nurse wasn't much older than y'all and while I'm sure she's seen just about everything in her line of work- a handsome young cowboy sans underwear was more than even she could bear. She asked him if he had a girlfriend."

"Oh, really." Rachael knew what she'd be buying him for a belated birthday gift. He was sorely mistaken if he thought she'd let this go after learning about that.

"Don't worry. He was quick to say he was dating a beautiful girl." Mrs. Baxter put her arm around Rachael's shoulders. "And that you are. In ranching Rachael, these types of things come with the territory. Try not to fret over it. He's only been seriously injured twice in eighteen years."

"I guess that's not so bad." Rachael looked around. "Where's Mr. Baxter?"

"He went to help Tristan and Maysie. You know him, he worries about leaving them alone for too long." She gave a knowing look.

Chapter Eight

Rachael's phone rang.

"It's my mother. I better take this."

Mrs. Baxter nodded in agreement.

"Hi, Mom."

"I heard about Travis."

"I'm at the hospital, now."

"How is he?"

"I'm sure he'll be fine. It's a nasty cut though. He may have a few broken ribs."

"He is a cowboy, honey."

"Until today it just seemed so glamorous."

"Not to mention super masculine." Her mother added.

"That, too."

"That's life. Can I speak with Ginnie?"

Rachael held the phone out to Mrs. Baxter. "Mom wants to talk to you."

"Hi." Mrs. Baxter paused, listening. "Well we've certainly seen better days, and worse too." Mrs. Baxter sat nodding her head and laughing from time to time. "I'm afraid she's getting a crash course in Ranching 101 today. First the injury and then the whole no underwear thing. It's been a tough day on poor Rachael."

Isn't anything personal around here?

"Okay. I will make up the guest room for her if and when we get released tonight. Take care." Mrs. Baxter handed the phone back to Rachael. She patted her knee. "Most cowboys don't wear underwear, sweetie to hear Mr. Baxter tell it, it has something to do with chafing. I personally think it's because they wear those

jeans so darned tight. There's no space for anything else." She
smiled. "Mr. Baxter has always called his jeans Stranglers, instead
of the name brand. Another favorite is his 'anti-theft pants'."

"So you're saying this isn't something I can change."

"Probably not." Mrs. Baxter thought about it for a moment.
"Except dress slacks on Sundays."

"I hope you're right. He's like an unrefined ruffian and I
never realized it."

"You're going to have to reform many of his ways. That's
marriage to a man."

"Don't tell me he drinks out of the cartons and all that other
nasty guy stuff."

"He does. Milk, juice, you name it. I like when he uses the
last of the cereal and puts the empty box back. He always blames
Maysie, but we both know it was him. I think he does that just to
annoy us."

"Don't share all of my secrets, Mama." The nurse appeared
wheeling Travis into the room. He looked groggier than before.
She helped him into the bed and laid him back at a more
comfortable angle. He was out in less than a minute.

"We're just waiting on the results of the chest scan?" Mrs.
Baxter asked her.

"Yes. The doctor will read them and be in shortly. We
should have you out of here in an hour or so." The nurse left and
closed the door softly behind her.

"Travis told me y'all are looking at going to school in
Gainesville. Are you excited?" His mother prompted.

"There's so much to plan between now and then."

"Going off to school together is exciting. With the two of
you it seems the natural progression of things. He knew he liked
you the moment he first saw you playing in the creek on the ranch.
He said you were catching tadpoles."

"Really? What else did he say?"

"He came home that day and told me he'd met the girl he
was going to marry. He told me how pretty you were, with the
longest tanned legs he'd ever seen. Blonde, wildly curly hair. He
hadn't planned on taking you air boating. Your aunt had mentioned

you, and he politely said he and Maysie would be glad to show you around. Then he caught sight of you and everything changed. He couldn't make plans to take you out on the water soon enough. Of course I never told Maysie any of this. I suspected y'all would become close friends and my Maysie never could keep her brother's secrets."

Rachael nodded her head in agreement. If Maysie had known all along that Travis had liked Rachael, she would've revealed all from day one.

"Things always work out the way they're supposed to, Rachael, and in God's timing."

"I'm beginning to grasp that concept more and more."

"I hope he'll be well enough to play football in a few weeks. It being his senior year and all." Mrs. Baxter commented.

"I hadn't considered that." Rachael added.

"He'd be so disappointed if he couldn't."

"I'm bruised up, not dead." He grinned his cocky smile, eyes still closed.

"Look, he's awake." His mother feigned shock.

"How long have I been out?"

"Thirty minutes or so. Not long." His mother advised.

"So what did y'all discuss?"

"You mostly." Rachael teased.

"Should I be nervous?"

"It's our little secret." His mother stood and went over to tenderly hug him.

The doctor came in a short while later carrying a chart.

"Well Mr. Baxter it looks like you'll live to ride another day."

"Good news."

"You don't have any broken ribs, but there is some bruising and those stitches will need to come out in the next ten to twelve days. As for medication, I've brought you a prescription for both a pain killer and an antibiotic. Follow up with your family doctor."

"We'll do that next week." Mrs. Baxter nodded.

"We're all finished here then. A person from the office will be in to discharge you shortly and you'll be free to go."

After the doctor walked out, Mrs. Baxter produced a plastic bag from the gift shop downstairs.

"I picked you up a clean pair of pajama pants and an extra-large t-shirt." She jokingly handed the bag to Rachael who quickly shook her head back and forth, refusing the bag, thrusting it back on Mrs. Baxter.

"No, thank you. Nearly seeing his backside once was enough."

"The way I see it…it's going to be your backside in a few years." She shook her finger at Rachael.

Rachael laughed at her joke and bounded out of the room to wait in the hallway outside. Another nurse appeared with some paperwork, more meds in little cups, and a clipboard.

"Can I go in?"

"Sure. He should be finished by now."

Rachael followed her into the room. She had to laugh at the lime green t-shirt with fruit across the front.

"It was all they had. Part of some healthy eating initiative." Mrs. Baxter defended her choice. "The pants are even better." Mrs. Baxter signed and initialed the last of the discharge papers.

Another nurse came into the room, a large man this time, wheeling another wheelchair. He assisted Travis out of the bed and into the chair. Travis was wearing a pair of hot pink pajama pants covered in limes.

Rachael burst out in giggles. Mrs. Baxter fought back fits of laughter, as well.

"I'm so happy the two of you can bond and have a good laugh at my expense." Travis chided.

"That's what you get for going without britches, Son."

"Tough luck man." The male nurse commiserated with Travis. "Gored by a cow and forced to wear pink pants. That's what I'd call a rough day."

The male nurse, Rodney, wheeled Travis toward the exit doors. Mrs. Baxter excused herself to go outside and bring around her SUV. When she pulled under the porte cochere, Rachael hurried forwards to open the passenger side door. Rodney supported him as he stepped into the vehicle. Rachael went over to buckle Travis up. If the seat belt caused him any discomfort he didn't let on. She reclined the seat a little to take some of the pressure off the wound. She remembered how sore she'd been since her riding accident on Creamsicle, and while her ribs looked nowhere near this bad, she remembered how much it hurt to sit upright.

Rachael gently closed the door and climbed in the backseat behind Travis and his mother. She felt relieved to hear him snoring lightly. He was resting peacefully at last.

"I didn't know he was a snorer." She whispered.

"Don't worry about waking him, honey." His mother laughed at Rachael's quiet tone. "Once these Baxter men fall asleep, you can't wake them!" She patted her son's leg. "As for the snoring, be glad he doesn't snore like his daddy. Now that man snores."

Rachael rode in silence for a while.

"Your mother knew we'd be late and asked me to bring you home tomorrow. Would you like to sleep in our guest room?"

"That would be nice. Thank you. I'm beat and now that he seems okay, I think I might actually be able to sleep." Rachael yawned.

"Me, too." His mother seemed more relieved than even Rachael was. Rachael wondered why. She caught her change in tone. Mrs. Baxter continued, "I was worried he may have bruised internal organs, his kidneys or lungs, but the scan showed all is well."

"I only knew about the x-ray."

"The other scan was done before you arrived."

"What time was he injured?"

"Around eleven o'clock this morning."

"JJ said it happened in the morning. Why didn't anyone come and get me sooner? Or call?" Rachael found it difficult to hide her aggravation.

"These hard-headed Baxter men. They didn't call me until around two o'clock. When I got here and saw it for myself- and found out that it may have involved some organs, I was not happy.

I called JJ and asked him to go pick you up. I didn't think you should drive yourself."

"Thank you for thinking of me. When Travis is better I'm going to talk to him about that. If I'm going to be in his life, I need to be one of the first people he calls. Not the last."

"Absolutely."

Rachael was fuming. So much for sleeping well. Her mind was in gear now and all she wanted to do was straighten Travis out. They pulled into the driveway and up to his house. Mr. Baxter must've been waiting up because he appeared on the front porch within half a minute to help haul Travis inside.

Rachael jumped out and opened the car door for them. Travis awoke and gingerly stepped out of the vehicle. His father carried at least half his weight across his stout shoulders. Mrs. Baxter raced up the front steps and onto the porch to hold the front door open for them.

"On second thought," she pointed toward the family room, "let's put him in the downstairs guest bedroom. He can't make it upstairs."

They assisted him through the downstairs to the bedroom suite. It had its own bathroom. Rachael pulled the blankets back and stacked pillows up at an angle so he wouldn't be lying flat. She helped to cover him after his father got him settled. She sat on the edge of the bed while Mrs. Baxter brought him a glass of water and some crackers on a plate along with a banana.

"I'll be back with a pair of socks." She disappeared upstairs.

"Come and get me tonight if you need anything." Mr. Baxter patted her head like she was one of his own children, bent to kiss her goodnight on the forehead, and disappeared upstairs as well.

Mrs. Baxter returned and handed Rachael a pair of socks.

"He likes socks when he's sick, ever since he was a little boy." She kissed his forehead.

"Okay."

"You can sleep upstairs in one of the guestrooms. I also put a stack of blankets and a pillow on the couch in the living room.

Your choice." She turned and walked slowly toward the door. "And honey, if you fall asleep in here it's okay this once. I don't think he'll be any trouble tonight." She smiled.

"Goodnight, Mama." He slurred out.

"Goodnight, baby."

Rachael stood and checked his breathing. He was already back to sleep. She went out to the kitchen to get a glass of water. On the couch in the living room she found the blankets and pillow, as well as some small pajamas. Neatly folded on top there was a short handwritten note.

"I picked you up a matching set. Figured you'd be more comfortable. Mama B."

Rachael unfolded the shirt and bright pink lime clad pants. She went to the bathroom and slipped them on. What they lacked in style and design they more than made up for in comfort. The pants were unbelievably soft, and the t-shirt loose and roomy. She went to check on Travis one more time. She made herself a pallet at the foot of the bed.

"Don't be ridiculous." He drawled out. "I can't even lift my head." He patted the bed.

"I'm bringing my own blankets and sleeping on top of the sheets." She joked.

She went back out to the couch and grabbed her blankets. By the time she came back in, he was out of bed stumbling to the restroom.

"Don't fall! Should I go get your dad?"

"I've got it." He shut the door.

Rachael listened for a loud thud and was relieved when none came. She continued listening. The flush of the toilet was followed by running sink water and apparent hand washing.

He may drink out of cartons and lack other refinements, but at least he washes his hands!

She heard him brushing his teeth, then spit and rinse. He opened the door and came out climbing back into bed. He moved very slowly and this time opted to lay on his side, right side facing up.

Rachael covered him up.

"Only the sheet please." He patted the bed. "I get hot and these pants are making me sweat."

"Okay."

Rachael went over to her side of the bed and climbed in on top of the comforter and sheets. She covered herself with the small afghan off of the couch.

"Don't let the sun set on your anger." His green eyes twinkled in the light shining in through the window. "My father always says that."

"What anger?" She lied.

"I'm sorry about not letting my dad call you earlier. I didn't want you to worry."

"We'll talk about it later."

"No. I want to set things right now." He mumbled. "I know I hurt you and next time I'll call you first no matter how bad it is."

She rolled to face him on her side. She touched his cheek with her hand.

"I hope there won't be a next time, ever again. I love you, Travis. I don't think I can ever be without you. The thought of losing you frightens me. I'm so happy you'll be okay."

"Me too." He fell back to sleep.

Chapter Nine

Rachael crept out to the kitchen table well before sun-up, lured out of bed by the smell of freshly brewed coffee.

Mr. Baxter stood in the kitchen fully dressed. Rachael could never remember a time he wasn't up and dressed well before the rest of the house. Did he sleep in his jeans and boots?

"Mornin', Rachael. Coffee?"

"Yes, sir."

Rachael pulled out a chair at the kitchen table. He came over and pulled out a chair next to her setting her cup of coffee down in front of her. Next he opened the fridge and brought over some sweetened coffee creamer.

"Mrs. Baxter and Maysie like this one. It's some sort of caramel milk-like stuff."

Rachael grinned as she poured it in her coffee.

"Thank you. Sweet coffee is a girl thing."

He sipped his own black coffee and set it back down.

"So I was told that yesterday was upsetting for you. Travis' injury gave us all quite a scare." He paused waiting for her to speak, but how did you tell your boyfriend's father that you thought the family business was a dangerous one?

That I'm not even sure…I want my boyfriend…to continue in that line of work?

Maysie entered the kitchen smiling widely. She was dressed to go riding and Rachael didn't doubt with whom. She wore slimming skinny jeans and a t-shirt, half boots with teal and pink leather crosses.

Mr. Baxter narrowed his eyes. "Going riding with Tristan?"

"I hope so. One calf ran off yesterday and tore through another fence line. I think it's separated from its mama."

"You don't think its mama went and found it- perhaps they mammied back up this morning already?" He questioned.

"Perhaps, but this calf was little and I for one wouldn't want to risk it." Maysie looked to Rachael for help but found none.

Rachael had no idea what they were talking about. They were speaking some cattleman language she didn't understand.

"Okay. Go on but be back before noon." He warned.

"Yes, sir."

"Maybe Rachael would like to join you. Take the edge off of Creamsicle."

Maysie looked to Rachael with pleading eyes.

Please say no...please say no.

"Normally I'd love to go, but with Travis being hurt and all, I don't want to leave him." It was the truth after all.

"No later than noon." Mr. Baxter reminded.

"I know. And Daddy, this isn't a date, this is business."

"I may be a lot older than you Maysie, but I'm no fool. That being said it sure as hell better not be a date." He smiled at her over his cup.

"Oh. It's not. Back-riding looking for a calf. That's all." She came over and hugged her father goodbye. "Bye Rachael." She skipped out the front door, heading across the yard toward the barn. The sound of Tristan's horse trailer rattling told them all he'd just pulled in the gate.

"I think we need to get you in the cowpens. If you were to get a feel for it, you'd see it's not the dangerous experience you're imagining it's."

Yikes...

"What's a head catch?" She asked.

"Squeeze chute or head catch, it's the same thing. It's a piece of equipment where cattle are given medicine, vaccinations, and even branded. They enter it one at a time. A gate is lowered at the back and there are steel bars at the front to hold their head and neck firmly in place to prevent them from moving. It usually works well and prevents them from injuring themselves, as well as us.

Yesterday was a freak accident. Braford cow swung her head around catching Travis. Another guy had her mugged to the side. She jerked her head, pulled it around, and caught Travis."

Mugged...the only mugging I understand is that which takes place in a dark alley and involves thugs.

"I think I've got a lot to learn."

"It'll come. Someday you'll be marrying a cattleman, if Travis gets his way."

"I know."

Travis lumbered into the kitchen and came over to pull out a chair.

"What are you doing out of bed?" Rachael jumped up to assist him.

"You can't keep a good man down, honey." He sat down.

"Shouldn't you be back in bed?" She asked, more commanding than asking.

"I'm starving."

Rachael walked over to the refrigerator and opened it. In minutes she located bacon, eggs, and English muffins. She produced a carton of orange juice and poured Travis half a mason jar full.

"Can she cook?" Mr. Baxter asked skeptically.

"Either that or she secretly has me insured already. Maybe she's trying to do me in." Travis teased.

"Be careful, Travis. I may never cook for you again."

"That might be a blessing. I can't be sure. I haven't tasted it yet."

"Well someone is feeling better." Mrs. Baxter stepped into the kitchen. "Poor Rachael, his aggravating ways are back."

"Not if he keeps picking on my cooking." Rachael narrowed his eyes at him, holding a spatula poised to swat him.

"In my defense I've only ever seen you make macaroni and cheese- and various microwavable, not to mention delectable, meals."

Rachael wadded up a kitchen towel and pegged him with it, landing it softly on top of his head.

"I can scramble an egg."

Mrs. Baxter came over and got out a medium sized glass bowl along with two fry pans.

"Ignore them. I do most of the time. Travis is grouchy when he doesn't eat but he's just teasing you."

"I know better than to take him seriously by now." Rachael grinned.

Rachael used a whisk to mix the eggs and added a splash of milk. She laid the strips of bacon in a pan and turned it up to medium. She returned to the fridge for butter and preserves for the toast. Her egg pan was ready, she poured the eggs in scrambling them to a perfect golden. Within ten minutes she had breakfast ready to serve.

She carried a plate of toast to the table, already buttered. She set the table with plates and silverware. There were already napkins in the center of the table. Finally, she carried over the platters heaped high with bacon and scrambled eggs.

Travis served his own plate with an enormous quantity of bacon and eggs. Guy was starved. Mrs. Baxter made her eggs, bacon, and toast into an egg sandwich. Mr. Baxter fixed his plate, as well as explained how he couldn't have as much due to high cholesterol.

Travis made a big deal over his first bite. He chewed and chewed.

"Tastes great, other than the egg shell left in there." He winked.

"Stop messing with that girl!" Mrs. Baxter scolded him. "There weren't any shells. He's just playing." She cut her eyes at her son. "If you keep it up she'll kick you to the curb."

"They're actually really good." He patted Rachael's knee and leaned over to kiss her cheek.

"You won't be getting any kisses today after that last comment." She pouted.

'We'll see about that." He swiftly laid one on her pulling her in for a squeeze.

"I think he's fine. Can you run me home after breakfast?" Rachael asked Mrs. Baxter. "I need to go feed the animals."

"You're going to abandon me in my hour of need?" Travis whined.

"You're just fine. Your mouth is obviously on the mend." Rachael stood to clear the table.

Mr. Baxter kissed his wife goodbye and headed out for work. Travis excused himself to go shower. Mrs. Baxter and Rachael tidied the kitchen together. When they finished Mrs. Baxter grabbed her keys and pocketbook. Rachael grabbed a plastic grocery bag from the laundry room placing her dirty laundry in it.

Travis walked in dressed for the day.

"Where are you going?" Rachael inquired.

"I'm going to ride with Mama to run you home."

"I don't think that's a good idea. You need to rest." Rachael frowned

"I will. On your couch. I can't lay around here all day-doing nothing. I'll go insane."

"Okay but you better be wearing pants."

"There's no chance of me getting injured. Like I told you- I hate the darned things."

"Pants." Rachael glared at him. When he made no move to get any she added. "I've been thinking of embracing my hippie side. Becoming a bra burner and all that. These things are so restrictive. I need to feel free." She wiggled her shoulders like the weight of the thing was binding.

"Fine!" He bellered. He stomped over to the stairs.

"You have several packs of unopened *pants* in your top drawer." His mother called from the kitchen.

Rachael walked into the kitchen, shaking her head.

"You're going to be good for him."

"I hope so."

They waited for Travis who stalked into the kitchen. He was normally never moody, but this injury sure had set him off. Rachael decided it might not be a good idea to battle with him over anything else today. Whatever came up, for the rest of the day, she'd let it slide.

He rode in the front seat, brooding. Mrs. Baxter drove and Rachael sat quietly in the back. When they pulled into her long driveway and up to the house everything looked quiet.

"I'll run him home later."

"Keep him. He's never a pleasant patient. He can't stand to be out of commission."

"That explains a lot."

Rachael helped him out. He held her hand, stopping just short of the front door.

"I'm sorry. I was really playing at breakfast, but my mother is right. I hate to be out of commission. I'm a grouch."

"It's perfectly understandable." She reached up and kissed his nose.

"Would you really have gone hippie, as you put it?"

"Yep. I don't want a repeat of yesterday. That wasn't fun. You're a taken man now and you better remember it."

"I like this take charge, bossy girl. It's hot."

"Shut up." She smacked his hand.

He laughed his way into the house. Inside Aunt Margaret and her mother lounged in the living room. Michael and Levi could be heard cheering at some game down the hallway.

Rachael's mother rose from the couch and came over to gently hug Travis.

"We were so worried."

"Thank you, ma'am, but I'm doing much better now. Rachael's been taking really good care of me."

"Her father called last night. I told him about it. He too sends his prayers for a speedy recovery."

She led Travis to the recliner and helped him into it.

Her cell phone buzzed in her pocket. She pulled it out and looked at it.

Amber...

'I had the baby last night. He was so perfect. An angel. Be home tomorrow if you'd like to visit me.'

Rachael's eyes filled with tears. She handed the phone to Travis. He read the message and conveyed its contents to Mrs. Harte and Aunt Margaret.

"Excuse me, I'm going to go feed the animals." Rachael stood.

She stepped out the back doors and crossed the tall Bahia grass field to the barn. Taffy and ole' lonesome George stared at their feed pans longingly.

She went into the tack room and opened the feed bins. She scooped each of them a scoop of feed placing it into a smaller bucket. She carried it out to the paddock, climbed over the fence, and poured it in their pans. She returned to the barn and grabbed them each a block of hay from the bale of Coastal in the corner. She put them in the hay bags tied onto the fence.

She walked around the corner of the barn and turned on the water spigot. She traced the hose to its opening where water spewed out onto the ground. She lifted it and carried it to the trough filling it to the top. She stood staring at the water.

Amber has given birth to a baby. A baby she'll never know.

"Want to talk about it?" Travis leaned against the blackboard fence. In the bright sunlight she could see his color was still paler than it should be.

She walked back around behind the barn and turned off the spigot. She coiled the hose up on the hose wheel where it belonged. She walked over to scratch Taffy's head and ole' lonesome George's neck where they both lifted their necks for a pat.

She climbed back over the fence and jumped down from the top rail to the ground. She put both arms around Travis and hugged him tightly. He hugged her back kissing the top of her head.

"We could have a baby someday."

"I'm sure we will." He answered. "Someday."

"I can't imagine ever giving one up the way Amber must be doing today."

"I can't either, but adoption is a beautiful thing. Imagine the family that is taking him home. What a blessing and a joy he will be to them, Rach."

"I'm glad we won't have to make that decision. Even if we found ourselves having a baby sooner than planned, I'd be okay with it. Not that I want to be a mother anytime in the near future, but I realize it goes with the territory- when we get married I mean."

"Well, I'm glad you know that much. I'd hate to have to explain the birds and the bees to you." He joked with her.

"I hate when you make me laugh when I'm sad." She giggled up at his cocky smile and ruffled his spiked dark hair.

"I'm counting on that humor to keep us going- maybe even get me out of trouble from time to time."

"We'll see about that. You better not be planning on getting into too much trouble."

"No guy plans on getting into trouble, it just sort of finds us."

"Let's get you off your feet."

"Sounds good to me."

Rachael led Travis into the sitting room where she set up a few pillows behind his back. He leaned over to take off his boots, wincing a little.

"Lay back. I can do this." She put his booted foot between her knees and pulled the first one off. She did the same with the other one, setting the boot on the floor next to the first at the foot of her couch.

"Maybe I should get hurt more often."

Rachael covered him with the blanket, ignoring his comment. She went to the kitchen and got him a glass of ice water. She opened the cabinet above the stove and grabbed the small crate of medicine her mother kept there. She located the ibuprofen and grabbed him three, remembering the doctor's instructions. He hadn't taken anything since last night and this was no time to be tough.

She went back to the couch and handed him the pills. He took the offered meds and the water as well.

"Now get some rest. I have to do Michael's laundry."

"Michael's laundry? Isn't he old enough to learn to do that himself?"

Rachael contemplated that. "I guess. I started doing it when our mom went to work to help out around here. I wanted to maintain some normalcy for him." She turned to walk away and stopped. "Do you do your own laundry?"

"Point taken."

"He's several years younger than you, too. Maybe it's time you started doing your own laundry." Rachael advised.

"Why should I? My mom does it now and in a few years it'll be your job. That's woman's work."

She whirled around. The way he was holding his belly and laughing she knew he'd been playing with her once more.

"Trouble does find you, Travis Baxter. Your humor may just be your only saving Grace."

"I'm counting on it."

Chapter Ten

All of the girls wanted to visit Amber if she was up for company. So Rachael called her house at around ten o'clock the following morning. Her mother said they'd need to wait one more day. She'd been released from the hospital and was home resting. Amber was exhausted from the ordeal.

Rachael politely ended the call and called to inform the others. They rescheduled and opted for a shopping day instead.

Maysie's car pulled up out front and she honked the horn. Armed with two hundred dollars in cash from her mother, and a list of school supplies for herself, she was impatient to get the shopping underway. Rachael grabbed her purse, called for Michael, and skipped out the door. Seated in the car already, Shannah rode shotgun. Maysie wore a huge smile.

"She's been like that since her ride with Tristan yesterday." Shannah jerked her head in Maysie's direction.

"He's such a gentleman, the way he opens all the gates for me on his horse and stuff."

"He should. That's what he does, he's a cowboy." Shannah added.

Maysie's eyes sparkled. "Yep. He is."

"Oh, barf." Shannah made a puking gesture with her hand.

"Just because you find yourself manless, don't be a hater." Maysie smiled sweetly.

"You're right. I'm a man hater now." Shannah confided. "We've got to find me a date for homecoming."

"School hasn't even started yet! Homecoming is like ten weeks away." Rachael did the quick math on her fingers. "Okay, nine weeks away."

"Exactly, and I can't go alone. The other guys at school are nerds or stalkers at best. I need a guy no one knows, someone intriguing."

"And hot. He's got to be gorgeous." Maysie amended. "Maybe tall and dark, maybe with a secret past."

"It sounds like you're describing Batman. Let's be serious here." Shannah commented.

"Why can't he be all those things? Just picture it. You show up to homecoming with some really good-looking guy, tall, dark, alluring. He's personable and friendly, the life of the party. Everyone wonders 'who's that guy'? Girls are drooling over him…but he is elusive."

"Does this sound like the lead character from a famous book? Is he an angel?" Shannah chided.

"Joke, but I know the perfect guy."

"Is he under nineteen years of age? Because I don't want some college aged guy." Shannah narrowed her eyes at Maysie. "What's your definition of *guy*?"

"He's eighteen and he's our cousin. Second cousin. He lives in North Florida. He'd be a perfect gentleman. You'll see."

"Don't look at me." Rachael held her hands up in the air. "I've never met him."

"You asked for our help. Do you want it or not?" Maysie asked.

"Okay. Let's look at a picture of him."

"Be my guest. He's one of my friends online. Check him out." Maysie handed Shannah her phone.

Shannah took a moment to locate the app. She opened it up and clicked on friends.

"Name?"

"Wade. Wade Baxter."

Shannah searched Maysie's friends, then gasped. "He *is* gorgeous!"

"Told you." Maysie chirped.

Shannah handed Rachael the phone.

"Yep. He'd work. So how do we get him here?"

"They're coming to buy some bulls over in Kenansville later this month. I'll introduce y'all then."

"Works for me." Shannah answered.

Rachael couldn't believe the striking resemblance between Wade and her own Travis. Equally good looking and tanned. The only difference between the two appeared to be the curve of their mouths and eye color. Wade's eyes were blue where Travis' were green. Rachael handed the phone back up to Maysie.

They turned up the radio to their most recent favorite pop tune. First they stopped off at a huge store where they needed to buy the list of school supplies that both Maysie and Rachael's mothers had printed out earlier this morning. Paper, pencils, blue and black ink pens. Spiral notebooks and folders with pockets. Some with brads and some without. Three ring binders.

"I've never quite gotten the whole half-inch, one-inch or one and half-inch binder thing. They should all be the same size. What difference does it make? It's a binder conspiracy." Shannah protested throwing one of each size into the cart.

"I don't think it's a conspiracy." Maysie contested.

"No, really it is. Look at this. If they were all the same size you could recycle and reuse. These things virtually last forever. My carbon footprint probably consists of twenty of these things at this point. It's ridiculous."

"So just reuse them already." Maysie interjected.

"I would," she frowned. "But they're the wrong sizes. Some are the big ones and some small. This year I need the one-inch."

"You've never been one to just follow rules. Use the others, and if anyone says anything tell them it's your green initiative." Rachael offered.

"You're right. I'm going to do it." Shannah put the binders back on the shelf.

Maysie looked at Rachael. The entire Gabe break-up was really bothering Shannah, but apparently she didn't want to talk about it. Both girls shared a look and decided to not bring it up. If she didn't want to talk about it…it was clearly off limits.

They were halfway through their list of items when they spied Honey at the end of the aisle. From behind, her hair had lost its luster and her hipbones stuck out on either side.

"What up with the *super skinny look* she's got going on?"

"After Misty the other day- it looks like it's contagious."

Honey had always been the friendlier of the two, so everyone headed in her direction to say hi.

"Oh, hey, I came out to grab school supplies, too."

Came out from what? A cave?

Her eyes were sunken in and deep shadows looked like purplish smears under them.

"Going to the dance auditions this week?" Maysie asked.

"Nope. Misty and I quit. We're getting a little old for that. We're running with a different crowd now."

Rachael thought back to the guys they were hanging out with at the beginning of last year when she ran into them at the party on Justin's family's ranch. If they were a part of the crowd they were running with, these girls were in with a bad crowd. They'd given Rachael the creeps even then.

"Sorry to hear that. We'll miss you." Maysie said, careful not to include Misty in her sentiments. While they'd all miss Honey, no one would miss Misty. Her rude comments and bad attitude made her a chore to be around.

Shannah shot Maysie a look that said *don't get too carried away here, sista.*

"I have to go." Honey pulled a pair of Versace sunglasses out of her purse and slid them on. She sniffled and wiped her nose. Without as much as a backwards glance, she walked away.

"What's wrong with her?" Maysie inquired.

"She looks like a zombie." Shannah said in earnest holding her arms out in front of her and dragging one foot along behind her. "Arrr. I'm Honey, former pageant princess turned walking dead."

Rachael laughed. Maysie frowned.

"Stop it." Maysie chided. "These girls are in trouble and we have to help them. They're sick."

"Yeah. In the head. And you can't help someone who won't help themselves." Shannah snipped. "Didn't you see the way she was sniffling?"

"Maybe she has a cold." Maysie sighed.

"Or a coke habit." Shannah whispered.

"As in cocaine?" Maysie looked upset.

"Let's check out and go somewhere we can talk." Rachael offered and smiled pleasantly at the elderly woman standing nearby with her mouth ajar. "Hi, ma'am. Nice day we're having isn't it?"

She grabbed Maysie's hand and pulled her toward the registers at the front. Shannah wheeled the cart behind them. At the register they spied Misty standing with another creepy looking chick no one recognized.

"They're multiplying." Shannah acknowledged.

Rachael helped Shannah unload their supplies onto the checkout counter. Maysie waved to Misty who did her best to ignore her. After the episode between her and Travis at his birthday, Rachael was surprised she made no move to come over and confront her. Maybe she'd decided he was finally off limits.

Rachael paid the cashier and put her wallet back in her purse. On the way out to the parking lot, Shannah handed her thirty dollars. They loaded the car and Rachael locked it back up.

"Come with me." Rachael motioned for them to follow.

The three headed to the Wings-n-Eats a few doors down in the same strip mall. Inside it was quiet. It was well before lunchtime, and they were the only people in there other than a couple of construction workers grabbing a bite to eat before work.

"Could we have that corner booth?" Rachael asked.

The waitress nodded, leading them to the booth in the corner.

Rachael ordered an order of fries and three sodas. Maysie looked like she could pass out. After their sodas arrived, she took several sips and the color returned to her face.

"Coke?" Maysie questioned.

"Travis thought it was meth."

"As in crystal?" Maysie asked.

"Is there any other kind?" Shannah said sarcastically.

"We've always loved Honey. Sure Misty has never been nice, but Honey. Come on, Shannah, she was your friend, too."

"Obviously I care for her, but if she's on that there's not much we can do. That's nasty business."

"I don't even know what it is really. A street drug obviously, but aside from that I'm clueless." Rachael confessed.

"Here's all you need to know. Meth is a methamphetamine. It's highly addictive and very popular out where we live. It's been offered to me before and I just steer clear of it. It's bad news." Shannah offered.

"And the sniffles?"

"You can snort it, inject it, or even smoke it. Look at her nose, the redness around her nostrils. The sniffling. A few scabs. Nasty." Shannah's face said it all.

"The emaciated look." Rachael grimaced.

"That too. The scabs on her arms. People pick at their faces, arms, etc. I don't know why, but they do. Travis is probably right. It's gotta be meth." Shannah surmised.

"What do we do?" Maysie asked.

"Her parents must've noticed. Who wouldn't?" Rachael advised.

"She's pretty deceitful. Maybe they think it's something else."

"I must intervene. I've known both of them since grade school. If Misty wants to carry herself down so be it, but I won't stand idly by and let her destroy Honey with her."

"What are you going to do?" Rachael asked.

"I'm going to tell her mother and then, if they do nothing, I can at least know I tried." Maysie stood up and threw some cash on the table.

Rachael and Shannah looked at each other. While they both thought this was possibly a very bad idea, they knew trying to talk Maysie out of it was out of the question.

"Let's call your mom. Maybe she'll come join us." Rachael said to Maysie's back, practically chasing her across the parking lot.

Shannah sprinted up alongside her.

"Rachael's right. Let's call Mrs. Baxter. She's levelheaded and always knows what to do."

"Call her." Maysie unlocked the doors and everyone climbed in.

Rachael dialed her and put the phone on speaker. When Mrs. Baxter picked up Rachael greeted her.

"Hi, Mrs. Baxter. It's me, Rachael." In the time she and Travis had been dating she'd never called Mrs. Baxter's personal cell phone.

"Is everything okay?"

"Well, we're not sure. I'm with Maysie and Shannah. We just bumped into Honey and Misty and another young lady. And well, they didn't look healthy."

"Travis told me about Misty and her appearance. I called her Mom. The poor girl is suffering from some sort of thyroid condition. She's lost a ton of weight and is even losing some hair. They're really concerned."

"That's just it. There was this other girl…and now, Honey, too. They all looked…" Rachael searched for the right adjective.

"Like zombies. Walking dead. All scabbed up and sickly." Shannah interjected.

"That's something different entirely." Mrs. Baxter paused, "So you think it's drugs?"

"We do. And Maysie wants to tell Honey's mom." Rachael said.

"That could go either way. She may be angry or concerned, but since Honey is your friend, you should do the right thing here." Mrs. Baxter commented. "I'll call her mother and see if she's home. Give her a heads up that you're headed her way."

"Okay." Rachael murmured.

A few minutes later, Rachael's phone rang. She answered.

"Okay. She is at home and said she'd welcome you stopping by." Mrs. Baxter paused for a moment and then added. "You don't have any proof, so be very careful what you say."

"We will." Maysie added.

"Are you sure we should be doing this?" Shannah asked aloud.

"If I ever look that bad- or you think I might be in trouble- please intervene on my behalf. I may not appreciate your efforts right then, but down the road I'd thank you." Maysie pulled up to Honey's house. It was a large estate home set back from the road. A grand white colonial house with rows of Live Oaks on either side of the driveway. The circular drive in front was empty with the exception of a minivan parked out front.

"Must be her mother's car."

"You guys can wait here if you'd like." Maysie offered. "This was my idea and I don't want to put you in the middle."

She climbed out and walked purposefully toward the front door. She rang the doorbell. Moments later, Shannah and Rachael joined her.

"We rednecks stick together." Shannah winked.

The door opened and Carolyn, Honey's mother, stood smiling at them.

"Come in, girls. Please come in."

She was Honey's twin, just a generation or two older. Same vibrant smile, beautiful skin, and dazzling hair.

They went into the front parlor where they all took a seat. Maysie took the lead in the conversation.

"Thank you for having us into your home. We ran into Honey today and she told us she was quitting the dance squad."

"She told me the same thing recently. She's lost a lot of weight and was sick this summer, she doesn't think she can uphold the commitment and stay healthy, too. She's exhausted and needs a break."

"We're her friends, and when we saw her today we were concerned. She was with Misty and another friend, both who looked ill and in all honesty, emaciated."

"I wasn't aware of that. I haven't seen Misty around here all summer. I didn't know they were still hanging out. Thank you for telling me. Did you recognize this other girl?"

"I don't know her." Maysie confirmed. "Neither does Rachael or Shannah."

Carolyn's face was tight and worry creased the corners of her eyes. Her slumped posture and overall demeanor conveyed concern and in some way ... defeat.

"Well, ladies, I've got an appointment in town. I appreciate you coming by today and I'll tell Honey you stopped by to say hello."

She stood and walked to the front door, stopping long enough to embrace Maysie as she walked by. She looked briefly as if she could cry but didn't. She closed the door gently behind them.

Maysie got into the car and put the roof down.

"What do you think?" Rachael asked the other two.

"She knows." Shannah answered. "She's worried. Obviously she'd asked her to stop hanging around Misty- and Honey is still doing so behind her back. She's a mom with a kid with a problem and she doesn't know how to fix it."

"Hopefully now she takes some drastic action to fix it." Maysie shook her head.

"I've got the definite feeling Honey won't appreciate our intervention." Rachael commented.

"Even so, we did the right thing." Maysie declared.

The girls drove the remaining distance home. They still hadn't done their back-to-school clothes shopping, but none of them felt much like it after their chance meeting with Honey. Then, there would be tomorrow's visit with Amber...

Rachael thought back to Travis and his comment about their friends finding themselves at a crossroads last year...a point where they begin to make decisions that could affect the rest of their lives.

Rachael thought of herself and her own situation. Sure, her own father was in prison, but overall she led a happy, fulfilled home life. Her mother was loving and understanding, always there to listen to her thoughts and make sure she never went without.

Her aunt was like a second mother. Then, there was Michael, a slightly annoying but all in all typical good little brother.

She also had Travis, and through him an entire second family who loved her. She decided she was fortunate in just about every way.

What makes a girl like Honey, who seemingly has it all...a good family, loving parents, good looks and even money, turn to a self-destructive lifestyle?

Rachael waved goodbye as she walked up to the house. The front door was locked and she found a note from Michael. He'd gone to Levi's for the day fishing. He'd be back later that evening. Rachael decided this would be the perfect day for a nap. She went down the hall and lay across her bed. A while later she awoke to the sound of a car outside and an incessant pounding at her front door. It was late afternoon. She'd slept for over two hours.

She peeked out her bedroom blinds at a small blue compact car she didn't recognize. The door stood open, the engine still running. The pounding on her front door continued.

"Open the door, you stupid..." The girl yelled in a loud voice.

Rachael knew she'd locked the front door, but wasn't sure about the back doors leading onto the back porch. She picked up her cell phone and dialed Travis. He didn't answer.

She didn't recognize the car or the voice of the girl pounding on the front door. She saw a guy walk around the side of the house, past her window. He was tatted from neck to hand and she'd never seen him before. She went out into the hall and slipped into the bathroom, locking the door. She thought about calling 9-1-1 but knew the sheriff's department could never get out here in time. Instead she called the Baxter house.

Travis answered the house phone on the first ring.

"It's me. I'm in the bathroom. There's some scary dude here with a girl. They're pounding on the door and yelling." She whispered.

"Slow down, Rach. Just stay where you are." Rachael heard Travis yelling for his father. "Stay on the phone."

Rachael listened. She heard the back door open. She heard the distinct voice of the guy inside the house. They walked through the kitchen and front rooms.

Rachael lowered the volume on her phone and silenced the ringer. Her hands shook. She climbed into the tub and lay down on her side. She heard the man saying something she couldn't make out. Then, the slamming of the backdoor.

"Answer me, Rachael. Are you okay?"

"I am." She whispered.

"I'm on my way." He hung up the phone and dialed her back on her cell.

"I'm almost there."

"Okay." She wept.

The car drove out of the driveway. The engine faded further into the distance. Several minutes passed. Rachael heard the sound of a siren coming up the road. Pounding on the front door alarmed her once more, but common sense told her they weren't back. She climbed from the tub and crept down the hall.

"Miss Rachael?" JJ hollered. "You okay in there?"

Rachael wiped away her tears and opened the door.

"Hi, JJ." She greeted him. He must have been working on a property nearby. He stood fully clad in his official game warden issued uniform. His truck parked in the driveway, lights flashing.

Travis pealed into the driveway racing up to park behind JJ's truck. He jumped out and sprinted up to Rachael. If his stitches were still sore he wasn't showing any signs of it today. He looked her up and down, his brow furrowed.

"Are you okay?"

"I'm all right, just scared me is all."

"What happened, Miss Rachael?"

More sirens could be heard coming down the main highway that bordered her property. Two sheriff's deputies flew up the driveway. They both climbed out and came up to join in the conversation.

"I was napping when I heard a raised voice at the front door. Luckily I didn't go answer it. She was yelling and calling me names."

"Did you recognize the voice?"

"Not at all."

"What happened next?" The shorter deputy asked.

"I saw a man go past my bedroom window and walk around the back of the house. I didn't think the backdoor was locked so I went into the bathroom and locked the door. I dialed Travis and hid in the tub."

"Did they come in the house?"

"I know for sure the man did. I heard him in the house. He came in through the backdoor. I'd left it unlocked."

"Okay. Don't touch anything. We're going to dust for prints- see if we can lift anything off of the back door." The deputy advised.

"Okay." Rachael nodded feeling a little confused.

"Are your parents at home?"

"No, my mom and aunt are at work."

The deputies disappeared around the back of the house. Travis draped his arm around Rachael's shoulders.

"You okay, baby?"

"Just shocked. Who would want to do such a thing? I didn't even know them."

"Did you get a good look at the car?"

"A small blue compact car. Some sort of older Honda."

"That helps." JJ wrote the description down. The taller deputy returned to stand beside him.

"What else do you remember," he asked.

"The guy had tatted arms. Shoulder to fingertip." Rachael thought for a moment. "He was kind of grungy."

"Anything else?"

"That's it."

Mr. Baxter pulled up to the house and climbed out. Mrs. Baxter was with him. Both came over to hug Rachael. Mrs. Baxter held both of Rachael's hands.

"I was just telling Mr. Baxter about Honey and your visit with her mother earlier today."

Rachael nodded her head.

"What visit with her mother?" Travis clenched his jaw.

"Maysie, Shannah, and I ran into Honey with Misty and a friend at the store. Maysie was worried about Honey's appearance and thought we should go talk to her mother."

"Tell me you guys didn't." Travis' face tensed.

"We did. I didn't want Maysie to go alone. They've been friends a long time. She didn't say anything bad. Just that she was concerned and all." Rachael thought about the comments about Misty and the other girl having the same look. "Well, she did say that Misty and the other girl had the same ill and emaciated look to them."

Travis rubbed his eyes and forehead with his right hand.

"Is there anything else, Miss Rachael?" JJ questioned.

"Her mother hadn't realized Honey was still hanging around with Misty."

"Thank you." The deputy returned to the car.

"Going over there was stupid, Rachael." Travis muttered.

"Travis." His mother uttered. "They were concerned."

"What Travis means to say Rachael is that Misty has been rumored to be running with a well-known meth ring." Mr. Baxter worded his thoughts carefully. "They aren't the kind of people you want to get involved with."

"I was just being supportive."

"We know, dear, and it's always important to do the right thing. You girls did the right thing, but because of it you may have drawn some unwanted attention." Mrs. Baxter patted her hand.

"It wasn't the right thing." Travis spat. "I hear a lot of things about certain people. Let it go in one ear and out the other. You can't save them all and some of them don't want to be saved."

Travis was nearly yelling.

Rachael didn't understand. Wasn't it Travis who just a few short months ago told his parents about Misty himself?

The deputy walked back over and handed Rachael his card with some numbers written on it.

"Your case number is written along the top and my cell on the back. If you remember anything else let me know. We pulled some prints off the back door, but we may get nothing. They could just be your family's fingerprints, but we'll run them just in case."

Rachael thanked the deputies. They both pulled away.

Shannah...

"Should we check on Shannah?"

"JJ called her on the way here. She's fine. Her father turned the dogs loose ... literally. No one will go up to that house."

"Let's call your mom." Mrs. Baxter walked Rachael inside.

Rachael dreaded making this call. Travis was right. They'd let their concern for Honey blind them to their own safety, but who'd have thought someone would come to her house looking for a fight? Or maybe worse.

When Rachael made no move to do so, Mrs. Baxter made the call for her. Mr. Baxter had a seat on the couch, while Travis walked out onto the back porch, hands on his hips looking out across the pasture.

Mr. Baxter nodded toward the porch and Rachael knew she would need to go out there- eventually.

She stepped down onto the stone floor of the back porch and took a seat in a nearby rocking chair.

"I'm sorry I called you guys stupid. That was wrong of me." Travis said his back turned to her still.

"Apology accepted." Rachael fumed. He was right. It was stupid, she wouldn't deny it, but they'd done the right thing and in the end it had consequences.

He turned around and came to stand in front of her.

"I don't think they'll be back, but for now, you should lock the doors, front and back, as well as the gate."

"I'm not an idiot."

"I didn't say you were. You're used to it being safe around here and for now, it's not." He leaned down in front of her. "You aren't dealing with rational people here. This circle has been known to employ some unique tactics. For now, I'd suggest putting Taffy and ole' lonesome George out in the pasture with the less refined moo's, as you like to say."

"They'd kill my pets?"

"Poison them, maybe. I don't think they will, but I've heard some pretty awful stuff." He clasped her hands when it looked like she might cry. "No more trying to rescue Honey. You've done what y'all thought was right and make that it. Promise me."

"I promise."

"The fact that you never turn your back on a friend and always do the right thing. You love people in spite of their flaws and shortcomings. You're intelligent and fun. These are the reasons I love you, the reasons you'll make a wonderful life partner and wife someday. All of these things make you ... you. When I get scared for your safety, I don't think clearly and say stupid things."

"Let's go let them out." Rachael jumped up and led the way to the barn.

She went in and petted them both lovingly wrapping her arms around their necks. She went to the back gate and swung it open.

"Don't think of this as goodbye. They're going to like this new freedom."

Rachael watched as both Taffy and ole' lonesome George walked over to the gate and sniffed the air, winding the other cattle off in the distance.

"Go on. Be free." Rachael held her head high, determined not to cry.

Ole' lonesome George used to enjoy escaping to greener pastures all the time. He leisurely walked through the gate and immediately went in search of the sweet clover blooming nearby. Taffy stepped through the gate, jumped and bucked running down the fence line, enjoying her newfound space.

"Does that look like a sad cow to you?" Travis asked.

"Nope. You're right. She looks happy!"

"She is happy. Maybe she'll get bred." He closed the gate and snapped the chain in place.

"Bred!!!" Rachael exclaimed. "She's just a baby!"

"She's over two years old, comin' three. I'm just about to pull the bulls off these cows but there's still a chance. Another two weeks."

"Two weeks?"

"Yep. She's cycling, Rach." He held his hand out to her blank stare. "It's the cow birds and the bees. Come on."

"Oh." A knowing look crossed her face. "No wonder she wouldn't stand still for her pedicure last week. She had cow PMS."

Travis shook his head. "You're a mess. She's a cow. She doesn't get cow PMS."

"How do you know? It's possible. I'm going to research it."

"Go ahead." He shook his head again as he led the way back up to her house.

Her phone vibrated. She pulled it out of her pocket.

"Hi, Dad." She answered.

"Hey, honey. Your mom just called me. Are you all right?"

"I am now. Travis and his family are here with me."

"That makes me feel better. From now on everything must be locked and I don't want you or Michael home alone. You'll both need to spend the last two days of summer with friends."

"We will. I can't believe school starts on Monday."

"Me neither. You'll be a senior."

"Don't remind me."

"Try to enjoy it. Adulthood comes too quickly. You're still a kid, try to remember that."

"I won't forget. I love you, Dad."

"I love you, too."

"Put Travis on the phone." Confused Rachael held the phone out to Travis.

"My dad wants to talk to you."

Travis took the offered phone.

"Yes, sir. Yes, sir." He just kept answering and nodding his head. "My thoughts exactly. Okay. Will do."

He ended the call and handed the phone back to Rachael.

"What was that all about?"

"He asked me to bring over a few of our more aggressive male dogs."

"Dogs?"

"For around the house."

"Is that necessary?"

"After today, you have to ask?"

"So who is to say I won't get bitten?"

"They like women. Maysie feeds the dogs, well, her and mama. They know me. We'll introduce them to Michael. Your dad is right- that's just what this yard needs is a few biting dogs."

"Won't someone else get bitten?"

"We'll post a *beware of dog* sign on the gate."

"I don't know about this."

"What yard out here doesn't have biting dogs? Ours are loose now, especially after today."

"Just seems so archaic."

"My dad turned our male dogs loose every time I had a guy campout. He didn't want any guys venturing up to the house to hang out with my sister and her cute friends. I'll remember that for when we have a daughter." He gently squeezed her hand. "It was an effective deterrent."

Chapter Eleven

Monday morning rolled around sooner than anybody would've liked. For homeroom this year Rachael had Mr. Richardson. He was typically the remedial math teacher. While she'd never taken any of his classes, she'd heard a few less than positive things about the man.

Around campus he was pretty much known as a creep. He liked to sit all the pretty girls in the very front row, especially those who wore shorts and skirts. This morning was no exception to that rule. He allowed all of the students to file into class choosing a seat wherever each one chose. Then after the second bell he asked everyone to stand. One by one he pointed to the students and motioned for them to go to their new assigned seats, which he chose for them.

Having heard about his reputation and affinity for nice legs, Rachael had selected a pair of jeans to start her school year. As a result, she found herself safely seated in the third row. After hand selecting their seats, he handed around a clipboard and had them write their name on it.

"You'll find a number on the corner of your desk corresponding to the numbers on the clipboard. Of course, that is assuming you can all count."

Man's a freak.

Everyone exchanged glances and began writing their names on the clipboard one by one. They passed it around the room. While Rachael was in the third row, she was still close enough to the front to see Mr. Richardson's desk clearly. It was piled high with paperwork, towering stacks covering every inch of available space. He appeared to be someone who never threw anything away. She was sure his desk could be featured on some hoarding reality show. If it were that cluttered on day one, what would it look like by the end of the year?

He sat reading his paper. From where she sat it looked like the business section. Every few minutes he lifted his head, cleared his throat and uttered a terse, "No talking." Then he'd return to reading. He sipped coffee from a mug that was white on the outside and black on the inside. Rachael studied it closely, not sure whether it was painted black on the inside or merely stained from years of not washing it.

His face was long and his eyes dark. He had a smattering of salt and pepper hair that could only be described as the classic comb-over. If Rachael were asked for an adjective to describe Mr. Richardson it would have to be weasel-like. While Rachael knew it wasn't a kind comparison, he certainly looked like a weasel to her.

Class was almost over when a student arrived at the door. Whoever it was had to knock because of the new locked door safety initiative put into place in most public school districts. Mr. Richardson picked up the clipboard, perusing the names. He spied a girl in the front row and narrowed his eyes.

"Martha. Grab the door." He commanded

Martha didn't respond verbally, but quickly jumped to get the door. Her long, tanned legs were the apparent reason for her front row seat placement. She briskly walked over and opened the door to the classroom. Alex stood there carrying her backpack. She looked rushed and a little out of sorts. Rachael was just relieved to have someone she knew well in her homeroom class. She waved at her from across the room.

Mr. Richardson looked over at her. He made a quick assessment and looked down at the clipboard once more.

"Miss Jennings." The girl in the last seat of the front row looked up pointing to her own chest. "Yes, you, please move to the third row in the available seat next to Miss Harte. New girl- you take Miss Jennings seat."

Pervert.

Rachael shot Mr. Richardson a nasty look. A quick assessment of Alex's mid-thigh length khaki shorts and cute pair of Tom's no doubt had landed her in the viewing area. Alex walked over, pulled out her chair, and plopped down. Mr. Richardson motioned for her to come up and obtain the clipboard from his desk. Alex ran up to fetch it and scribbled her name next to her assigned seat. She handed it back to him.

He quickly had his nose buried in his paper again and read until the bell chimed signaling the end of the period a few minutes later.

Rachael walked over and helped Alex grab her stuff.

"How was your visit with Amber yesterday?"

"It never happened. Her mom had to reschedule us. She keeps pushing it back, day by day."

"So she doesn't want y'all coming around?"

"I guess not. Either that or Amber isn't ready for company yet. That's completely understandable considering all she's been through."

"Gotta be tough."

"Gotta be." Rachael thought she better warn Alex about Mr. Richardson and his lecherous fascination with young girls with nice legs. "Real quick, watch out for Mr. Richardson. I hear he's a creep. He sits all the girls with short skirts and nice calves in the front row."

"I heard. I got my schedule just this morning. That's why I was late. I was in the office changing drama to art. I took drama last year and while it was cool I don't want another entire year of it."

"I get that. Did you hear Misty and Honey quit the squad?" Rachael asked.

"I did. With Amber gone and the two of them, we're down from six seniors to three."

"I hadn't thought of it that way. It's just Maysie, Shannah, and me, if I make it."

"You'll make it for sure now." A mischievous grin played across her lips, "The juniors will take over."

"I bet you will." Rachael was almost to her next class in the main building. "I've got English next."

Alex nodded, looking reluctant to walk away.

"What's wrong?" Rachael prompted.

"That." Alex looked over to where Fred stood talking with possibly the prettiest blonde Rachael had seen since starting school at EMHS.

"Who's that?"

"Shh. Tell you more later."

Fred and the blonde made a bee line for the two of them.

"Hi, Rachael. This is Elena, our exchange student."

"Nice to meet you, Elena." Rachael smiled. "Where are you from?"

"Sweden." She answered just as the bell rang.

"Great to meet you. I've got to get to class, but I'm sure I'll see you around."

Rachael turned and opened the door to English. Inside Maysie waved at her from across the room. She'd saved her a seat. Rachael plopped down in the chair.

Mrs. Marsden passed out the syllabus and asked a guy in the front row to come up and read it to the class.

"Did you meet the Swede?" Maysie scribbled on the bottom of her syllabus. Rachael nodded, but never turned her attention from the front of the room deciding that getting into trouble for note passing on the first day might not be a good idea. Maysie took the hint and they didn't speak about it further until after class.

Outside Travis waited for them in the hallway.

"What is his mom thinking?" Maysie protested as soon as they stepped foot in the hall.

They continued toward their lockers on their way to the portables across campus where their next classes were located.

"Whose, Mom?" Travis interjected.

"Fred's. She took in an exchange student." Rachael answered.

"Oh. The Swedish girl? She seems nice enough." He smiled, cutting his eyes at Rachael.

Clay and Adam walked up behind them to join in the conversation.

"I was thinking it wasn't such a bad idea. Maybe we could take a few in, right Travis? A Brazilian, maybe Norwegian." Adam teased.

Rachael saw green and realized she was jealous. She glared at Travis.

"Speak for yourself, man. No exchange students in our house." Travis said, playing it safe.

"Good answer, Travis." Maysie surmised. "See Travis is well-trained. What's wrong with Fred?"

"Well-trained?" Travis raised his eyebrow.

"Well-trained. Rachael has you well-trained."

"She does, does she?" Travis looked over at Rachael.

"I never said that!" Rachael cast Maysie *the shut up look*. "I'd never say anything so ridiculous."

"Um, hum. So how long have I been in this training program, Rach?" He teased.

"I didn't say that." She could kill Maysie.

"It starts the moment you start dating." Maysie clarified. "Tristan is in training and he doesn't even know it yet. Of course, we aren't actually dating, but by the time we are he'll be like a Doc Bar cutting horse." Maysie paused briefly and then waved over her shoulder. "Tootles trick pony!"

Rachael couldn't help but laugh out loud.

"So you think that's funny?" Travis cast her a sideways glance.

"Admit it. She's hilarious."

"We're out of this conversation, man. I think it's about to get heated around here." Clay and Adam walked off cutting across campus toward the two hundred building.

"I'll remember this conversation." He threatened in a teasing manner. "We'll see about well-trained. How do you know I don't have training of my own in mind for you?"

He bent in and gave her a kiss on the cheek, turned walking back toward the two hundred building. Rachael watched him go, making her stomach turn a flip as she contemplated his comment further. She darted off to class and decided in future she'd have to pick up the pace a bit. While the teachers would cut her some slack today, being the first day and all, she wouldn't be so lucky the next time.

A few hours later Rachael was relieved it was lunch time. Shannah stood in the bagel line waiting for her coveted everything-bagel and cream cheese. Rachael had long ago foregone the everything-bagel, convinced the onions and garlic stayed with her until mid-afternoon. She'd been dating Travis for a while now but wiping him out with the stench of garlic wasn't a priority for her. Shannah fixed her plate paying for three extra cream cheese packets.

"You gonna put all of that on one bagel?"

"Why not? I look at it this way. I've got a few good years before I have to start worrying about what I eat. So for now, it's everything in excess."

Rachael grabbed a taco and a chocolate milk from the other food bar. The girls headed to their typical table. Maysie and Alex were already there with Fred…and the new girl.

"Who's the new chick?" Shannah vexed.

"Elena. Swedish exchange student."

"Fred's?"

"Yep. Be nice." Maysie paused, cutting her eyes at Shannah, "She seems super sweet."

"Since when am I the mean girl?"

"Just the gruff, sometimes ill-tempered, and long to warm to new friends girl."

"Okay, I'll give you that." Shannah conceded.

The girls quit talking as they sat down. Today the table was absolute silence. Alex was jealous of Elena. Fred was mesmerized by a combination of her beauty and foreign accent. Shannah just kept looking over at Rachael raising her eyebrows when she thought no one else was looking. Only Maysie seemed oblivious to it all going on around her, and began chatting nonstop about the dance tryouts.

"I can't believe there'll only be three seniors this year. Three! Count them. One-two-three." She pointed to each of them at the table. "Eight juniors. A few sophomores. And two freshman plan on trying out."

"I like to dance." Elena spoke.

Alex widened her eyes.

"That's fantastic! And you're a senior too. Maybe you should try out." Maysie offered.

Shannah kicked her from under the table.

"Ouch." Maysie protested.

Then a knowing look donned on Maysie's face, but it was too late to take back the suggestion. Elena jumped on it like a kid at the fair jumping on the carousel.

"I think it's a great idea. Elena's a great dancer, classically trained. We've got that in common." Fred added.

Lunch ended and Alex offered to escort Elena to her next class. Fred insisted on going along as well. After Fred, Alex, and Elena disappeared out of the cafeteria, Shannah unleashed her redneck side on Maysie.

"What were you thinking?"

"I plead temporary insanity."

"Hold up." Rachael held up her hands. "If she's a dancer why shouldn't we encourage her to try out? If Fred and Alex's relationship is strong, it shouldn't matter that his family has taken in an exchange student. She's sweet and nice- and we've got to be fair to her."

"So you're telling us if Maysie took in a blonde, five foot eleven super model from Paris and moved her into the Baxter house- in the room next door to Travis'- you'd be like- Oh. That's cool." Shannah smirked. "There's no way. You can't fool me. I know you'd be all over that girl like gravy on a biscuit."

"Maybe you're right, but this isn't my situation. It's Alex's, and as her friends we have to help her cope. I think we should embrace Elena like Maysie is doing."

"Okay. If you say so."

"I've got to get to French." Maysie waved.

"I've got Spanish Lit."

"College level IB class?" Shannah asked.

"Yep."

"Me, too." Shannah surprised her with her answer. "Hey- I've got some smart classes, too."

They both laughed as they walked down to Senora Wilder's Spanish Literature class. It was Siglo del Oro Literatura, whatever that meant, but they were both prepared…armed with Spanish dictionaries. They set them out on their desks alongside pens and the first book on the reading list, some sort of Spanish poetry written circa the sixteenth century. Rachael leafed through it in the bookstore the day before and found she could barely read any of it. It wasn't exactly full of Spanish vocab words she'd learned in Spanish one through three, unless of course they'd be ordering some food or asking the whereabouts of the nearest restroom.

The bell chimed and Senora Wilder fluttered in wearing her sombrero and high heeled boots.

"That's a look." Shannah muttered.

A flurry of late arrivals strolled into class. Most of them Rachael recognized as regulars at their high school. While the school was good sized, you pretty much knew everyone by name and face after three years, even if you didn't necessarily hang out with them. Among the regulars, however, there was a new face. He was a tall, athletically built guy with dark-brown wavy hair and ice blue colored eyes that caught even Rachael's attention. He was strikingly handsome with what Rachael thought of as soccer hair- kind of messy- kind of styled. He could've stepped out of the shower and run out the door- or he could've spent hours working to get just that look. His skin was naturally tan and he was about six feet tall. Of course, he caught Shannah's attention as well.

"Ruh row, raggy. Who's dat?" She said in her best Scooby voice.

Rachael slapped her knee under the table.

"I'm just sayin'. Ain't blind or dead over here, girl." She whispered.

He chose the desk next to Shannah's, setting his stuff down. He flashed his pearly whites and took a seat.

"Class, this is Romero, our Spanish exchange student. He'll be with us for the year. Try to make him feel at home."

"It's like a hot exchange student invasion." Shannah muttered.

Rachael stared straight ahead doing her best not to crack up.

Senora Wilder continued, "This year our school is hosting twice the number of exchange students as we did in the past. As always, we're looking for students and their families who would be willing to host these students. As a result of our program's growth, I find myself with a few more in need of host families."

Shannah looked over at Rachael and nodded her head. Rachael mouthed the words 'bad idea'.

"Anyhow, if you'd be interested please see me after class."

Rachael had a sinking suspicion Shannah would be the first student in that line, but when the bell rang, and she merely packed up her bag, Rachael was confused.

"What? I want to date him, not move him in! Ain't dead or blind, didn't say I was stupid and a moron." She teased.

Outside the girls strolled, talking about the invasion of exchange students. It didn't take long for Romero to jog up to them.

"Ladies, I was hoping you could show me where the three hundred building is."

While Shannah's typical response would've been along the lines of "What, they didn't give you a map?" today's response was a "Sure thing."

Rachael watched as they headed off in the direction of the desired building. Travis frowned as he walked up.

"Who was that with Shannah?"

"Romero. From Spain."

"Exchange student?"

"Yes. And his situation is a sad one. He's displaced and needs a host family." Rachael tried to sound convincingly sad, wiping an invisible tear from her cheek.

"I'm well-trained, not a pacifist." He grinned.

"Like I'd ever take in an exchange student." Rachael almost added…especially a good looking one like that, but thought better of aggravating him too much.

Chapter Twelve

The first couple of weeks passed. Rachael and Michael seemed to find their rhythm once more. One afternoon, Michael sat complaining.

"Why do the teachers pile on the homework from day one?" Michael grumped at the dining room table where he'd started his math assignment.

"I don't know. I always figured they're trying to set the tone for the rest of the year."

"I don't think being a hard ass right out of the gate gets you anywhere with your students."

"Watch your language, Michael!"

Rachael walked over and picked up his book. It was a geometry book. She opened the front of it and read the names of the previous students who'd had this same book. She ran her finger up the list and stopped at one name.

Travis Baxter.

"This was Travis' book?"

"Yep. Sophomore year." Michael snatched it away and set it back down.

"What's wrong with you?"

"Nothing. I'm just trying to get some work done here."

"Okay, moody boy."

Rachael walked into the kitchen. She unloaded the dishwasher, putting the silverware away first. Next she moved on to the glasses, plates, and bowls. She was carefully putting them away when she heard chuckling coming from the dining room.

She poked her head in to check on Michael. "What is so funny?"

He whipped his head up and looked like a cat caught eating the family goldfish.

"Nothing. This teacher, Mr. Sanchez, he's funny. Total jokester."

"If you say so. I never found him all that amusing." Rachael shook her head and returned to her chore. She'd had Mr. Sanchez- and he was very stiff- maybe a little bit boring, but never funny.

A few minutes later she heard more giggling. She knew better than to believe it was just Mr. Sanchez. She crept around the other side of the wall to the foyer where she could clearly see into the dining room, over Michael's shoulder.

Michael had the book opened to the index at the back of the book. Among the pages where the answers to the even numbered problems were, there was a white page completely covered in drawings. Along the top it read *The Journey of a Redneck Debutante*.

She crept closer and saw it was similar to a comic strip- and the girl who was the main character throughout was her! There was the first one with her standing in a creek catching minnows with a shocked look on her face as a herd of stampeding cattle approached from behind. There was one with her sitting on an airboat- hair blowing widely about her face- bikini two sizes too small. Her personal favorite was one of her fishing with a tiny bass latched onto her finger. The caption read "Ouch! Bass have teeth?"

At this point, Michael realized she was peering over his shoulder. He slammed the book closed.

"What's the problem? I thought they were cute!"

"Okay. But don't tell Travis you saw them."

"Why not? There's nothing wrong with them."

"I think it'd embarrass him."

"It's kind of stalker-like." She teased. "Of course, I'm joking. It's sweet. He chronicled our every meeting."

"Not all of them I hope. Geez Rach, don't make me barf."

She punched her brother's arm. "I want it." She said.

"I need the book, you can't have it. How else am I supposed to do my homework?"

"I'll cut it out carefully. No one will ever know it was taken out of there."

"Okay. But if I get fined or something, you're in huge trouble."

"You're not going to get fined."

Rachael went to the kitchen and procured a pair of scissors from the crafting container located in the bottom of the pantry. She returned to the dining room and carefully cut along the edge up the spine of the book. Since the page was blank and had no credits of any kind listed on either side, its absence would be unnoticeable.

"I think I'll frame it."

She glanced at the pictures from top to bottom. She stopped at the one from last year's dance. Had her chest looked that full in the dress? If it had, no wonder he offered her his jacket.

Poor guy.

She took the picture down the hall and found an empty picture frame in her aunt's hall closet. She'd always kept a few on hand. Rachael removed the back and slid the page into place. She had to laugh at the one of her getting sick down the side of a horse and the caption accompanying it. 'Moonshine might be the death of me!'

She did her own homework and decided to catch up on social media. She had a short note from Ellery in response to her recent post about senior year and going back to school.

Hi Rach-

I can't believe we're about to start our last year of HS either! TJ and I are great. No changes there. He got accepted to UF and we're super excited. Did you do your applications yet? LMK.

Love ya,
Ellery

Rachael responded letting her know she hadn't completed her application yet, but that she would get right on it. Rachael hit the send button just as she heard Travis coming up the driveway. She jumped up to go greet him. She thought about hiding the drawings but reconsidered.

She leapt to the front door and swung the door open. He wore a shocked expression.

"That was fast."

She threw her arms around him and gave him a bear hug and a kiss.

"Wow. What's gotten into you?"

"She found the drawings dude." Michael confessed from the dining room. "Not my fault. She found them all on her own."

Travis looked annoyed.

"It's not a big deal. I thought they were sweet. I had no idea you were such an artist."

"Yep. I like to draw." He turned and quickly changed the subject. "I brought you those male dogs we talked about. Care to join us, Michael?"

"Here I come." Michael jumped up.

Outside the dogs barked at them in the back of Travis' truck.

"They going to bite us?"

"Nope." He lowered the tail gate and let them jump down. They sniffed around circling the yard and then ran back to meet Rachael and Michael. The one male dog, Spike, licked Michael's hand sweetly, while the other one growled at him from nearby.

Michael looked at the growler, also known as Hank, and whistled to him.

"Hank's a little rowdy, but he'll warm up to you both."

Aunt Margaret and Mrs. Harte pulled into the driveway and up to the house. Both ladies got out. Hank barked at them, but warmed to them within fifteen minutes. Spike on the other hand looked like he wouldn't bite a robber if he were loading a moving van with all of their most cherished possessions.

"Hank." Travis called.

Hank came over and sat at his feet.

"Hank is my dog."

Rachael held out her hand for Hank to sniff. He did doubtingly and then settled back down at Travis' boot.

"I'm not sure he likes us."

"He will."

"You should probably stick around for dinner and make sure he doesn't take our legs off or anything." Mrs. Harte commented.

"Thank you, I will."

Rachael noticed a change in Travis. He was more bothered by her finding the drawings than he should've been. Something was wrong and she'd have to get to the bottom of what it was.

"Travis, I was about to take a walk on the ranch to check on Taffy and ole' lonesome George."

"Sure. They're probably at the molasses tanks."

Rachael grabbed his hand pulling him along with her. When they were near the barn she started talking. "I loved the drawings."

"I'm glad."

"Have you done any others?"

"I have. A bunch actually." He grinned over at her. "Not all of you. Hate to disappoint."

She jerked her head around to look at him. "Of bunches of girls?"

"No." He laughed. "Animals mostly. You're the only female human subject of my artwork."

"Well, that's a relief. I'd hate to have to burn all the others."

"You've been spending entirely too much time with Shannah."

"Maybe. I don't think I've ever threatened to burn anything before."

"I better watch out. If we get into it when we're married someday you're gonna go all pyro on me and burn my clothes on the front lawn. Crazy redneck woman."

He squeezed her hand to let her know he was joking, but his eyes lacked their typical smile.

"What's wrong?"

"Nothing."

"I'd believe that if I didn't know you so well."

They crossed through the fence line and continued toward the barbed wire fence in the distance. At that fence, Travis held the second strand down for her with his sneaker while simultaneously holding the top strand up to prevent it from catching on her top. He followed her through the wire and took her hand once more.

"If you won't tell me, I'm going to try to guess." She looked at him. "You're mad at me."

"Not at all. You'd know it if I was mad at you."

When he still said nothing, Rachael decided to let it go. He never held back with her, and she knew whatever it was he mustn't be ready to discuss it.

In the distance she could see the molasses tanks coming into view. The smell of cattle manure greeted her from where she was.

"I think this is close enough."

"That stink isn't poop. It's the liquid feed in those large tanks over there. I think we should build a house out here after we graduate college. Wake up to that smell every day."

She knew better than to think he was serious.

She saw Taffy grazing near the tanks with ole' lonesome George beside her.

"How did you know they were here?"

"I've been checking them every afternoon since we put them out here. I knew you'd be worried."

She turned and kissed him, standing on her tiptoes in the deep grass. He wrapped his arms around her and returned her kiss. He reached his hand down and brushed her blonde hair away from her face kissing her forehead.

"I love to draw, but I was born a rancher's son. Drawing cartoons is something I've done since I was little. It's fun."

"There's no reason you can't do both. A drawing, artistic cattleman."

"I know, but I gave up on the dream of doing it for a living a long, long time ago."

"Would you have liked to have gone to school to study art?"

"Maybe in another life."

"You still can."

"No, I can't and that's okay."

"Why not take some art classes, too? There's nothing wrong with that."

"I guess not. That's just another reason I love you Rachael Harte. You make me feel like anything is possible."

"Anything is possible- if you want it to be."

"Come on. Let's go jump in the creek. The water's up."

"I'm going in fully clothed."

"Suit yourself. I've got on shorts."

"That better not be all you're wearing, Mr. No-britches."

"I've got those on too. You wanna check?"

Rachael jumped back a few feet shaking her head.

"Nope. I'll take your word for it."

"Thought so. Wimp." He took off his shirt and threw it on the ground. He slipped off his sneakers, followed by his socks.

"I'm not a wimp. I'm just maintaining clear boundaries."

"For now." His eyes gleamed in the afternoon sun. "Let's race to the creek. I'll give you a head start."

"I'm not that fast!" She exclaimed.

"I know." He winked at her. "But I am." He paused, "You better get going because I'll give you fair warning…when I catch you- you're getting kissed, good."

Rachael wasn't sure what getting kissed good entailed but she took off at a sprinter's pace. The jeans she'd chosen to wear were a bit of a hindrance. She moved as quickly as she could. The trees lining the tree bank were getting closer and closer. She felt the wet soil beneath her feet and jumped in. Another figure flew into the water passing her. She disappeared below the surface. When she came up for air, he was there.

He grabbed her in an embrace and kissed her.

She ran her hand down his side where his cut was almost completely healed, tracing it with her fingertips. Next, she continued her exploration down his sides to his strong waistline stopping there.

"I can't stand here."

"I know." He smiled into her eyes, "But I can."

Rachael had to hold onto him to keep her head above water.

"Do your ribs still hurt?"

"Not at all. We're tougher than that." He bent his head and kissed her again, and again, until it began to turn dark. Crickets chirped and bullfrogs croaked near the water's edge.

"Let's get you home."

Chapter Thirteen

Dance tryouts finally arrived and Rachael was a flurry of nerves. After last year's embarrassing, yet deserved, suspension off the team, she knew she had to go in there and give it her all. It was her senior year and dancing was just a part of the overall school experience she'd always pictured.

As seniors there was a good chance Maysie and Shannah would be named captains! Rachael was ecstatic for them. While Shannah would protest at first, she'd step up to the role and do a kick butt job. Maysie would accept the position with poise and grace, in typical Maysie fashion. That was one thing you could always count on from her.

Rachael walked to the locker room where she put down her book bag. She opened her locker and tugged out her dance bag where she'd stowed it earlier the same morning. She unzipped the bag and pulled out her tights and favorite pair of Capezio slip-ons. For today, she'd brought a pair of tight jazz shorts with matching Lycra top. She glanced around the locker room and still saw no sign of Maysie or Shannah.

Some of the other younger dancers came filing in and greeted her. Alex and Sidney opened their lockers next to hers and quickly began getting ready. Rachael considered her competition. It wasn't often that a veteran dancer would get cut, but it had happened in the past. According to Maysie the last time was her freshman year and she remembered it had caused an uproar—especially among the parents and sponsors. When a sponsor's daughter gets cut, you not only lose the dancer, the program loses the money, too.

This thought increased Rachael's uneasiness. *What if I go in there and dance my heart out- and they just plain don't want me back?* It was a real possibility at this point.

Mr. Greene, the band director, was nice enough, but he'd made it clear how displeased he'd been with her skipping practices and such. While he'd told her he'd love her to try out again in the future, Rachael had no way of knowing if he'd meant it or not.

Rachael heard the door slam behind her and watched as Elena came into the locker room. She was received coolly by the handful of other dancers who made no move to acknowledge her in any way. Rachael was especially surprised at Alex, who not only ignored her, but disappeared into the bathroom with a hairbrush, hair tie, and bobby pins to put her hair up in a bun.

Rachael grabbed her own hairbrush out of the bag and a hair tie; then turned to welcome Elena.

"Hi, Elena. There's an empty locker over here beside mine if you want it."

Elena nodded and came over to set her dance bag down. She looked nervous, almost sick. She quickly changed in silence. Rachael seized the opportunity to use the restroom and do her hair.

In front of the mirror, Alex applied some gloss and did a final once-over of her outfit. "Don't be too nice to her, Rachael." She whispered.

"Why not? She's an exchange student, new to school, with very few friends. She hasn't done anything to us."

"Not yet. But I think she likes Fred."

"I think she likes him as a friend. Give it a week or two- you'll see. She'll make friends and you'll see you don't have anything to worry about. He adores you."

"Maybe you're right."

"Besides, I've been that new girl. Remember?"

Alex laughed. "At least none of us is having her followed into the locker room or anything."

"I held my own." Rachael attested.

"And you had Redneck Shannah. Who's going to challenge that?"

The girls finished up and went out into the locker room where Elena was finishing lacing up her dance boots. Rachael had to admit to herself that Elena was fit, super pretty, not to mention blonde…and sweet. What eighteen year old senior wouldn't be affected by that …living in his house…under his same roof?

Okay, maybe she should worry, but I can't tell her that.

"We're going to walk down to the dance room. Would you like to join us?" Rachael offered to Elena and another underclassman who'd shown up for auditions.

"Sure." They chimed.

Rachael glanced around and still saw no sign of Shannah or Maysie.

"They must be down there already." Alex pointed out, reading her thoughts.

"I hope so. I didn't see them today except for lunch and one class with Maysie. She never mentioned auditions. I guess she figured I was nervous enough already."

"She was probably right."

The girls walked across campus toward the football locker room, weightlifting room, and personal trainers' and coaches' offices. At the far end, they saw the doors to the dance room standing open. Shannah stood talking outside to Romero.

"Who's that?" Sidney asked.

"He's got to be new." Alex added.

"He's an exchange student." Olivia offered. "Romero from Spain."

"Romero from Spain." Sidney sounded intrigued.

"Sorry ladies, but it looks like he's into Shannah."

"Looks like." Alex smiled. "She's got that feminine beauty with a little bit of jock appeal going for her. Not every girl can pull that off."

"I liken it to some type of animal pheromone." Sidney chimed in.

Everyone looked at her cracking up.

"Pheromone?" Rachael sounded doubtful.

"Exactly. Pheromone. Some people just have it. I've watched her since last year. Guys are just drawn to her, pulled in by some unseen force. It's gotta be pheromones."

"I wish I had some pheromone." Olivia griped.

"Luck of the draw. Pheromone. Some got it. Some don't." Sidney, the obvious pheromone expert advised.

Shannah saw them approaching and excused herself from Romero to go inside the dance room. When Rachael and the others stepped inside the dance room, her heart lurched forwards and hurtled headlong toward her feet. There must have been twenty-five girls in the dance room ahead of their group of six. Many of them were new freshman. Rachael should've assumed there would've been more this year than in year's prior. Dance was becoming huge at their school. There was a handful of sophomores and a bunch of juniors, like Maysie said, who'd already tried out at the end of last year and would assist in the audition today. Alex quickly walked over to join them. *Whatever happened to only two freshman planning on trying out?* At this rate Rachael would be lucky to have a spot at all. But, still, there might be hope. In addition to the two existing openings, there were also now the spots previously occupied by Misty and Honey. That would make four openings- total.

Today Maysie was all business. This was an entirely new side to her Rachael had never seen before. No wonder she and Shannah hadn't been in the locker room this afternoon. By the looks of it they'd been down here getting things ready for the try-outs. Both of them acted as if they'd never seen her before, which was understandable.

They can't play favorites. This is an audition.

Rachael spied another girl coming in through the opened dance doors behind them.

Amber...

She walked over to where the girls sat in circles chatting excitedly. She was dressed in new dance clothes, her figure much fuller than it'd been the year before. She wore a smile and held her head high.

"Here." Rachael and Alex slid over making room. "Sit with us."

"Surprise." She whispered.

Rachael, Alex, Sidney, and Olivia hugged her. Shannah nodded her *what's up, girl* from across the room where she talked quietly to Maysie.

"Time to get started." Shannah came over to address the group. "I'm Shannah."

If the girls thought there was going to be more to her speech than that they were mistaken! She wasn't big on public speaking or small talk. Shannah led them through a series of stretches and warm-up exercises. Most of the girls were experienced dancers and they showed it. Next, Maysie took over the audition explaining things. The first thing she did was ask the girls to line up in straight lines, eight to a row. There were four rows across the studio.

"This year Mr. Greene, the band director, has selected Shannah and me to be your captains. We're going to teach you a challenging routine that is typical of one we'd use during football season and at competition. Of course we're not on a field, so it will be in a confined space. Most of you are freshman and probably haven't danced with a high school band before so blocking and marking is something we'll teach you in the course of the next few weeks at practice. Therefore," Maysie paused and walked across the front of the room like a military general inspecting his lines. "Today will be primarily focused on dance, technique, and skill."

Maysie and Shannah taught the routine which was ten minutes in length, shorter than the average halftime routine yet longer than a typical dance. It combined movement and direction changes, leaps, and triple pirouettes. The descriptive word that came to mind for Rachael was grueling. Shannah must've thought so, too, because Rachael caught her looking her way one time and she mouthed the words 'what up with this, Maysie'?

Rachael nearly laughed but had to maintain her focus. After the longer than necessary routine, they received a water break. Some of the girls went out for water and didn't return. Rachael hated to admit as much, but she was relieved. Undeterred, Maysie asked them to line up again.

"And then there were sixteen." She grinned at them.

Rachael watched her strut across the room and thought all she lacked was a crop, one of those short handheld whips carried by riding jockeys.

"Look around you, ladies. Dancing is hard work. Summer vacation has ended. Practice is practice. If you make it, be on time, dressed and ready to dance. A list will be posted on the band room doors tomorrow. Thank you for coming."

The remaining girls grabbed their stuff and walked away.

Rachael approached Maysie and Shannah reluctantly. "Is it safe to say hi?" She joked.

"I don't know. Even I was scared about fifteen minutes ago." Shannah shook her head.

"Sorry, girls, but Mr. Greene said to make it tough. He's tired of the quitters and problems and all that other stuff."

"You accomplished that," Shannah commented. "We've never had girls actually not finish the audition."

"If they can't commit to finishing the audition, how can we rely on them to finish the season?" Maysie grinned.

"I'm sorry. I was one of those losers last year." Rachael admitted.

"No. You were suspended. There's a difference."

"That's worse!"

"No. Just a life lesson. Let's go grab pizza." Maysie smiled. "And Travis isn't invited. He's gotten on my last nerve lately."

Shannah and Rachael exchanged looks with Amber. They decided to let the newest sibling war slide.

Everyone was so excited to see Amber. It was just like old times. Rachael had to catch a ride with Shannah and Maysie to the pizza parlor since Travis drove her to school this morning, while Amber drove her own car separately. At the pizza restaurant they grabbed a booth and ordered the 'works' veggie pizza.

"Sorry I didn't tell y'all I was coming to the audition today. Things have been a little crazy for me."

"Well, yeah. We get it." Shannah commented leaving the obvious unsaid.

"We're just glad you're back." Maysie added.

"Me, too. My mom told me last week if it'd help me I could go back to public school with you guys and have a normal senior year with friends."

"We're glad she did."

"But I'm not allowed to date right now. I didn't want to anyway. I'm pretty messed up- adding a guy and dating to my situation wouldn't be good."

"Just know we'll be here to support you every step of the way, every step." Maysie reached over and patted her hand.

Rachael sat quietly pondering the audition. She knew Amber was thinking the same thing. Neither of them mentioned it, though, and Rachael decided to stick to safer topics of conversation like shopping and the remainder of the school year.

"My big goal is to lose the weight. I had to go out and find some dance pants that fit this booty." Amber sighed.

"You look fantastic." Rachael complimented.

While catching up with Amber was always fun, this afternoon the conversation dragged a bit. It was very difficult to find anything to say that wouldn't touch on the subject of guys, your figure, or anything that would in some way make Amber feel uncomfortable. Even something as simple as school gossip about who did what at a party, or who hooked up with who, suddenly became off limits. Rachael and everyone else felt like they were walking on eggshells around her. Her situation had forever changed everything.

A little downhearted the girls climbed into Maysie's car and headed for home.

"It'll get better, guys. It will."

Shannah...the redneck voice of reason.

"You're right. It's just so new. I'll never call myself chunky or curvy again in her presence. Like she said she's got forty-five pounds to lose. She's just had a baby! A little over two months ago...and today she was at a high school dance audition." Maysie laid it out in black and white.

"How do you move on from that? I can't imagine. I think it's worse now than before." Rachael added.

"Worse how?" Maysie asked.

"Worse as in- if you had a baby and kept it, well, you'd be planning that life. The life of being a mother. Now what? Try to return to normal teen life?" Rachael frowned.

"She's right and the whole dating thing. How do you even begin to address that?" Shannah shook her head.

"I don't think she needs to address anything. People have babies all the time. All the time." Maysie commented.

"Not at seventeen!" Shannah yelled.

"Sure they do!" Maysie countered. "I may get married first. And maybe I'll be nineteen when I have my first child. College isn't for everyone and waiting until you're thirty to have a child isn't for everyone, either."

"Wow! I wasn't talking about you, Maysie, and whatever you've got planned. It wasn't a personal judgment statement or nothing. Chill." Shannah defended herself. "That's entirely different and you know it. You can't compare graduating high school, getting married, and then getting pregnant to what poor Amber has just gone through. You've got an example here of what I call: planned and unplanned. There is a huge, ginormous difference!" Shannah spat.

Rachael had a feeling this argument was going nowhere good and fast. She decided to intervene. "You're both right. It's okay to get married young and start a family. College isn't for everyone. And it's also okay that things happen, unplanned things, and we grow to overcome them."

"So says Dr. Rachael from the backseat. Everyone's expert on teen love and relationships." Maysie muttered.

"What's your problem?" Shannah turned facing her. "Tell Rachael you're sorry for being a wench! I don't know what crazy pill you took today, but we're not having it."

Maysie pulled over on the side of the road and threw the car in park. "Get out!"

Shannah and Rachael looked at each other confused. Rachael decided there was no point in arguing. She grabbed her bags, both the dance bag and the book bag, and climbed out. Shannah grabbed her stuff as well.

"If I didn't think you were going mental I'd kick your butt right now, but instead I pity you." Shannah slammed the door.

Maysie spun her tires and drove away.

"What was that?" Rachael watched her race off.

"I'd say she threw us out."

Both girls laughed their butts off.

"Really, it's not funny- but it kinda is." Shannah held her belly. "Maysie's got a little booty kicker in her yet."

"I guess, but what is she so fired up about?"

"I don't know, but something sure as heck is bothering her. Trouble in paradise with Tristan would be my guess."

"Mine, too."

"So what now?" Rachael asked.

"My dad's working and your mom and aunt are too." Shannah offered.

"Travis." He's our only hope.

Rachael called Travis and told him she was stranded at the corner of University Parkway near I-75.

"Stranded?"

"Stranded. As in Shannah and I need a lift."

"What happened?"

"Just come get us. Twenty-five miles from home would be a long walk."

Rachael and Shannah spent the next fifteen minutes sitting at the nearest service station debating on whether to tell Travis the truth or lie through their teeth. At first Shannah concocted an elaborate tale.

They'd gone for pizza with Amber. She'd offered to run them home and blown a tire on the way. She'd called a tow truck and after it came- her mother came to pick her up.

"And what? Her mother came and left us here? Without a ride?" Rachael shook her head. "Travis will never buy that."

"Okay take two." Shannah offered. "We caught a ride with Romero and he ended up being a total butthead, so we were stranded and needed a ride."

"Yep. That will go over well with my boyfriend. He'll get arrested for beating Romero to a pulp."

Travis pulled into the parking lot wearing a scowl. He threw his truck in park and climbed out.

"You okay?"

"Perfectly fine." Rachael kissed his cheek.

"What happened?"

"Your sister's gone postal." Shannah hopped in the backseat and closed the door.

Way to go easy there.

"She left you guys?" Travis looked like he might rupture a vein in his neck or something.

"Not left exactly. We all had a disagreement over, I'm not sure what exactly, and she kicked us out."

"Of the car?"

"It's okay. I called you. We survived."

"Come on." Travis tossed their bags in the back.

Rachael climbed in and he closed the door behind her.

He drove home, a little faster than usual, dropping Shannah off at her house on his way. After Shannah was out of the vehicle he started. "She's been in rare form lately."

"So I'm sensing."

"She's ticked that there is some double standard in our house, and I can't say she's wrong. But in the end she's a girl, and girls can end up in bad situations that guys can't."

"Whoa. You may want to rephrase that last statement."

"Why should I? It's true. We can date. At the end of the day nothing bad could happen to me, but a girl, well she could end up...like Amber."

"Maysie's not allowed to date Tristan seriously because of that? That's stupid."

"I don't know for sure, but that's part of it. He's older and naturally he'd have more experience and be used to a more physical relationship. So in a nutshell, yes."

"And you're okay with that?"

"Okay with what? A girl having more dating restrictions?"

"Yes. Well are you?"

"I guess I am."

"I thought your parents were worried about the age gap and all that bullarky."

"They are- and what's that age gap exactly?"

"If she is eighteen and he's twenty-four, the gap is six years." Rachael fumed.

"You're looking at it as a number. I'll tell you what the difference is between her and Tristan. He's had relationships. Lots and lots of relationships. He can drink. She hasn't had her first drink yet."

"So what? Your parents said they could date down the road and they will."

"I'm sure, but in the meantime she's pushing for more and more. Now she doesn't want to even go to college. She's going to ruin her life getting married too young." Travis spouted.

"Is that what you'd say about us?"

"No. We're different. We're not abandoning college, for one. And two, you're not so clouded in your thought processes that you just kicked two friends out on the side of the road."

"Well I'm not happy about that, or about your parents' double standard, or the fact that you support it."

"Now you're defending her? I'm not the one who kicked you out, remember? I came to your rescue."

"And for that I'm appreciative, but when we have a daughter…your double standard is going to change, Sir."

"You go right on living that dream." He spat through clenched teeth.

"Okay. Pull over." Rachael put her hand on the door.

"You're not walking home." He made no move to stop the truck.

"Am too."

"Fine." Travis pulled over and let her climb out.

She grabbed her stuff and slung it over her shoulder. She started walking down the side of the road. She was less than a mile from home now.

Travis pulled in behind her, following at an idle. He put his flashers on. Rachael rolled her eyes at him and stuck out her tongue. Just to annoy her further, he rode up alongside her with the window down.

"Nice day for a walk, beautiful lady. Would you like a ride?"

"Nope."

"Suit yourself." He continued driving beside her until her gate was less than fifty yards away. He drove ahead.

"Good riddance." She kicked some rocks and gravel from beside the roadway. She saw him turn in and get out to open the gate.

He stood behind the gate, gorgeous smile, green eyes, and spiked hair, holding it open for her. "Look at her go. Grace and beauty rolled into one. That's one good looking woman."

She passed through the gate. "Go home, Travis." She tried to sound angry.

"Bye, baby." He called shutting the gate, chaining it, and locking it.

"I got my stitches out." He'd left his truck parked outside the gate, and jogged to catch up with her.

Her anger turned to concern.

"I'm still not done talking about the double standard, but let me see your side."

He pulled up his shirt. The purple scar was already beginning to fade. Rachael stopped, running her hand down it.

"Looks so much better."

"And I'm cleared to play football in a week. Can't wait."

"Good."

He reached over and held her hand, walking her up to her house. She didn't protest.

"Should we go look for your sister?"

"She's a big girl. In the past I might have, but she's got to find her own way. It may surprise you, but I won't even rat her out over today's little incident."

"That's cool. You won't have to by the time Shannah's done with her. The weird thing is she respected your sister more for actually getting ticked off for once."

"Shannah's a funny one. No one's victim, that one."

"That's for sure."

"How was the audition?"

"Okay, but a lot of girls…and only four slots."

"What's meant to be, will be. If you don't make it, I'll let you dance for me around the living room once a week."

She smacked his hand away. "That's not the same and you know it."

"It's even better, for me anyway." He looked at her dance outfit. "About this outfit, it's nice, for around the house."

"It's a dance outfit. Everyone wears one, to practice, and especially to an audition."

"I was just hoping for a little more ... material." He paused pointing to her thighs and backside. "Like here and here."

"Not going to happen. This is the look, like it or leave it."

"Oh I like it- I just don't want anyone else liking it."

"Too bad."

"Can I come in?" He smiled.

"Are you going to behave? As in no talking about your sister and Tristan. No talking about my small dance costume. Nada."

He made the sign of the cross.

"Okay. Entre si vous plait."

"Oui." He stopped just inside the foyer. "Where's Michael?"

"He went home with Levi because he knew I'd be late. I have to go get him."

"So we just walked home, why?" Travis smirked.

"To get my car. I like to be independent." She grabbed her keys and set down her bags. She ran down the hall to get her wallet off of her dresser. When she came back toward the kitchen, Travis had helped himself to a piece of pound cake. He stood eating it in the kitchen, sipping on a glass of milk.

He'd cut her a monster wedge, as well, and poured her a small glass of milk.

"I can't eat this whole piece." She eyed it. She picked up her fork and took the first bite.

"I was banking on that. I didn't want to be a pig and go for two pieces. I'll finish it if you can't." He picked up his fork and dug in on the opposite side of her plate. He scarfed down in four bites what would've taken her six or more.

He went to the fridge for more milk. He lifted the carton up to his mouth, poised waiting to swig.

"Hey! Not in my kitchen."

"I was just testing. Seeing how much you'd let me get away with, now that you know all my bad habits from Mama."

"Not much."

"We'll see." He grabbed his glass and carefully refilled it. Then he looked over his shoulder flashing a wicked grin. "You know the way I see it. Once we're married, your spit's my spit, baby."

"Gross! You're sooo gross!"

Travis laughed, "I'm a guy. Now who's training who?"

Rachael should've known that conversation would come back to bite her in the proverbial buttocks.

"One little step at a time. I'm molding you and you don't even know it."

"Why are you so aggravating today?" She questioned.

"I don't know, but I'm enjoying it. I've told you before I like it when you get feisty with me."

"Bye. I'm going to get Michael." Rachael strode out of the house.

Travis followed her to the door and locked it behind himself. He walked out and climbed in the passenger seat.

"Football better start soon. I don't think I can handle any more of your pent up energy- or whatever this is."

"Maybe that's it."

"I've figured you out. No hunting and no football makes you, well," She thought for a moment, "you get bored."

"We could never be boring. Nope, this is just me enjoying your company and annoying the heck out of you in the process."

"Truth? You aren't really annoying me. I could do this with you every day of the week."

"Soon you will." He patted her thigh.

At the end of the driveway, they saw a small blue car speed past. He turned to look at her.

"Was that the car?"

"I'm pretty sure it was."

"Okay."

"Do you know who that was?"

"I do. And if it was him he just saw my truck here. I don't think you'll hear from him again." Travis looked straight ahead, his gaze intense.

"Who is it?"

"An old friend." Travis didn't elaborate.

"You were friends with those types of people?"

"You knew I ran with a rough crowd at one point."

"I didn't realize they were that rough."

"We were a few years younger and that's where I split. They got heavier into drugs and I didn't want to go there. Sure, I avoid them now, but I know them and they know me."

"So what if they pull his prints?"

"He doesn't have a criminal past, but he won't be back around now, that's for sure."

"I've gotta admit to being shocked here." She clenched the steering wheel and cast him a sideways glance. "I never thought you knew those types of thugs."

"He wasn't a thug when I knew him. Just a kid who got off on the wrong path and stayed on it. No matter what, I knew him before that. Now he knows you're my girlfriend, he won't mess with you." Travis explained.

"I don't get it."

"What's not to get?" Travis blew out an angry breath. "He's got no beef with me. If he showed up again he'd have one then. We used to be friends. If I saw him on the street I'd nod and say hi, not stop to chat- or exchange numbers- or anything. But let's be clear, if he showed up at your place again I'd kick his you know what."

"It's like you've lived...two lives."

"It didn't go that far, but I've always said you can ask me anything. And I meant it."

Rachael thought about this new conversation and the various questions it brought to mind. *Of course she had questions! Who is this guy, really?*

"Did you ever use drugs?"

"Nope, a lot of drinking though."

"But they used drugs, your friends I mean."

"Certainly. I've been around some drug users. That's why I knew Misty was on meth when she showed up at my birthday party. She was always a pot smoker, but meth is new for her."

"This stuff is completely foreign to me." Rachael blinked.

"And you thought my parents were thinking you might lead me astray? I ran with a wild crowd. Not going to sugar coat it." Travis sat quietly. "I don't want to go around it ever again. It's a bad scene."

"Did you get into fights in the past?"

"A few too many, but not now. You've got me trained." He teased.

"Stop saying that! I never said I had you trained...or in training...or any such thing."

"I don't know, if I'm going to be anyone's trick pony it might as well be yours."

Rachael turned on the radio to drown him out.

One more week. Football starts in just one more week. Let the countdown begin.

Chapter Fourteen

Rachael sat cross legged on her bedroom floor finishing translating her first Siglo de Oro poem. She scribbled her own translated notes above words and phrases just in case she needed to reread it for an exam, she wouldn't have to do all the work over again. Guess that was the benefit to having paid for the book yourself, you could take notes, highlight, and do whatever you wanted with it. She heard the front door, followed by Michael who jumped off the sofa to answer it.

Her bedroom door swing open.

"Hey, Rachael, it's Maysie and Shannah." Michael panted. "They said to bring your sleeping bag."

Rachael had completely forgotten! Every year on the night of the fall audition, the girls who made it on to the squad were blindfolded and driven to an all girls' slumber party. It'd only been four hours since Maysie had thrown her out on the side of a busy highway more than twenty miles from home.

This should be comfortable.

Rachael opened the hall closet and grabbed her sleeping bag. She put her books in her book bag. She shoved clothes for dance practice, along with pajamas and a change of clothes for school in the morning, in a separate bag. In the bathroom she grabbed her make-up bag and toothbrush.

In the foyer she heard Michael chatting nonstop with Shannah. Rachael smiled at his attempts to strike up a conversation with her. Maybe there was more to this pheromone business than she thought.

"Hey." She greeted them both.

"What up." Shannah nodded.

"We've got my mom's SUV. There are four of you that made it. You, Elena, Sidney, and Olivia. And two alternates."

"Alternates? We've never done that before." Rachael worried, *what about Amber?*

Mrs. Harte came out to wave goodbye to the girls. "Have fun!" She called from the doorway.

Inside the SUV, Maysie turned and handed Rachael the blindfold.

"So, you obviously know it's us. You don't have to put this on yet- just when the other girls get in." Maysie paused and looked like she might cry. "Sorry about earlier today. That was so unfair of me to do to y'all. I'm just so frustrated by the whole Tristan thing, and for what? It doesn't bother him at all. He's perfectly fine waiting to date me."

"Let me break it down for her." Shannah interjected. "She feels like if Tristan isn't willing to battle her parents over the dating thing, then he doesn't really care about her all that much."

"Or he's a total gentleman and mature. He's showing he respects you and your parents." Rachael offered.

"That's what I said." Shannah pointed out.

"Either way I have to wait to date him." She started the vehicle. "And I'm really sorry. Truly sorry."

"Shannah kick your butt? Did she land a roundhouse kick to your head and straighten you out?" Rachael teased.

"No, but the thought did cross her mind I'm sure of it."

"No, like I said, glad to see her getting tough." Shannah raised her eyebrows. "It's cool."

"What was cool is how Travis left it between us girls. He didn't rat me out or anything. I'd have lost my car for a month!"

"Yeah. Well while I thought it was okay once- don't do it again." Shannah warned.

Rachael sat and considered the list of girls who made the squad today.

Elena, Sidney, Olivia, and herself. She wondered once more...*what about Amber?*

"What about Amber?" She whispered.

"She's an alternate. Her score wasn't as good as everyone else's. That's just how it turned out." Maysie admitted.

"Who were the judges?"

"Other squad members, plus Shannah and me. We had the final say, but the numbers don't lie." Maysie obviously regretted the outcome of the audition scores.

Rachael considered the members of the squad who'd been there assisting in the tryout. There was Jen, Lisa, Marcey, Tina, Jody, Savannah, Caitlin, Selena, Gina, and Alex. She thought back to the slumber party and the girls who'd been there, and their moms.

"I don't mean to sound rude, but are you sure it was judged fairly? I mean with a couple of the girls having moms who obviously dislike Amber?"

"We already considered the same thing. We'd hate to think they would let their mothers' feelings about a girl affect how they judged a dance tryout." Maysie fretted.

"That'd suck." Shannah commented. "But there's no way to be sure."

"Amber really needs this." Rachael said quietly.

"We know, but what can we do?" Maysie lamented.

"Did you call Mr. Greene?"

"He said the scores stand the way they are. Four slots, but he added two alternates, which is new. They'll practice with us and learn all the routines, cover when a girl misses. That sort of thing."

"So an alternate has to learn most every position?"

"Pretty much. It'll be a challenging position for Amber and Riley, she's a new freshman."

"Do they get to come tonight?" Rachael asked.

"Absolutely." Maysie answered. "Put on your blindfold, this is Fred's house. Oops, I mean…Elena's house."

Rachael situated her blindfold over her eyes and waited. They were back in less than thirty seconds. Rachael could hear Fred cheering for Elena. He kept talking and sounded somewhere close by.

"We got it from here. Thanks Fred." Shannah's less than pleased voice could be heard just outside the SUV.

Elena climbed in next to Rachael. Seconds later the SUV was on the move once more. Absolute silence surrounded them. They drove a short distance and picked up someone who was giggling profusely. Rachael decided the nervous giggler could be none other than Riley. She was always happy.

They continued their journey and picked up the three other girls. Olivia and Sidney were first. The distance between their houses was so close, they must've lived in the same neighborhood. The last stop was Amber's house. Rachael could hear her mother walking her to the car. She helped her sit down and kissed her cheek hugging her.

"See you had nothing to worry about. This is just what you needed." She whispered in her ear where only Rachael seated next to her would hear. "A fresh start. God always provides." She gently closed the door.

They rode a long ways. Olivia sneezed and Sidney coughed- purposefully. Riley started to giggle.

"Silence." Shannah commanded.

Everyone laughed.

They turned into a driveway, which was bumpier than normal. Their destination had to be Shannah's house at the back of the orange grove. The sand road would be filled with potholes where the large trucks constantly loaded out fruit from early December to late March. Today, however, it seemed exceptionally unsmooth- and rough.

They drove and drove- and drove. Then drove some more. Rachael was beginning to wonder if they'd ever make it there. When they finally stopped, they commanded them to remove their blinds.

In the fading sunlight, Rachael saw they were in the woods. A nice cabin with a wrap-around porch greeted them.

"Welcome, ladies, to the Dance Retreat."

"Wow!" Riley said. "Are we alone out here- in the middle of nowhere?"

"My mom is here with us." Maysie smiled. "Don't be a chicken. Let's go."

Rachael looked around and saw a wide river flowing quietly a hundred yards behind the cabin. The cabin itself was large, made of logs, with cypress furniture on the porch. It was refined and rustic at the same time.

"Pretty river." Sidney commented.

"The Myakka. It's high right now, there's been a lot of rain."

"Can we swim in it?"

"Canoe. You could swim, but there are plenty of gators out here." Shannah answered.

The girls grabbed their sleeping bags and went inside to get set up. Mrs. Baxter was in the kitchen where she finished the final preparations for what smelled like a spaghetti dinner complete with salad and cheesy garlic toast. The kitchen was decorated with pigs-pig trivets, pig cookie jars…even pig plates dotted the table.

There was a large family room and living room where mounted bucks, hogs, and other wild life adorned the walls. The lamps and chandeliers were made from antlers. Upstairs there were three bedrooms, all decorated in various game motifs. There was a turkey room, a white tail buck room, and finally- a duck room.

"Gobbler, White Tail, and Mallard. This is the ultimate hunters' retreat." Shannah surmised.

"Is this the Baxter's?" Rachael asked.

"No. It's Tristan's."

"Wow."

"Score." Shannah rubbed her hand along the buckskin throw adorning the foot of the bed.

"I guess if you're into hunting." Rachael was a little overwhelmed by all the woodland creatures.

"You better be into hunting if you're going to stay with Travis." Shannah cocked her head to the side.

Rachael wandered back downstairs to the living room where the other girls rolled out their sleeping bags and claimed floor space. She set hers out and sat down on it.

Maysie kicked off the evening's events by talking about the practices which would begin the following week. Shannah was still upstairs looking around.

"Could someone go fetch her?" Maysie asked.

"I'll go." Rachael disappeared back upstairs.

She found Shannah laying across the mallard bedspread. She patted it next to her.

"What are you doing? They're waiting on us."

"Girl, I can't help but think about the whole Amber thing. It's like she needs this, more than we need it, she like really needs it. Freakin' scores." Shannah griped.

"And I'm not entirely sure the other girls weren't biased."

"So what do we do?" Shannah complained.

"Announce me as the alternate." Rachael offered.

"No. That's not cool. You need it, too." She stared up at the ceiling. "I remember your trouble with Melinda last year."

"How about we call it the swing position?"

"Sounds weird."

"No, hear me out. We had this in my productions in West Palm. These girls were the most advanced dancers. They had to learn everyone's part because on a moment's notice they were required to step in and perform any part." Rachael explained.

"That's alright, I guess. I think we could sell that."

"So, it's not that you didn't make it. It's that you were chosen to do this. I wanna be that girl. The swing dancer. At our studio it was a huge thing to be chosen."

"What happens when a girl isn't out sick that week?"

"Well, if a girl misses even one practice- she forfeits her spot that week."

"I guess that works, kinda brutal though."

"Maysie will love it, her new toughness. She'll be the enforcer."

"I still don't know." Shannah rolled onto her side contemplating the situation.

"Announce me as the swing." Rachael knew this was the right thing. "I'll own this thing. I think it's cool."

"You sure?" Shannah asked.

"Yep. Besides I need the challenge of learning all those roles."

"You're a real friend." Shannah smiled up at the ceiling.

"What are you looking at?" Rachael stared at the ceiling fan spinning around and around. There was something dangling from the chain.

"That gobbler beard. Think it's a six or a seven?"

"OMG. Are you kidding? I didn't even realize that's what it was." Rachael jumped up. Maysie's yell from downstairs brought her upright once more. "We need to get down there."

The two bounded down the stairs and made their way to the living room.

"We've been waiting." Maysie teased.

"We were working on something."

"Okay. Share." Maysie stepped back opening the floor to them.

Shannah took the lead.

"This year we've decided to introduce two new positions on the dance team. The dance swing. This member of the team will be required to learn every part in each routine. She will be required to learn the blocking and marking for each song. Her role will be to fill in for anyone who is absent, even once during a rehearsal week. First I will announce the swing positions. Drum roll please."

The girls patted their hands on the wood floor in front of them.

"In swing positions we have: Rachael Harte and myself."

Rachael's head swung around. Her mouth hanging open.

"Due to the strenuous nature of the swing role, I've opted to take one myself."

Maysie looked utterly and completely baffled.

"In the regular dance roles we have Riley, Amber, Olivia, Sidney, and Elena."

Everyone clapped and the party began. There was an enormous dancer piñata filled with chocolates and lollipops. Afterwards, the girls ate dinner and played a round of *Dancing with the Stars* where Michael, Travis, Mr. Baxter, Fred, and Tristan posed as the stars. Then a team consisting of three girls each had five minutes to teach them a routine. Mrs. Baxter, Aunt Margaret, and Mrs. Harte served as the judges.

The worse performance of the night was performed by Mr. Baxter who found himself forced to dance a hip hop routine. He was a full count behind in every move and while the effort was there, he lacked any real skill. Fred wowed the audience with his tango with Sidney and Alex. The years of polish and dance technique was impressive. Michael was cute and youthful in his ballroom routine with Elena and Olivia. While he'd never taken a single lesson, he held his own and the judges gave him all sevens. Tristan was the big shocker with his sock hop. With Amber and Riley as his guides, and Maysie scrutinizing his every move from the sideline, he didn't miss a step.

The last team to go were Travis and Rachael who danced the waltz. Rachael had only danced with Travis once in the past two years, but knew he could waltz better than any cotillion partner she'd ever had. When they finished the judges gave them all tens.

After the dance competition, the older dancers shared insights with the newest members. Rachael excused herself to walk Travis outside. Maysie and Tristan followed behind them, leaving Shannah inside to oversee the final event of the evening.

Outside Maysie came over and hugged Rachael, not letting go.

"You're the best friend ever." She paused. "I can't believe what you did for Amber."

"She would've done the same for me. She needed it." Rachael felt uncomfortable taking all the credit. "The real surprise was Shannah. We hadn't planned that part."

Shannah appeared out on the porch in the moonlight. "If y'all are gonna come over here and hug on me, I'm going back inside." She announced.

They both ran up to her and bear hugged her.

"Ok." She pulled away. "Give me some air. I'm not the touchy feely type." She fled into the safety of the house.

Rachael walked Travis to his truck. "This is role reversal, me walking you out."

"I know. All the pressure's on you to kiss me goodnight."

"No pressure. There'll be no kisses tonight." Rachael looked over to where Maysie walked Tristan to his truck. She hugged him goodbye, he climbed in, and she shut the door.

Travis looked like a puppy thrown out of his dog house. "Not fair." He protested.

Rachael turned and waved over her shoulder. "Bye Travis."

Maysie met her on the porch. They waved to the guys as they drove out of the long road and their taillights faded into the night.

"I've kissed him, you know." Maysie stated matter-of-factly.

Rachael didn't know what to say. "Really?"

"Yep. We didn't mean to, but it just sort of happened on my birthday."

"That's good." *Or was it?*

"We talked about it- and it won't happen again. It hasn't since, but he's the one. Some things you just know."

Rachael thought about it and the double standard. There were just some things that were between girls and this was one of those instances. In her gut she knew they'd be married someday. Tristan and Maysie were just one of those things that were meant to be.

"Let's go inside." Rachael opened the door, the sound of laughter greeting them as they entered.

Fred and Alex passed them on the way out. Fred looked tense and Alex looked annoyed. Rachael closed the door behind them.

Mr. Baxter sat with Mrs. Baxter at the table eating some dessert, while some of the other girls packed up the rest of the food and put it away in Tupperware containers. Rachael heard Michael in the living room talking to Riley and Olivia, the two freshman to make the squad.

Rachael heard him offering to take Riley four wheeling...*four wheeling?*

Rachael listened earnestly for her response. When she said she'd love to, Rachael was shocked.

"Four wheeling?" She walked into the kitchen to help Mrs. Baxter, who'd gotten up from the table to assist in the cleanup.

"He's growing up." She smiled at Rachael.

"I guess so. But four wheeling? I hadn't pegged Riley for the off-roading type."

"You'd be amazed what I've seen girls show an interest in for a guy they liked." Her own mother nudged her with her elbow. "I can remember showing an earnest interest in race cars. I really had no idea about them, but I went out and bought every book. I studied night after night. Before too long, I was an expert on race cars. Really and truly. Your father faked an interest in wine. Now he loves the stuff. It's all good."

Did Mom just say that?

Rachael said goodnight to her mother and aunt, then returned to the living room. She lay down among the rowdy crew and slept horribly.

Around two o'clock Shannah rolled over and muttered, "This wood floor just don't have no give. My butt feels like a plank."

"Mine too." Rachael whispered. She looked over to Maysie's bed roll. It was empty. Rachael sat up. She scanned the room in the darkness. "Where is she?" Rachael asked.

"Where do you think she is?" Shannah hushed her.

"We have to go get her." Rachael spat.

"She's a big girl." Shannah whispered.

"You're either going with me or you're not, but I'm going to get her." Rachael demanded.

She climbed out of bed and tiptoed across the room to the front door. She slipped on her sneakers and waited for Shannah to join her.

She clomped out onto the front porch.

"I'm here. Geez." Shannah grumped.

"Where are they?"

"His house is back up at the entrance." Shannah explained.

"I was blindfolded, remember?"

"Oh, yeah. Follow me."

Shannah crept off of the porch and down the driveway toward the ranch road weaving its way through the front of the property.

"How far?"

"Three quarters of a mile."

"That's a long ways in the dark."

"Yep, Magellan. It is." Shannah chided.

"We have to go. What is she thinking?" Rachael questioned.

"She's in love with the boy. So she's not thinking." Shannah suggested.

They walked down the narrow road, sticking to the rutted path beat out by trucks and jeeps. The moonlight lit their way. A few raccoons and hogs crossed their path and while Rachael squealed in fear, Shannah merely managed to roll her eyes at her.

"Haven't you ever been fire hunting?" When Rachael uttered 'no' she answered "That's a shame. Those critters are good eatin'."

Rachael couldn't be sure if she was playing with her or not. For now, Shannah was her guide into the darkness, down a long road leading to nothing but more darkness.

Just when Rachael thought she might give up, a screech owl hooted from the woods nearby. Rachael nearly jumped onto Shannah's back.

"Get control of yourself. That was an owl. Not Freddie. Travis has got to get you into the woods at night a little more often."

The two kept walking until a light came into view in the distance. It was a bright light hooked up to a power pole. Rachael recognized the doublewide as Tristan's house from her previous meeting here after her trouble with the law last year. His porch light was on, and Rachael figured Maysie must be inside.

Rachael squared her shoulders, as did Shannah. Both looked like warriors preparing for battle. They held their heads high and marched up onto his porch. It was at his door that Rachael lost her nerve.

"What are we doing?" She whispered.

"We're dragging her hussy little butt back down the road. That's what we're doing." Shannah paused, poised- ready to knock. "Come on! You're the one who drug me out in the middle of the night."

"I know." Rachael looked around. "Okay. Knock."

Shannah pounded on the door, rather loudly, and stepped back.

They immediately heard footsteps and jumped away from the door. Tristan opened the door wearing nothing more than camo pants.

"Okay, bucko. We know she's in there, so send her out, and there won't be any trouble." Shannah threatened.

Tristan shook his head and laughed. "I don't know who you're looking for, but if it's Maysie she's not here." He swung the door wide when it looked like Shannah might charge the family room. "Be my guest."

Shannah went in and took a look around.

"She's not here." She announced. "Place is clear."

Rachael stood dumbfounded. "She wasn't at the house and she disappeared in the middle of the night. We kind of figured…she must be here."

He grinned. "Let me grab a shirt and shoes. I'll bet I know where she is."

He invited them in to have a seat and they gladly accepted. While mosquitos didn't bite as badly this far into the night, they still had more than ten bites each and were trying to avoid any others.

"I feel like a jerk." Shannah admitted.

"Tell me about it. What is she doing gallivanting around in the middle of the night?"

"Who knows?"

Tristan came back down the hall and handed them each a flashlight. They walked out onto the porch, following Tristan across his front horse pasture. The grass was still dry, the morning dew still a few hours away.

"What are you doing up this late?"

"I have a house full of teenaged girls on the river. Couldn't sleep." He wiggled a brow in their direction. "Who knows what y'all could get into?"

A large barn rose up out of the darkness. It was pitch black with the exception of a small light on in one window at the far end. Tristan opened the door and a large yellow lab raised its head to greet them, before laying back down to fall instantly back to sleep.

"That's Jed. Watch him, he'll take your hand off if you're not careful." He teased.

He held his hand to his lips and walked up to a large stall at the back of the barn. There, curled up on the hay in the corner of the stall was Maysie. Nearby, a mare lay on her side.

"That's Belle. She's due to foal any day. Maysie refuses to miss it. She's been over here after school for the past two days." He smiled at her warmly.

Rachael couldn't decide which he liked better, Maysie or the horse.

Belle lifted her head and stood up sniffing his hand.

"She's my mare, but she loves Maysie better. I think I like her better, too." He unlatched the stall and walked over to pick Maysie up. She wrapped her arms around his neck, snuggling in.

He carried her back up to the house and out to his truck. The other girls slid in the backseat while he buckled the still sleeping Maysie in shotgun. When he started the engine and drove back down toward the cabin, she smiled over at him.

"You're going to get us into trouble coming over here to see these horses in the middle of the night."

"Only ten months to go." She fell back to sleep.

Tristan pulled into the driveway of the cabin and walked around to carry her inside. He set her on the porch and kissed her nose. He walked back past her friends and nodded his head.

"Ladies." He paused after stepping past them. "I appreciate your concern where Maysie is concerned, but mark my words. I plan on marrying that girl. Like she said. Only ten months to go. Now if you'll excuse me I need to get home. Goodnight."

He climbed in behind the steering wheel of his truck and drove off.

"Wow." Shannah turned and stepped onto the porch.

"I guess he told us." Rachael giggled. "I feel badly that we went over there expecting something bad."

"Not something bad. Now he knows." Shannah said cockily.

"Knows what?"

"He's on our radar. That's all. We've got our eyes on him."

"And his horse barn." Rachael teased. "Cause that's where the bad stuff is going down. The horse barn. Next time Travis comes over we need to call out the posse. Especially if he steps foot into our barn, or there's a colt being born. That's enough right there to hang him." Rachael joked.

"They shared that one kiss."

"She told me. So what? Travis and I've shared many kisses. That doesn't mean anything."

Shannah looked at her and frowned. "There are kisses...and then, there are kisses." She raised a brow. "The kind of kisses that there's no turning back from. The kind of kisses that lead to the other...STUFF. Theirs was that kind of kiss. Since you're still holding onto your seven year plan," Shannah paused, "then, you haven't shared that kind of kiss. If so...you'd have only one of two options, break up and cool your jets a while. Or move the wedding day up. That's the kind of kiss we're talking about here."

"She made it sound like just another kiss. Their first kiss."

"It was their first kiss and it was their last. It was that kind of kiss. The kiss to end all kisses."

"She said they won't kiss again."

"Probably not. She knows it's dangerous for them."

Shannah walked in and snuck back into her sleeping bag. Rachael closed the door softly behind her. She tiptoed across the room toward her sleeping bag, careful not to step on the squad underfoot. She thought about all of her kisses with Travis and how they'd progressed. While he kissed her, and kissed her good, she now realized he was holding back with her. They'd never shared what she now knew was that kind of kiss. *A kiss only reserved for−*

Well, Rachael wasn't sure. What was the word? Married people? Lovers? She had a seven year plan. *Where does that kind of kiss fit into my plan?*

Tristan was honorable. He made it clear he planned on marrying Maysie. That until then, there'd be none of that. He was more refined and considerate than Rachael had ever thought possible.

She saw Maysie laying on the couch. The other side wasn't occupied and Rachael decided her current position on the floor needed rethinking. She grabbed her blanket and pillow and made her way among the bodies to the couch. She crawled on it and covered herself up to her neck. The cabin was chilly.

"Thank you." Maysie whispered. "For worrying after me, but you don't need to. Tristan and I have an understanding. He has given my dad his word and that's iron clad. I even threw myself at him and nada. He kissed me the once, a birthday present, and that's it. Now I have to wait, but some things are worth waiting for. He said I'll be the death of him yet. By the way," She propped herself up on her elbows. "This is my house. I already redid the kitchen with the pigs. Mama helped me. Next, I'll tackle the man cave and bedrooms. He so needs a woman's touch. I mean look at this place. Antler light fixtures. As if I'd ever allow it." She plopped back down.

Rachael smiled sweetly. "I'm happy for you."

"Go to bed already." Shannah protested from the floor where she tossed a couch pillow at Maysie's head.

Rachael stared up at the ceiling, unable to sleep. She glanced at her watch. Four o'clock in the morning was way too early to call her father. It would scare the daylights out of him. Rachael contemplated the kiss conversation. Why hadn't Travis kissed her like that? The dangerous kind of kiss Shannah described. The one where you either got married or broke up. Then, there was the other option, but Rachael refused to consider that. It wasn't an option for them. Maybe her seven year plan had been flawed. What normal couple could make it seven years? At this rate Maysie and Tristan would be fortunate to make it a year.

The way they were headed they'd be married by next summer, just after graduation. Was there something wrong with that?

Rachael tossed and turned.

*

Eventually the sun came up and still she'd never slept. She went to the bathroom and dressed for school. She brushed her teeth. Outside she heard a familiar truck and ran out to greet Travis, hauling her bags with her.

"Thought you might need a ride."

"Sure do." She jumped in.

"You look like you slept well."

"Not a wink. Let's go." She griped.

"Okay." He backed up and turned around. He kept looking at her and grinning widely. "Something wrong?"

"Nope."

"I know you well enough to know when something's wrong."

"Nope. There's nothing."

He put his hand on her knee and drove to school.

"Are you holding back on me?" She blurted out.

"Holding back, how? Like not telling you something?"

"No. Like not being fully complete with me."

"Complete? What do you mean?"

"Shannah was talking about the kiss. This dangerous kiss. The kiss that ends all kisses- that kind of kiss."

"Are we talking a goodnight kiss? Is it that kind of kiss? I wouldn't ask you for what other guys are calling a 'goodnight kiss'. Definitely not. That's something entirely different."

Rachael heard a couple of dancers last year talking about *the goodnight kiss* in the locker room and she knew she wasn't interested in that. It had nothing to do with kissing and in her mind was disgusting.

"Forget it."

"No. We won't forget it." He pulled over, getting frustrated. "Am I holding back on you? Yes. Everyday. Do I want to? Definitely not. Do I have a choice? No, I don't. But if you want me to kiss you like that, I will."

Travis reached across the seat and pulled her to him. He kissed her gently on her mouth nudging her lips apart, he teased her tongue more urgently, and dove in deeper…kissing her until she could think of nothing else but him. The smell of him and the feel of him on her skin, soft and hard, gentle and rough, all at once. He lifted his head and looked into her eyes tracing his way to her ear with tender kisses.

"Does that answer your questions?"

"Yes." She whispered.

"If I kissed you like that for a while, every time we were alone, do you see how that would be dangerous?"

"I do."

"So yes, I'm holding back on you. And yes…it's nearly killing me, but for now I don't have a choice."

"It gives me something to look forward to."

"That's the cowboy way." He threw the truck in drive and sped down the road toward school.

Chapter Fifteen

Romero and Shannah walked down the sidewalk toward the practice field. The percussion section could be heard warming up while the saxes riffed their way through some scales. Rachael and Maysie walked behind them, observing.

"You think he's the one?" Maysie asked.

"I don't know. They're worlds apart." Rachael answered her.

"Literally. Like Spain and the United States apart. There's no bridge wide enough to span that gap."

"I was talking more about her redneck, country girl ways and his wild, free spirited soccer slash European lifestyle."

"I know. I picked up on that, too. He's studied all over the world."

"He's worse than a sailor or a pilot. He's what I'd call well-traveled." Rachael commented.

"You're not talking about trips or general vacationing here, are you?"

"I just think that a guy like that is really looking for more of a good time, kind of like Ty. I learned my lesson there. I hope Shannah's careful."

"We'll make sure of it." Maysie promised.

Mr. Greene stood at the podium speaking into the microphone. It'd been several weeks since the auditions. Rachael had made the right decision. Having to learn everybody's part was difficult, but was working wonders for Rachael's thighs.

If only I'd develop Shannah style abs too. Maybe shed a pound of boob.

Rachael blinked up into the bright sunlight. It was blinding at this time of day, the rays coming across the field at an angle. The band director was a little edgy. They only had the field for half an hour due to football practice sharing the same space. The football players lined up in the area beyond the end zone and went through a series of stretches.

Rachael watched Travis. He was surprisingly flexible. She couldn't believe he could actually reach his toes. Rachael scanned the bleachers and saw Romero sitting in them watching Shannah lead practice.

Everyone took their positions for the opening number. All of the dancers were in attendance. She already learned the routines, as in plural, and was relieved to be able to stand out for the next thirty minutes.

"This alternate gig really has its advantages." Shannah winked.

"I know. Who'd have thought?"

Mr. Greene walked off the field, asking Rachael to run to his office across campus for a clipboard with some music sheets on it. She agreed and hurried off. The band room was nowhere near the football fields or dance room. Due to an overall lack of musical talent, Rachael had never really frequented his office. She could hear them rehearsing each morning during homeroom from Mr. Richardson's classroom down the next hall.

Today the building was silent, with all of the band students out on the field. Rachael briskly walked to Mr. Greene's door and opened it. She located the clipboard on his desk at the back of the room in the unlocked office, right where he said it would be. She grabbed the clipboard and the accompanying sheet music off of the desk. She closed the inner door behind her.

She crossed the music room and walked up the steps to the main door. She'd left it open a crack. She grasped the handle, prepared to pull it open and paused.

Outside in the hallway she heard a girl walk by, sobbing. She opened the door and looked out. A sophomore she recognized as Samantha walked down the hall, visibly shaken. Rachael knew her but not well. She briefly rode the bus with her prior to having a

163

car of her own or riding with Travis. She always seemed sweet and upbeat before.

Rachael closed the door and continued up the hall behind her, heading in the opposite direction of where she needed to go. When Samantha sensed her coming behind her she hit a jog and disappeared around a corner. Rachael could've sprinted to catch her, but decided she needed to get back to practice. She whirled around and bumped right into Mr. Richardson. He had an apple in his hand and took an oversized bite, chewing it.

"Rachael, what brings you over here this late in the day?"

"I had to get Mr. Greene's clipboard. He needs it on the field."

"You're turned around, aren't you?" He pointed down the hall in the opposite direction. "The fastest way to the field is that way."

"Oops." Rachael walked around him. "I must've gotten turned around."

She glanced back over her shoulder. His dark eyes bore into hers. She was lying and he knew it. Rachael hoofed it outside moving as quickly as she could. She cut between a few portables, taking a shortcut that looked similar to what she now knew were called game trails, edged into the grass by students through the years. She emerged near the weight room taking the sidewalk leading out onto the field.

"What took you so long? I thought I'd graduate before you made it back." Shannah quizzed.

"Long story. I'll tell you in the car."

After her run-in with the creep, practice drug on and on. What Rachael thought of as personal break-time, turned into the longest practice in the history of practices. When they were finished, Maysie and Rachael headed out to Maysie's convertible. Travis would be practicing another hour or more and Rachael needed to get home. She'd thought about driving her own car, but loved riding with Travis in the mornings. The only downside was not having her own car at the end of the day.

Michael sat on the picnic tables waiting for them under the trees. He put his books inside his backpack and stood to walk over to them.

"Hey." Rachael waved.

He smiled back at them.

"He seems to be adjusting to high school well." Maysie whispered.

"I think so. He's gotten in a good rhythm. He does his homework everyday while we are at practice. It'll work well until spring comes- and he's got baseball every day."

"He'll be fine. He's a freshman now. Who would've thought this day would come?"

They got Maysie's car and Michael called shotgun. Rachael merely shrugged her shoulders in response. Seated inside the car, Maysie cranked it up and put down her roof.

"Let's blow some of this heat out of here."

No one argued with her there. The inside temperature of the car must've been over one hundred degrees. Sitting in the Florida sun, in a parking lot, for over eight hours, would be enough to heat up any vehicle.

A few blocks from school they stopped at a light.

"So where'd you disappear to during practice?"

Rachael nodded her head toward Michael in the front passenger seat.

"I'm not a baby. Whatever it is, I can handle it." He argued.

Rachael considered what she'd seen. "I went to the band room to get some music for Mr. G. Then on my way out I saw Samantha, the sophomore with the red hair walking past. She was sobbing. Seriously...crying her eyes out. I followed her to check on her, but she started running, to escape me."

"That's weird. School had been out for a long time at that point. I wonder where she'd come from."

"Well that's the weird part. The only teacher over there was Mr. Richardson. I nearly bumped into him coming down the hall."

"You mean Mr. Creepy?" Michael teased. "Come on, Rachael. It's no secret among the guys how he puts the hot chicks with short skirts in the first two rows. Who could blame him, right?"

"I got a bad vibe off of him, like he was the reason Samantha was crying." Rachael confided.

"I hope you're wrong." Maysie interjected. "I've had him for a couple of classes, never had an issue with him."

"I hope I'm wrong, too."

Maysie dropped them at home and drove away. Hank and Spike ran up to greet them. Hank had warmed to them over the last few weeks and Rachael no longer lived in fear he'd take her right arm off every time she stepped outside her own home. Michael walked around the back of the house to fill the dogs' water bucket.

Rachael went inside to start her homework and work on some sort of plan for dinner. She looked in the freezer and located a bag of frozen chicken breasts. She pulled it out and set it on the counter. She procured a thirteen by nine glass baking dish from under the counter. She laid the chicken breasts in it. Next she found an unopened bottle of barbeque sauce, opened it and spread it over the frozen chicken. She opened the oven and set the auto oven to three hundred fifty degrees and sixty minutes.

Dinner made easy.

Rachael grabbed a can of candied yams and put them in a small casserole dish. She sprinkled them with sugar and cinnamon. She melted half a stick of butter in the microwave and poured it over the top. She set it in the oven as well.

Tonight was Aunt Margaret and her mother's late shift at the resort. They wouldn't be home for several hours. Rachael liked to have dinner made early and all of her homework done.

She peeked out the window overlooking the backyard where Michael played with the dogs. While they were full grown, they still behaved more like a couple of puppies. They loped across the yard, fetching sticks, and rolling. Michael ran from them calling 'puppy, puppy'.

Rachael walked to the dining room and got out her own homework. She didn't have all that much to do. Math evens, a page of vocab, and some Spanish reading that could better be described as translating. Rachael worked diligently, until she realized she could no longer hear Michael in the back yard. She walked to the back porch and opened the French doors. She looked across the lawn. There was no sign of him or the dogs.

She glanced at the oven. Dinner only had ten minutes to go. She walked over and switched the oven to off. While it had been set to auto oven and should shut off on its own, she didn't want to risk a fire. If she didn't open the oven door, the chicken would finish cooking anyway.

She stepped out onto the back porch.

"Michael?" She called.

There was no answer. She crossed the back yard and went into the barn. Hank lay on the cool cement floor, sleeping. He didn't even lift his head to acknowledge her presence. His front paw twitched like he was chasing something in his sleep. Rachael walked over to the stairs and climbed them to the hay loft. At the top of the stairs, she stopped at the sight of Michael and Spike fast asleep in the hay.

Outside she heard an unfamiliar car engine pull into the yard. She glanced out of the front hay loft double boors and spied a small truck sitting in front of her house. Spike sat up and perked his ears up, hearing it as well. He cocked his head to one side listening.

The vehicle honked its horn. He tore past Rachael and down the stairs barking. The commotion woke Hank as well, who went out to bark at the stranger.

Michael sat up and yawned. "Didn't Maysie lock the gate on her way out?"

"Obviously not." Rachael answered. She turned to go back downstairs.

"Where are you going?"

"To see who it is. We can't let Hank bite them."

"I think they're bright enough not to get out of the truck." Michael laughed. From the top of the barn they could see the two male dogs circling the small truck, teeth bared and hair standing up along the ridge of their spines.

"Let's hope so." Rachael padded her way down to the first floor, still barefoot. She crossed the yard heading back toward the house. Michael ran up beside her.

"I'm coming with you."

They walked through the back doors, locking them. Then they passed through the house and opened the front door. From there they could see the passenger in the truck was Honey, while the driver was the super thin blonde.

Honey rolled down her window a crack and motioned Rachael to come over to the truck.

"It's me, Honey!"

Rachael told Michael to wait at the front door where he was poised, ready to call 9-1-1 if need be. After the recent events she couldn't be sure whether Honey's visit was a friendly one or not. Rachael went out to see what they needed, their vehicle still idling in the driveway.

When Rachael got to the truck, she saw a body slumped across the front seat, laying in Honey's lap.

Misty!

"We didn't know where else to go. We found her like this."

"Is she breathing?" Rachael screeched.

"Yes, but she won't wake up. If I called for help we'd get in trouble. Help us Rachael."

Rachael, not knowing what else to do, called for Michael to grab Hank. She opened the truck door and Honey helped her pull Misty out of the truck. Honey was wobbly on her feet, barely able to stand herself. She staggered. Rachael directed her to grab Misty's feet while Rachael got the heaviest part, her upper torso. They carried her to the house and laid her down on the couch.

"We have to call an ambulance. She needs medical attention." Rachael grabbed her own cell phone out of her purse and dialed. She returned to Misty trying to wake her.

Honey went back outside to tell the other girl. Rachael heard the vehicle driving away.

The 9-1-1 operator answered the call.

"What's your emergency?"

"A friend of mine just showed up at my house with a girl, passed out, and I can't wake her."

"Is she breathing?"

"Yes, but she's not responsive at all."

"Do you know her name?"

"Yes. Her name is Misty. I know her from school."

"An ambulance is on its way, ma'am."

Michael stood in the front doorway.

"Go shut the dogs up in the barn." Rachael ordered. He ran from the house and she could hear him calling the dogs.

Rachael got a wash cloth from the hall linen closet and dampened it. She came back over to Misty and placed it across her forehead. Her color was between ashen gray and white. Her lips were lackluster and other than her shallow breaths she looked…

Dead.

Rachael's hand shook a bit as she patted her arm. She said a silent prayer for Misty and her life. That the Lord spare her.

Rachael could hear the sirens coming up her driveway after what felt like an eternity. Michael must've greeted them outside because he was suddenly there opening the door, propping it open. The EMT had a stretcher. Rachael stood and moved out of their way. They took her pulse and put an oxygen mask on Misty.

Her eyes didn't move, not even a flutter. She was completely oblivious to everything going on around her.

One of the first responders came over, along with a deputy, to ask Rachael some questions. She provided them with Misty's full legal name, her age, her weight, etc. She called Mrs. Baxter to get her parents' contact information. Mrs. Baxter answered on the first ring. Rachael rushed through an explanation for her call. She handed the phone to the deputy who arrived on the scene. He recorded all of the information. When he finished he handed the phone back to Rachael.

Since Misty was no longer a minor, no guardian was needed to obtain permission to take her to the hospital. Rachael and Michael sat in her house, speaking with the deputies, the same two who'd been called out to their house a few weeks earlier.

"The blonde was the same girl as before. The other girl with her was Honey."

"Since your friend Misty isn't a minor and obviously went with them willingly, as well as used some sort of substance knowingly, they haven't broken any laws here. I'd still like to contact them though."

Rachael thought back to Honey's debilitated stagger and the glaze covered effect of her eyes. She provided the deputy with Honey's cell phone number and home address so that the officer could follow up with her himself.

"Any idea where they'd come from?" He questioned.

"No. We're not close friends. They brought her here and just dumped her out." Rachael said in disbelief.

"Not getting caught in possession or under the influence was more important than saving a friend's life." The deputy stood up and gave Rachael his business card again. "Just in case you've lost the other one."

"No, sir. I still have it. Thank you."

Rachael and Michael stood to walk the deputies to the door. The EMT's and ambulance departed earlier, and must've been nearing the hospital with Misty by now. After closing the door, Rachael and Michael went into the kitchen and sat at the table, both too stunned by the afternoon's events to speak about it further.

"Go turn the dogs out, please. Just in case we have any more visitors today. I'll walk down and lock the gate."

Michael nodded, hesitating, "Let's do it together."

Rachael decided he was right, and while she didn't think they'd ever show up here again, she knew he must be a little scared by what he'd seen today. She was a few years older and she was freaked out by it.

Misty could've died…she could still die.

They walked out to the barn and let Hank and Spike out of the stalls. The dogs raced wildly around the yard trailing where all of the strangers had walked. Rachael and Michael continued up to the gate, closing, chaining, and locking it. They strolled back to the house and Michael excused himself to go play some video games.

Rachael watched him, worried he might have some questions for her.

"Michael?"

He paused, "Yep."

"Do you want to talk about it?"

"No. I think I figured it out. She did some drugs and was unconscious, so they dropped her off, like trash. They didn't even stick around to see if she was okay. It's not cool. No one deserves to be treated like that."

"I think they were worried about getting busted."

"Still, no excuse. That sucks." He turned and walked into his bedroom, closing the door behind him.

The sound of Travis' truck out front alerted Rachael to his presence. She walked up and opened the door waiting for him. He stepped into the foyer and hugged her gently to him.

"You okay?"

"I guess so. I was more worried about Michael but he seems to understand it, as best a fifteen-year-old can. What I don't get is why did they come here?"

"You're closest to Ted's house. I'm assuming that's where they brought her from."

"Ted's?"

"You don't want to know where it is, trust me. But she probably overdosed there. There's no phone or running water there half the time. These aren't the type of people who pay their utility bills. Even if they had cell phones, they wouldn't want to incriminate themselves, or be placed there."

"So they brought her here?"

"They didn't want her to die is my guess. Your house is closest and Honey knew you'd do the right thing." He opened the oven and looked inside. "Chicken?"

"Yes, it's chicken." Rachael opened a drawer and pointed to a pot holder and oven mitt. He picked them up and pulled the chicken and yams out of the oven, closing the door with his foot.

Rachael reached up and got down three plates. Travis tossed the pot holder and mitt on the counter, then he walked down the hall to Michael's door. She heard him rap on it.

"Not hungry." Michael responded behind it.

"It's me, Travis. If you don't come now, there won't be any left for you." He warned.

"Coming!" Michael swung the door open and attempted to push past him to beat him to the kitchen. Travis scooped him up and flipped him, beating him to the kitchen. Michael smiled from ear to ear. Rachael gave Travis a look of gratitude. Travis served their plates too full and set them on the table. Rachael poured Michael a chocolate milk, his new favorite.

"Is that chocolate milk?" Travis' eyes gleamed.

"Would you like one too, little boy?" Rachael teased.

"Yes." He pleaded.

"Okay. Chocolate milk all around."

They all sat down at the table. Rachael cut her chicken breast and found it a little tough…and dry.

"It's a little over cooked." She frowned at her first attempt at chicken.

"A little? My sneaker is more tender."

Travis kicked Michael under the table.

"Ouch." Michael rephrased his last statement. "It's good considering you were distracted and had to leave it in the oven, and the sauce and yams are great!"

"You don't have to be sweet guys. I know it's not the best chicken, but I'm getting better."

Travis took a huge swig of chocolate milk nearly choking on a hunk of chicken. "No, really, baby. It's good stuff." Everyone cracked up, so he changed the subject. "Are you going to go see her in the hospital?"

"I wasn't going to." Rachael thought about it. "If we'd ever been friends I'd go, but she hates me."

"Maybe not now. You've probably saved her life."

"I'll think about it, but I won't be heading up there any time soon."

"You wouldn't want to. The first several days are the worst!" Michael's eyes widened as he spoke. "First they'll be making her swallow charcoal and puke it out! She'll be in detox, maybe even a drug addiction or rehab center."

"How do you know so much?" Rachael marveled.

"Internet. I went back to look it up."

"Great. It will be fun to explain this to Mom tonight."

"You don't need to. The mom hotline is already in action. My mom called all the moms, including yours." Travis had nearly drained his milk glass trying to moisten the near chicken-jerky he chewed. "It's crazy how fast they all communicate."

"That's kind of a relief."

"Only in this situation. There are other things I wish the mom hotline wouldn't communicate." Travis winked at her.

"That's my cue to leave." Michael stood up and cleared his own plate, placing it in the kitchen sink. Rachael heard him grab the house phone and walk out onto the back porch. Travis stood and cleared both he and Rachael's plates, glasses, and silverware. He walked into the kitchen and rinsed them off.

"When were you planning on telling me about the true love waits conversation with Mama?"

"I wasn't. It's not something we need to discuss, is it?" Rachael toyed with her napkin.

Travis loaded the dishes into the dishwasher. Plates on the bottom, glasses on the top.

"I've never seen you do the dishes before." She observed.

"I'm nervous. Keeping busy." He rinsed the silverware. "Your dad called me."

"My dad?"

"Yep. I was on my way here. It was unpleasant."

"I can imagine. So let me guess, you asked your mom and dad to change our purity agreement, your mom told me…and also talked to my mom." Of course Rachael had known about the first parts of this equation for months now. Guilt over not admitting as much to Travis welled up inside her stomach, but she truly never expected her father to call him. *And why now? After all this time. He has to have known for a long time…*

"Bingo." Travis started washing the glass baking dishes by hand which were too large to fit in the dishwasher.

"So my dad threatened to kill you."

"Not exactly, but he told me to quit pressuring you and keep it, put away, so to speak."

Rachael covered her face to hide the crimson spreading from collar to hairline.

"We've never had it out. Now he'll call me next."

"Yep." Travis got out a dish towel. "Turns out you're having quite the afternoon already. I thought I should warn you."

Travis turned around and saw her seated at the bar, head laying on her forearms.

"Where do these go?"

"Under the counter, beside the stove." Her muffled response unclear.

He walked over and put his arms around her waist. "I owe you an apology, Rach. I'm sorry for pressuring you and I'm sorry for pushing. It won't happen again."

"No need to apologize. You haven't pressured me. Now to handle my father, are we back to chaperoned outings?"

"Nope. He said he thinks he made himself clear, and without sharing any details with you, he did."

Rachael's cell phone rang sharply. It was her father's ringtone. She answered reluctantly.

"Hi, Dad."

"Hey. Is Travis there now?"

"He is. He just told me the two of you talked."

"We did. Did he apologize?"

"He did, but really, Dad, he never laid a hand on me, or pushed me in that way."

"Asking his parents is pushing you, it may be a more upfront and straightforward way of going about it, but he did it- and in the end it made you uncomfortable."

"His mom told you that?" *The only thing that made me uncomfortable was her...*

"She told your mother." Her father paused. "So I have his word he won't bring it up again, and if he does, you'll find yourself in boarding school."

"Boarding school!" Rachael shrieked.

"Get married, or go to boarding school, those are the options."

Rachael couldn't believe her father was serious. He'd always been more laid back than this. What had changed?

"Have I made things clear?" He asked after a minute of stunned silence.

"Yes, sir." Rachael answered.

"I'll talk to you next week." He hung up.

Rachael turned her phone off and set it on the counter. She walked over and slouched on the couch.

"Are you sure you want to turn it off?"

"I don't think I can handle any more calls today. I'm done."

Travis came over and crouched in front of her. He held her hands.

"It's okay. We'll get through this."

"No. It's not okay. I can understand if you were like grabbing my butt and stuff. If you were all over me and wouldn't take no for an answer, but you've really done nothing wrong. For him to threaten boarding school, that's just crap!" Rachael shot upward. "I'm tired of it. Your mom means well, but she's gone and caused me all this grief. You asked to change your purity pledge, so what? They said no and you were good with that. It doesn't need to be some all-out council meeting about us not doing it! We're not doing it!" Rachael paced and yelled out to no one. "We're not. I hope y'all are happy. Maybe we should take out an ad."

"We can still date. We can still hang out together. I survived, you did too. It's okay."

"No it's not, because on the surface they're preaching trust, but behind the scenes they don't truly trust us. Not truly." The words stung.

"That's partly my fault. I'm the one who wanted a renegotiation. If I'd kept my mouth shut it never would've come up." Travis sat on the couch. "All I can say is I'm sorry."

"If you feel a certain way or have concerns, talk to me. I'm the one the concern involves, I'm the one it's about. I can help you through it. I'm glad you think I'm sexy. It may surprise you Travis, but I'm not scared of you in that way. I can't wait until we're married and we can be together. I really, truly can't wait!"

He looked confused.

"What I meant to say is I can wait to do it, but I'm so excited about it. Not that I literally couldn't wait."

"I've got it. And I won't talk to anyone about it anymore." He stood up. She rushed over and kissed him.

Rachael grabbed his hand and asked him to walk out to the barn with her.

"So what part of your pledge were you renegotiating anyhow?" She asked.

"I can't tell you. I gave your father my word I wouldn't discuss it with you again until we were engaged- or married."

"That's a pity. You had piqued my interest."

"I hope not too much." He squeezed her hand. In the barn, he glanced around. "It's too quiet out here without Taffy and ole' lonesome George." He glanced in the stalls where they were completely shoveled out. "Let's get you a horse of your own."

"A horse of my own? Are you kidding?"

"Nope. A horse of your own."

Rachael jumped up and wrapped her entire body around him, almost knocking him down.

"If I'd known I'd have gotten this response, I'd have gotten you a horse long before now." He pried her off of him and led her from the barn.

They walked around the front of the house where Rachael saw the horse trailer hooked up behind Travis' truck. It was Maysie's long sleek show trailer, not the typical stock trailer they used to haul their horses when they went to work cows.

"I was so upset earlier I didn't even notice the trailer." She skipped out to the rear doors.

Standing with her nose peeking out was a gorgeous mare. She was a buckskin. Black socks, mane, and tail. She wasn't very tall but was perfect for Rachael.

Rachael patted her nose gently and kissed it. The young mare nuzzled her back.

"She's sweet."

"That's why we chose her. She's been at Tristan's for a few weeks. He was working with her for you. I needed the right time to give her to you, seems like today was right."

"She's perfect. I think I'll call her Grace."

Rachael opened the gate and grabbed the lead rope. She stepped back so that Grace could climb out. Rachael ran her hand down her sides.

"Does she kick?"

"Would I give you a horse that kicks?"

Rachael walked around behind her running her hand along her back quarters and down her tail.

"She's so well groomed, so clean. I didn't think you washed horses."

"I don't. That's what girls are for. Maysie did it. She's been spoiling her rotten."

Rachael worked her way up to her mane. There was a tiny braid there and some purple feathers.

"Maysie." He said, shaking his head.

"The purple halter and lead rope? And don't tell me Maysie, I know you picked the last one for Taffy."

"I'll admit to that part." He put his arms round her waist and pulled her to him. "Purple is your favorite color."

"I love her." Rachael leaned up on her tippy toes and kissed his nose. "Let's take her to the barn."

She stopped long enough to knock on Michael's bedroom window. He opened his blinds and gave her a thumbs up. It didn't take him long to come out and join them in the barn. Within minutes he was armed with a brush and comb, setting to work grooming Grace a bit more. Rachael filled her water and gave her fresh feed and hay.

Chapter Sixteen

Homecoming week was finally here. It'd been a great football season and the homecoming game was oddly the last game. Rachael knew the week would be a busy one. She'd been picking Michael up after float decorating every afternoon. A few weeks earlier, Riley started carpooling with them. She'd needed transportation or she couldn't have remained on the dance team.

Michael, of course, volunteered his sister and four weeks later here they were. Today Rachael figured something was up. When they pulled up to Riley's house Michael jumped up and walked her to the door. Rachael craned her neck to see around the corner of her front walkway. He leaned in and pecked her on the cheek.

He sauntered back up to the car, a new hitch in his step.

"Is Riley your girlfriend?"

"Maybe she is."

"Has she been your girlfriend this whole time?"

"Since the third week of school." He confessed.

"You little turd! Why didn't you tell me?"

"She's my girlfriend. We're not getting married or anything."

"Is there anything you want to talk about?" She assumed a more motherly tone.

"Gross. No."

Rachael decided to aggravate him further. "Okay, but if you need to talk- I'm here for you."

"I'm getting all my advice from Travis."

"Travis knows, and he didn't tell me?"

"Brother knows how to keep a secret."

"I can keep a secret."

Rachael pouted the rest of the way home. Her cell phone kept vibrating in her purse.

"Someone's blowing up your phone."

"I know. Check it." She pointed to her purse on the floor of her car.

"No. Who knows what it is! I don't want to see that." He held his hands up like her purse may jump up and bite him.

"Get it out. My texts aren't that exciting, and yours better not be either." She shook her finger at him.

"Stop." He chided and reached in to pull out her phone. He looked at it and covered his eyes. "My eyes! My eyes! I think I might go blind."

"What is it?"

"Shannah in a dress." He teased.

"Shut up."

"No really, it's Shannah in a dress and she looks good actually." He handed the phone over to Rachael. Sure enough it was Shannah, in a dress, several dresses. "She's going with that long haired dude, Romeo, to Homecoming?"

"I guess so. And it's Romero."

"Either way, he's a pretty boy. I always see him in the locker room after he's been jogging or whatever, blowing his hair dry and styling it."

"He's nice, I think." Rachael felt a need to defend her friend's friend...or whatever he was.

Shannah and Romero had been hanging out since the beginning of the school year. She was really into him, but their relationship never seemed to progress past go.

"He's crazy if he doesn't date Shannah." Michael looked at the dress selections. "The blue one has my vote."

"Mine, too. Text her that."

Michael texted Shannah their choice. When they pulled into their gate, Maysie's car sat there waiting.

"She doesn't know the combination." Rachael acknowledged.

Rachael jumped out and opened the gate for them. Maysie raced through. She sped up to the house like she was competing in the Daytona 500. Rachael followed and parked behind her. Michael grabbed his bag and disappeared inside the house.

"What's going on?" Rachael greeted Maysie.

"Let's go out to the barn."

Maysie power walked in the direction of the barn. Rachael had to sprint to keep up the pace.

"What's wrong?"

Maysie stood in the barn with her hands on her hips. She looked like she might kill someone. "Romero! He's a total loser."

"What did he do?"

"He's got a bet on Shannah."

"A bet?"

"That he'll do it with her on Homecoming night!"

"What?"

"Travis told me! Just this afternoon."

That's two things he's kept from me recently. "Who else is in on this bet?"

"Gabe!"

"Are you serious? Gabe?"

"Yeah, and they think it's so funny. Gabe told Romero how Shannah is hot and all, but that he dated her for like, forever, and she wouldn't put out. They're friends the two of them!"

"And Travis knew all this and didn't tell me?"

"He just heard. You'd already left. He told Gabe it was super stupid and uncool, but guys are guys and they only want one thing."

"Some of them." Rachael amended.

"Oh no, don't fool yourself, they all want it. The difference is that some are willing to wait for it and others are not."

"Okay, I agree with you there. What do we do?"

"We have to tell her." Maysie determined.

"Obviously, but how?"

"We need to go to her house, now. Get your brother."

Rachael went in and called for Michael. He was dressed in workout clothes and sneakers.

"You've got to come with us, we need to do something."

"Is this about the bet Romero has that he's going to score a homerun on Homecoming night?" Michael made hinged quotation marks in the air around the word *score.*

"What happened to my innocent little brother who knew nothing?"

"What can I say? But you'll be glad to hear I didn't place a wager either way."

Rachael grabbed his arm towing him from the house. They piled into Maysie's backseat and drove toward the gate. Maysie glanced at the empty passenger seat.

"Who's that for?"

"Levi. He's jogging here."

Rachael saw him coming up the road. They pulled over and told him to jump in. They sped away in the direction of Shannah's house. When they got there, there was no sign of her training in her pole barn. Her jeep was parked out front though, and the girls knew she must be inside.

Rachael's hands shook. How did you tell your good friend she was about to go to the dance with a sleaze bag? He was a tool, plain and simple. Levi and Michael climbed out of the car and walked up to the door.

"Ladies, allow us to handle this. This is a man's job." Levi strode on to the porch.

"Definitely not." Rachael interceded. "If he's here, there'll be no fighting."

Rachael heard a clamorous banging from inside followed by the riotous noise of something getting knocked over. A loud thud of another something hitting the trailer floor.

"She must have heard." Maysie surmised. "She's tearing apart her room."

Rachael, Levi, and Michael put their heads to the door and listened.

"Sounds like she's dragging a huge trash bag up the hallway."

The door opened inwards and the three of them fell to the floor. They looked up and saw Shannah standing over top of them.

"I'm glad y'all are here. Help me with him." She pointed to Romero lying face down on the ground.

"You killed him!" Maysie exclaimed.

"No, merely tasered his butt." Shannah spoke.

"Really?" Michael sounded impressed.

"No. Not really. I kicked him and he hit his head on the bookshelf."

Romero's eyes flipped open and he came to. He lifted himself onto his elbows.

"Look. We want no trouble from you, pretty boy." Michael did his best to make his biceps look big by putting his hands under them on either side of his ribcage.

Shannah's dad pulled into the driveway and stepped up onto the porch.

"Is this the creep?" He directed his question to Shannah.

"It's him."

Shannah's father gave Romero the once over. He had what appeared to be the starts of a black eye and a concussion.

"I'll run him home." Her father showed an amazing amount of restraint. He looked like he wanted to kill this kid, but since Shannah had seemingly already handled it herself he just needed to get the guy home.

"Why are y'all here anyway?" She asked.

"We were going to tell you about the bet and rescue you." Maysie grinned.

"What bet?" Shannah asked.

"If you didn't know about the bet, why did you beat Romero up?"

"He got a little too friendly." She narrowed her eyes. "What bet?"

Rachael looked to where Shannah's father had loaded Romero in his truck and was safely pulling down the driveway. She nodded to Michael and Levi.

"You guys can go for your jog. Stay around here though. We'll be ready to go in an hour."

The boys trotted off, heading down the driveway toward the main road.

"Romero had a bet he could sleep with you. And the worst part is Gabe was in on it."

"Gabe!" Shannah fumed. "I'm glad I didn't know that part or I may have really tasered his butt."

"Well, you didn't, and that's a good thing." Maysie chimed.

"Maybe if we drive really fast we can catch my father."

"Not a good idea." Rachael surmised.

"I can't go to the dance now. I'll be a joke."

"Not if you have the best looking date there." Rachael walked inside prompting the others to follow. "Sit."

She opened the fridge and got each of them a diet cola. Between sips of soda Shannah spewed a continuous stream of expletives. Maysie looked up to the heavens and uttered a silent prayer.

Rachael stood in the kitchen, hands braced on the edge of the counter.

"I've got it."

"Can't wait to hear this." Shannah sighed.

"Travis' super, hot cousin."

"Yippee. Now we're thinking." Maysie clapped.

"Think again, girls. I never even got to meet him. Of course that was my fault. I didn't want to because of the jerk. I didn't want to mislead him. Let's be realistic girls. The dance is on Saturday. Today is Thursday."

"We know what day it is. We're not goobers." Maysie griped.

"Don't push me, Mays. I'm still not happy about that little walking episode earlier this year."

"Stop, both of you." Rachael picked up her cell phone. She called Travis and explained everything. When she hung up she said. "Okay. He said he thinks he'll do it."

"Okay- so I've got a date, but how do I get back at him for the bet?"

"I've got just the plan." Maysie winked. "Tristan's got this friend who cheated on his wife. She used peppers, as in habanero peppers."

"In her cooking? I'm not about to drop off some enchiladas later." Shannah sounded a bit testy.

"We're not going to cook with them, Shannah."

A knowing look crossed Shannah's face. "Oh. I've got it."

Rachael was stumped. "Got what? What are we doing with the peppers?"

"But how do we get the pants?" Shannah asked.

"Are y'all speaking in like some redneck girl code or what? What pants?"

"His pants."

"For what?"

"The peppers."

"We're going to pepper his pants?" Rachael asked.

"His tux pants."

"Isn't that illegal?" Rachael asked.

"It's not going to kill him or burn him, really. More annoying than anything." Maysie advised.

"Maybe Rachael's right, no putting habanero in the crotch of his tux pants. Prison isn't on my *to-do* list."

"Back to the drawing board." Maysie looked longingly. "Okay. I've another pants idea."

"Great." Rachael rolled her eyes.

"We loosen the button on his pants."

"That's better. No one gets hurt, no singed male parts, and all that. I could get behind that." Shannah grabbed a bowl of grapes from the fridge.

"He'll only be embarrassed. No harm done."

"Unless he's like the cowboys and doesn't wear drawers." Rachael said the words and regretted them as soon as they passed her lips.

"TMI." Shannah commented.

"No. She's innocent here. Poor Rachael found out when Travis was in the hospital. He's been forced into boxer servitude since and he's not pleased." Maysie clarified.

"Okay, no pants." Shannah added. "Anything involving pants is off limits."

The front door opened. Michael and Levi walked in. They'd been eavesdropping on the front porch, both of them completely free of sweat.

"Why don't y'all leave it to us? We'll take care of it and I promise you it doesn't involve any fighting." Levi suggested.

The girls nodded their heads.

"But make it good. Don't let me down." Shannah jumped up and gave them each a high five. "A little redneck retribution is always a good thing, as long as it's legal."

"Nothing illegal. I swear." Levi held up his hand. "But when someone messes with one of our own, we can't just let it slide."

"We've got it all under control." Michael grinned.

"I don't know that this is such a good idea." Rachael worried.

"Don't fret it, sis. Travis will help us."

"Even better. Great, now I'm seriously worried."

"Don't be such a wuss." Maysie challenged. "What he did was horrible. Doesn't he deserve a little embarrassment?"

"I guess."

Michael and Levi snuck out the front door.

"What happened to the good ol' days when someone wronged you and you could just beat 'em to a pulp?" Shannah reminisced.

"You did that ... today." Rachael acknowledged.

"But I didn't know about the bet. If I'd known about that I wouldn't have been so...merciful." Shannah seemed to be reconsidering their strategy.

Rachael decided to take control of the situation before she found herself spray painting Romero's driveway or something equally awful. "I think the best way to get even with him is to be the most stunning girl at the dance with the hottest date. And besides, Wade is fine."

"For sure. Like Redneck Fine!" Maysie added. "Just your type."

"Skoal can in his butt pocket?" Shannah asked hopefully.

"This boy's no stranger to a dip can, camo cap, tight faded Wranglers, work boots. Just your type, Redneck Fine." Maysie raised her eyebrows up and down.

"I could go for that. And he's not a creep, right?"

"You won't have to kick his butt for getting too friendly, if that's what you mean." Maysie teased.

"Okay. I'm in. As long as he's Redneck Fine and not Redneck Crazy. I've got enough crazy for the two of us."

"I'll take care of the nail appointments." Rachael smiled. "My treat."

"I've got hair." Maysie added.

"Y'all want to see my dress?" Rachael asked.

Maysie picked up Rachael's phone and scrolled through her pics.

"It's awesome!" She squealed.

She turned the screen and handed it to Shannah.

"That's cool. Pink camo."

Rachael couldn't believe she'd chosen the dress for herself, but Travis would love it. A pink camo strapless dress.

"I'm pairing it with a pair of hot pink heels." She added.

"Only you could pull that off." Maysie admitted.

"Hey, now, I could've pulled it off too, but not in pink. Maybe Mossy Oak. No pink though." Shannah pouted.

"If we had more time we could've all done it!" Maysie cheered.

"Maybe not." Rachael shook her head. "Pink camo on parade might have been a little overkill."

"Maybe if it had lace?" Maysie asked.

"Not even then."
                    *

The following morning school was abuzz with the news of Romero and Shannah's unfortunate split and the details about how she'd whipped his butt. Of course the story had grown, and now it involved an arrest. By lunchtime, Shannah looked like she might jump in her jeep and flee campus.

After lunch ended Rachael found herself convincing Shannah to not pound Romero in Spanish Lit class.

"The last thing you need is to get expelled."

"I guess." Shannah sounded indifferent to the possibility of expulsion. She forged ahead of Rachael, down the sidewalk, and toward class.

When they arrived and took their seats, there was no sign of Romero in the classroom. Everyone else seemed disappointed too. Shannah's friend, Tracy, patted her on the shoulder as she walked past and took her seat behind them.

"Too bad, girl. Could've been a showdown in Lit Class."

"Right?" Shannah answered.

Senora Wilder came into the room and greeted the classroom.

"Hola estudiantes."

"Hola, Senora Wilder." The class responded.

"Unfortunately for us Romero has decided to change his language focus to French Literature and has gone over to join Mrs. A's class."

Tracy whooped and hollered. A few other kids whistled.

Senora Wilder did her best to quiet them. "I know how sad you all must be, but I'm sure you'll still run into him around campus."

"Wimp." Shannah whispered.

Rachael ignored her and got her book out, along with her spiral notebook containing her most recent notes and questions about this week's reading assignment. Senora Wilder dove right into the subject at hand and Rachael was relieved it redirected Shannah. After class they had the Homecoming Pep Rally. All the girls went to change into their uniforms.

The Pep Rally was always a big deal for their school. This year it was extra special, seeing that they were seniors. They'd voted for Homecoming Court the previous week. The six guys receiving nominations were Gabe, Travis, Clay, Romero, Jason, and Bobby, a star baseball player. The six girls receiving nominations were Rachael, Shannah, Maysie, newcomer and exchange student Elena, Honey, and Misty, who was still in the hospital. The news of her overdose had traveled the campus in less than two days and Shannah was convinced her nomination was nothing more than a pity vote- since no one in their right mind could've truly thought her Homecoming Queen material.

The Homecoming Court was announced at the Pep Rally and the crowd cheered, with the exception of Romero who received several boo's. Unaffected by his few haters, he strutted across the field, swagger in full force.

"Can you believe I liked that guy?" Shannah prompted under her breath from her dance line.

"I sure can. It was less than two days ago." Maysie returned, giggling.

"Let's call it temporary insanity. What would possess me to date a guy who spends more time on his hair than I do?"

"I wondered the same. How could a girl ever compete with those luscious locks of brunette?" Maysie commiserated.

Next, the principal announced the female nominees for Homecoming Queen. Shannah, Maysie, Rachael, and Elena just waved from their position on the field. After the principal finished, he and the administration did a skit where they were the Hulk and the other super heroes. They were defending EMHS from the Raiders who attempted to steal the championship trophy and reclaim the school's cheerleaders as their own. The pep rally let out just as the final bell rang. The principal dismissed everyone directly to their buses and the car lot.

Rachael watched as Romero joined the other soccer players and headed to the locker room. She glanced around and searched for her brother and Levi, both of whom needed a ride home. When she didn't see them she headed out to the parking lot, sure they'd catch up with her there.

Travis joined her on the sidewalk, grabbing her from behind, startling her.

"Wade should be here this afternoon. Want to go grab pizza?"

"Sure. Probably need to introduce him to Shannah before tomorrow." Rachael agreed.

"I was thinking the same thing. What kind of dress did you get?"

"It's a surprise."

"I kind of need to know what color shirt to wear."

"White shirt."

She thought about suggesting he wear pink, but she knew he'd scoff at the idea. Furthermore, she didn't want to tip him off about her dress.

They walked hand in hand out to the parking lot. Travis kissed her goodbye.

"Pick you up around six-thirty?"

"Yep."

Rachael looked and saw Michael and Levi sprinting across the parking lot.

"Get it done?" Travis asked.

"Yep." Michael grinned.

"Get what done?" Rachael chimed in.

"Nothing." Levi said. "But spread the word. Soccer practice started today and no one should wash their hair."

"Got it. You don't have to worry about us football players, we leave dirty. Besides we have a game tomorrow, no practice for us."

"Gross." Rachael commented. "You don't bathe before you come home? I'll remember that. That goes on my list of *Things Travis Needs to Change*."

"God made dirt and dirt don't hurt, baby."

Travis walked away, headed directly for a few soccer players he knew standing outside the locker room dribbling balls with their feet. Rachael climbed through the window of her car and buckled her seatbelt. Levi and Michael climbed in and did the same. Both were unusually quiet.

"Where's Riley?"

"She caught a ride with Amber today. Sleepover or some girl thing."

"Probably getting pretty for you for Homecoming."

"I hope she doesn't put on too much makeup. I hate that stuff, look all white like a ghost."

"Whatever you do don't tell her that, you'll hurt her feelings. Just tell her she looks gorgeous no matter what."

"I'm not a total failure, I know how to talk to girls. I've been under the tutelage of the master, remember?"

"How could I forget?"

Rachael dropped the boys off at Levi's house for the night and went home to feed Grace. When she pulled into the driveway she glanced at her phone. She had three hours. With any luck she could fit in a ride, shower, and still be ready in time to go to dinner with Travis. She texted Shannah, who said she was up for anything, and so their plans were set.

Rachael went out to the barn to clean Grace's stall. She was always so happy to see her. She whinnied at her approach. Rachael went in and patted her nose. Then suddenly she whinnied again, right next to Rachael's ear. It was deafening.

Rachael heard another sound, the rattling of a horse trailer coming up the drive. She knew it must be Travis and he'd know where to find her.

She got her bridle and reins out of the tack room. She put it on Grace and led her out of the barn into the sun. She brushed her down until she shined, slick and smooth. She heard two guys talking and turned to see Travis and a guy who could've only been Wade walking out toward the barn.

"Great minds think alike." Travis smiled. "We thought we'd go surprise Shannah and suggest a ride."

Rachael overheard from where she stood with her horse. *I know Shannah said she was game for pizza, but a surprise horseback ride?* She couldn't be sure how Shannah would feel about the change in plans, but she didn't want to refuse either. Wade had just driven in from North Florida and he was even more handsome in person than his profile picture reflected. He was not only Redneck Fine, he was all-around good looking, and could've doubled as Travis' slightly older brother. Rachael would guess him at nineteen, compared to Travis' eighteen years old. His blue eyes popped against the azure blue of his pearl snap shirt. The cuffs were rolled back exposing his strong forearms and masculine hands.

Yep. Shannah's gonna like this one.

He walked over where Travis introduced them. Rachael reached out her hand and shook his. His callused palms even reminded her of Travis'. There was just something about a hardworking man that made him all the more attractive.

"How do you like your mare? She looks like she's settled in nicely."

"She has. I named her Grace. She's the sweetest thing. Up until today I've only ridden her around the house here. I'm not sure she's ready for the real thing yet."

"She'll be fine." Wade commented. "My little sister, Katie, rode her everywhere for a year. She wouldn't hurt a fly."

"Travis bought her from you?"

"From my father. He called saying he needed a gentle one that handled well and was a smooth ride."

"I love her. She's fantastic."

Travis took the reins from her and they all walked toward the horse trailer out front.

"Excuse me a minute. I need to grab some sunscreen and a hat." Rachael sprinted inside, out of hearing range, and closed the door. She ran down the hall and dialed Shannah. When she picked up she yelled in a frantic whisper.

"Change of plans! Don't hate me."

"What's up?"

"We're coming over now."

"Now?"

"Now! They just showed up to go riding, with a horse for you too! I'm sorry. Throw it together, quickly."

"Is he fine?"

"Like super fine! Super cowboy, uber handsome, freakin' redneck fine!"

"Great. I haven't shaved!"

"Pull on a pair of jeans girl! We're riding horses! He won't see your legs. Do your hair, some make-up. But not too much. You want to look like we caught you by surprise. Surprised- but not too surprised. Got it."

"Okay." Shannah hung up. The nervous edge to her voice obvious.

Rachael appeared outside, wearing her cowgirl hat from Travis, lip gloss, and some perfume. She needed to look like she was inside taking some time on herself, not calling and warning Shannah.

She climbed in the front seat next to Travis and slid over to hold his hand.

"You smell nice." He gave her a strange look. She didn't elaborate.

"So tell me a little about Shannah. All I know about her is the picture I saw of her two years ago in the Citrus and Florida Cattleman's Magazines."

"In the magazines? Doing what?" Rachael couldn't imagine.

"She was Miss Teen Florida Orange Blossom Princess or something like that."

Travis just burst out laughing. Rachael smacked his thigh.

"Shannah? A pageant girl?" Rachael doubted it but Wade didn't seem like a liar.

"No. She really was. Her father wanted her to represent this area and citrus. He entered her against her will, and she won the whole darned thing." Travis advised.

"So," he smirked, "she's not the pageant type?" Wade sounded relieved.

"Not at all. I'd describe her as more of a real country girl. Very pretty and fit, a little bit rugged too, but not butch."

Okay, I'm digging a hole here.

"I'm good with not butch." Wade laughed. "In north Florida we tend to like the girls who sing soprano. Just like that famous AJ song says."

Travis just shook his head and laughed. Rachael had no idea what Wade had meant by his last comment, but she had the definite feeling Shannah would like him. He was definitely her type of guy. Outgoing and spirited, very confident. A guy without all of these qualities could never compete with Shannah's effervescent personality. She'd run right over top of him.

Maybe this was a good thing. Rachael considered Shannah's house and its proximity to her own.

I need to buy a little more time.

"Can we stop at the feed store?"

Travis looked at her suspiciously. "Does that need to happen now?"

"I'm out of hay and if I don't get it now…I may not have another chance. I don't have a truck and it dirties the trunk of my car."

He pulled in and they climbed out.

"I'll wait here." Wade commented.

Rachael walked inside.

"What's going on? You're acting strangely." Travis asked.

"You can't just spring this on a girl. Dinner was set for six-thirty. She wasn't even dressed, yet. If she had been, she would've been dressed for pizza, not riding."

"So we're buying her some time? Shannah? She doesn't care."

"Trust me, under that tough exterior, she cares."

"Are you really out of hay?"

"Nope."

"Come on." He grabbed Rachael's hand and towed her back to the truck and climbed in.

"No hay?" Wade winked.

"No hay. Rachael here's worried we didn't give Shannah enough time to get ready."

"Gotcha."

Rachael narrowed her eyes at Travis.

"And I'd just as soon tell her she doesn't need much time to get ready 'cause she's just that pretty." Wade stuck a toothpick in his mouth.

Travis backed the horse trailer out and they continued toward Shannah's house. Rachael fumed, not speaking another word to Travis. He sensed it.

"I tell Rachael that all the time. When you look as good as she does, all that other stuff is just gravy." Travis grinned, trying to soften her mood.

"Gravy's good, but some women just don't need the extra fixin's." Wade added.

"I feel like I'm at an all-you-can-eat southern buffet." Rachael squeezed Travis' upper thigh.

"There's two of us now, we're ganging up on you." Travis reached over and held her hand.

"Is this what it'd be like if you had a brother? Twice as aggravating."

"I know all about you, Rachael Harte." Wade spoke around the tooth pick. "From the first day he met you up until now."

Rachael cut her eyes at Travis.

"He does. He's the closest thing I've got to a brother."

"Why haven't I met you before now?"

"He didn't want the competition." Wade joked. "He's kept me hidden away, hunting trips and working cows. No ladies."

"Good. I'm glad to hear no women are allowed on those trips. Keep me informed Wade, keep me apprised of his every move."

"You better watch out man. She's got you branded."

"Roped and tied up too." Travis winked.

They pulled down Shannah's long driveway. Wade climbed out and went up to ring her bell.

"Should I go?" Rachael went to open the door.

"Does he look like he needs your help?"

"Guess not."

Shannah opened the door, obviously expecting Rachael. Her shocked reaction was visible from the truck. She quickly masked her jaw dropping response and turned to close the door, locking it.

Wade walked her to the truck and opened the back door for her. She climbed in and slid across. For the first thirty seconds silence filled the cab of Travis' diesel. Rachael had never heard Shannah speechless, but here it was…stunned silence…she said nothing.

She'd worn a pair of fitted gray skinny jeans with a pale blue tank top. Her hair was in a high pony tail that hung to the middle of her back. She even smelled good. She'd lined her lips and put on some mascara along with a little light pink shimmer.

"Wade, thank you for doing this." She blurted out. "You didn't have to, but I really appreciate it."

"No, thank you for inviting me. I graduated last year. This will probably be my last homecoming."

"Are you in school?"

"I am, in Tallahassee, but let's not discuss it in front of Travis. Tallahassee's a fighting word among us."

"Can't say I'm a Nole fan, either." Shannah confessed.

"You never know, you might come around. I've seen people change team loyalties for all sorts of reasons."

Rachael wasn't sure they were exactly hitting it off, but at least Shannah was talking. She seemed nervous.

When they pulled into the gate, Wade got out to open it and swung it wide for them to pull through. Travis looked straight ahead, grinning...and said not a word.

He drove through the gate and parked the truck and trailer off to the side. Shannah jumped out first to help Wade unload the horses.

When Rachael was sure they were out of earshot, she asked, "You think they're okay?"

"They're fine. Shannah seems a bit off though." Travis admitted.

"I don't know why." Rachael vented. "But she needs to pull out her A-game."

"I think Shannah always chooses really bad guys, and I think she does it on purpose." Travis whispered.

"Whatever. She does not." Rachael defended her friend.

"Has it ever occurred to you that maybe she chooses them because they're safe? The bad guys are emotionally unavailable to her, they only want one thing, and she can keep them at arm's length. Then they break up, so she's never really gotten close to anyone. Think about it. I'm right. Now she's faced with a really good guy. He'll treat her right. I bet she runs. If he lets her." Travis smiled and opened his door.

"What do you mean 'if he lets her'?"

"I warned him, yet he has wanted to meet her since two years ago. He likes her and won't give up easily."

"Must be a family trait."

"Must be."

Rachael slid across the seat and jumped down into his awaiting arms. She had to laugh at the sight of Shannah up on the side of the horse trailer.

"What are you doing?"

"Getting on. I'm a redneck, not a cowgirl." She protested.

"Nonsense." Wade walked over and lifted her down off of the side of the trailer in spite of her protesting. "Just put your foot in the stirrup like this." He lifted her sneaker clad foot into place. "Grab the saddle horn." He put her hand on the saddle horn. "And up you go."

He was so swift and methodical about it, she couldn't say no. Next thing you know, she was up on the horse, and he was handing her the reins.

Rachael looked at Travis who tightened his own girth strap, never looking up to make eye contact. Shannah and Wade rode off ahead of them. He swung up into the saddle and cut his eyes over at Rachael a few moments later.

He mouthed the words, "If anyone can handle Miss Shannah- it'll be that man. Come on."

They struck a lope and caught up to them across the pasture.

"Where are we exactly?" Shannah asked.

Rachael had been planning on asking the same. They were out past Shannah's house at a pasture even Rachael had never been in.

"This is our bull pasture." Travis explained. "We needed to ride over to check on the bulls Wade and his dad picked out in Kenansville. Make sure they aren't too stressed. They've been in here for a few weeks, adjusting."

"We'll leave them here until January and then move them to our place. They're all three's." Wade added.

"Three's?" Shannah questioned.

"Three year olds." Rachael explained. From her conversation regarding Taffy a few months back she understood that much.

"These are all bulls?" Rachael asked.

"Sure are." Travis and Wade looked at each other.

"What are they teaching in biology class these days?" Wade asked.

"Not enough, obviously." Travis answered.

Rachael looked more closely at the bulls and saw that where there would've been utters, if they'd been females like Taffy, there was something else entirely different. It reminded her of the trucks she saw all over town with the yucky stuff hanging from where the hitches were.

She knew she was turning red and decided to keep any thoughts she had in regard to the physical anatomy of a bull to herself.

She could hear Shannah and Wade talking about cattle breeds and bull breeding programs, pasture rotations, etc. She seemed genuinely interested in the conversation.

Rachael saw one bull with something wrong with its eye. Travis and Wade spotted it first and rode over to look at it more closely.

"Pink eye." Travis said.

"Yep, weren't all these bulls vaccinated against pink eye?"

"Thought so."

"Will it kill them?" Rachael asked.

"No, but it can be a pain to treat. Glad we rode out here." Travis nodded toward Wade. "We ready for pizza?"

"Ready if y'all are. Ladies?" Wade asked Shannah and Rachael.

"Sure are. I'm starved." Shannah added.

"You don't look like you could weigh more than a buck, maybe a buck ten." Wade smiled at her.

"Don't be fooled. I can put it away." Shannah challenged.

"I hear you can whip my butt, too."

"Maybe I can."

"I'd like to be on the receiving end of just such a butt whipping."

For once Shannah didn't say anything in return. If any other guy had said that to her, or even made the suggestion that she 'whip them', she would've gone crazy on him. But here was a direct challenge from Wade and she merely took it, not saying a word- not rising to the occasion- not putting him in his place.

Maybe Travis is right. There's no running from this one. He's got her beaten already, and she knows it!

Shannah and Wade raced their horses to the trailer. Of course he won, he was the much better rider.

"Are you sure he's a gentleman?" Rachael asked, riding side by side with Travis on Coal.

"He wouldn't lay a hand on her, but he's been on dates." Travis pondered his statement looking for the right words. "He's not as religious as I am, but he's had a good time and now he's looking for the right girl to settle down with."

"He's had a good time! How good of a time?"

"Let me rephrase." But before Travis could rephrase, Rachael was turned in her saddle shaking her finger at him.

"Did we set her up with a player?"

"I didn't say player. What, you think she can't handle him? She knocked a guy out two days ago, Rachael. I think she'll be fine. I was just saying he's not a monk. Okay? Not a monk, but not a lecherous creep either. And that's all I'm going to say about that."

"Looking to settle down." Rachael thought aloud. "Why do you country guys like to get married so young?"

"Because we know the obvious, all the good ones get snatched up early. It's slim pickins' if you wait too long to get married. Can't let the right one get away. Come over here." He beckoned.

"Are you intentionally annoying me today?"

"Yep."

"Then nope. I'm going back to the truck." She loped away.

Chapter Seventeen

The following morning was a blur of hair and nails. Shannah, Maysie, and Rachael sat in the salon with those wedge-like foam separators stuck between their toes while the nail tech finished their nails.

"I for one think this is ridiculous. Look at this torture we're having to endure. And what do you think the guys are doing?" Shannah spouted.

"They're out baiting hog traps and running dogs." Maysie chirped.

"That's what I'd like to be doing. Not having this popsicle stick stuck under my cuticles." Shannah griped.

"She's pushing your cuticles back and trimming them, not sticking a popsicle stick under them."

Rachael decided to change the subject. "Down and curled, in a sleek retro style. That's how I'm wearing my hair." Rachael blurted.

"Up with a tiny tiara. I'm a redneck princess tonight, girlies." Maysie added.

"In a knotted braid, at the back of my neck."

Everyone's heads whipped around. Shannah never opted for the coifed, classy slash refined look.

"Do you like Wade?" Maysie asked.

"It's too soon to tell for sure, but I do. I like him, a lot. He makes me feel, fragile."

Maysie squealed and clapped her hands. "Yippee! We'll all be Baxters."

"Hold your horses, Maysie, this isn't Dallas and we're all not moving up to the big house to live with Daddy in a few short weeks." Shannah spat. "But I will admit to really liking him even though he's not my usual type."

"Well he's clean for one. And I don't mean in the *he's taken a bath recently* sort of way." Maysie smiled sweetly.

"Clean?" Shannah almost sounded offended.

"Yep. No drug test or other types of testing needed."

"Meaning I usually go for the loser, looks like he could be a druggie or a total sleaze gigolo?"

"That sums it up."

"She's right." Shannah acknowledged. "He *is* out of my normal realm of losers. What am I thinking? I can't even find a single flaw. And I like them flawed."

"Flawed hasn't been working for you." Rachael commented.

"I know. Right? He's practically perfect." Shannah wrinkled her nose. "I've become one of you!" She faked horror. "Maybe I should cancel."

"No!!!" Rachael and Maysie cried in unison.

"I'm sure he has a flaw. A big one." Maysie chimed.

"Like what?"

Maysie and Rachael considered what would be bad boy enough for Shannah to want to date him, but not so bad that she'd rule him out entirely.

"Why does he have to have a flaw?" Rachael asked. "I mean for real. Why? Why can't he be what he is? An all-around really good looking guy with an amazing body, personality, and charm. He's a cowboy to boot. Don't you deserve perfect? Who wants flawed? Certainly not me."

"You know Rachael, you're right. I deserve a good guy, a good guy like Wade."

"Yes, you do." Rachael emphasized. "And he deserves for you to treat him right."

"Yes, he does." Shannah looked at her nails. "Do you think I could get some sparkle on these nails?"

"Rhinestones." Maysie nodded. "We all need rhinestones."

"No tiara though. I'm drawing the line there, only rhinestones." Shannah emphasized.

After their nails were polished and studded, Rachael had the nail tech write Travis on her pointer finger and dazzle it with some glitter. Maysie liked it so much she had Tristan's name put on hers as well.

"Got a rifle you could put on there?" Shannah joked.

"No firearms on your nails!" Maysie interceded.

"Joking."

Next the women set to work on their hair, working for hours to get it just right. By the time they were finished even Rachael felt half-starved and weak. Her mother came in to pick them up and cart them over to Aunt Margaret's to get ready. Since Wade and Travis were staying at the Baxter's, getting ready there was out of the question.

At her house they each ate a sub, some chips, and downed a soda for strength. Maysie set to work on all of their make-up. Her makeup tackle box was full of stuff that even Rachael didn't know what half of it was for. She picked through everything until she found the right colors for each girl. Finally, it was seven o'clock and the girls slipped on their dresses.

Maysie's ensemble was young and whimsical- everything she'd wanted. A sleek updo adorned with a small rhinestone tiara and matching rhinestone jewelry. It made her look like royalty. The black four inch, rhinestone studded heels, set the whole thing off. She looked at herself in the full length mirror behind the door.

"It's all about the shoes." She grinned.

Shannah's sky blue dress was slinky and feminine. It accentuated her flat abs and strong thighs. Her long lines were perfect in this dress. With coifed hair and silver strappy platforms, it was truly an elegant look.

"Bam! What a dress!" Maysie teased.

"Is it too much?"

"Nope, but we wanted you to be the hottest girl there, well look out Gabe and Romero!"

"Come on, Rachael! Hurry it up. The guys are here. I just heard a car door." Shannah fussed.

Rachael opened the bathroom door. She wore a simple, strapless pink camouflage gown. It was snug at the bodice and around her rib cage, but looser through the hips where it flowed freely about her to the floor.

"Gone With the Wind meets modern Redneck Glam!" Maysie called.

The sweeping blonde hair set in long flowing waves over one shoulder sat in contrast to the bright red lipstick.

The doorbell rang and Aunt Margaret rushed to get it.

"We want pictures!" Mrs. Harte exclaimed. "I've promised all the moms."

Maysie, Shannah, and Rachael made their way up the hall to the family room. The guys stood in awe.

Travis was the first to come over and hug Rachael. He gave her a wrist corsage with purple roses and Babies' Breath.

"Need a shawl? You might get cold." He teased.

"No. I'm fine and you'll be too." She kissed his cheek.

Maysie went over and twirled around in her dress for Tristan.

"I love it. Can't wait to take you hunting in that. The hottest whitetail to step foot in the woods, ever. Six months and counting." He whispered giving her a sweet hug and placing the daisy corsage on her wrist. It was huge and Maysie just loved it.

All eyes were on Shannah who walked over to talk to Wade. He gave her a kiss on the cheek. She held out her wrist where he placed red roses accompanied by tiny white tea roses.

"No wonder you won Miss Teen Florida Orange Blossom Princess."

"You saw that?"

"Two years ago." He smiled.

"My dad made me do it. I had no choice really."

"I'm glad he did. I wouldn't have agreed to drive four hours to go to a high school dance if he hadn't."

If Rachael wasn't mistaken, Shannah actually blushed. She hadn't thought it possible.

Mrs. Harte snapped numerous pictures. Rachael's lips and cheeks ached from smiling.

"I think I'm getting a twitch in my right jaw." Travis griped.

"Be quiet, Travis, and just stand there and look handsome." Aunt Margaret chided.

"Yes, Ma'am."

When the photo session finally came to an end, they walked toward the front door. Wade opened it and held it wide for Shannah. She passed through and he followed her, quick to take her hand and lead her to the waiting limo. The limousine driver held the door open as the three couples slid in.

Inside there were bottled waters and sodas, along with fruit and veggie trays. A cheesecake platter looked tantalizing, as well. Shannah spied a piece of turtle cheesecake, but Maysie shook her head with a look that said, *don't you dare mess up that makeup*!

Wade saw the exchange and grabbed the platter and a napkin. He fixed one of each type for them to sample. Shannah took one being polite and ate it daintily. Maysie looked on approvingly. Rachael poured herself a soda and handed one to Travis as well. Everyone chatted non-stop the entire way there.

"You look gorgeous." Travis whispered. "Stunning."

"Thank you. You clean up nicely too."

When they pulled into the restaurant and hotel down on the bay where the dance was being held, they were in line behind a few other limos waiting to unload.

Travis climbed out first and helped each girl out. When he got to Tristan and Wade he merely said, "I ain't helping y'all." Laughing, he walked away.

Rachael and Travis held hands as they walked up to the door. Rachael saw Fred and Alex coming up the walkway waving to them. Elena was behind them with Bobby alongside. When they met, they stopped briefly to say 'hi', and then proceeded inside.

"See, she had nothing to worry about. Fred is a good guy." Travis grinned.

"Yep. He is." Rachael agreed.

"I'm still not going to sign on for any exchange students." Travis warned. "So don't ask." He said to both Maysie and Rachael.

"I don't know. There was some French guy who needed a place to stay and Mama thought it'd be nice to offer…" Maysie winked conspiratorially at Rachael.

"And that's when I offered our house." Rachael added.

"Not funny." Travis griped.

"I heard Elena has a cousin coming and she needs a place to stay." Tristan gave Travis a look. "If y'all are taking in exchange students, why not her. A good European girl in need of a good home."

"Truce." Maysie threw up her hands.

"I thought so." Travis nodded.

"Were they always like this?" Rachael asked Wade.

"Since childhood. There were many times I had to remind him she was a girl and kicking her butt would land him in a load of trouble."

"Are you saying girls are weak?" Shannah jumped into the conversation taking Wade on.

"Not at all. I like a strong woman who's able to defend herself, but a man should never lay a rough hand on a lady."

"Well put." Shannah complemented him.

Inside they found their way to a back corner, the benefits of coming early…you usually got your choice of table. The music was an eclectic mix and the option to go with a DJ, rather than a loud band like last year, had been the right choice. The menu was a choice of either chicken marsala or sirloin tips, with asparagus and mashed potatoes. It was surprisingly good and Rachael found herself enjoying the evening more than even she expected.

Tristan, Wade, and Travis all got up to fetch the girls' drinks. In their absence, Rachael, Maysie, and Shannah all slid over to sit closer together. From where they sat, they could observe everyone. The buffet line was still full of students holding their plates, patiently waiting their turn. The oversized dance floor held a cluster of over-eager dancers in the center. The types that started dancing, as soon as the doors opened, and danced until *Shout* played, closing the dance as the final number.

When the guys returned to the table, they were forced to sit down three in a row. If it bothered them they didn't let on. Song after song played. Travis excused himself from the guy talk and came over to lead Rachael out onto the dance floor. He pulled her close against his warmth as he twirled her around the dance floor. She laid her chin on his shoulder and breathed in the scent that was uniquely him.

"I think she likes him." Rachael said.

"I think you're right. I was sitting over there thinking these may be the couples we're surrounded by for years. Maysie and Tristan, it's a forgone conclusion they'll get married. You and me. Then there's Shannah and Wade- it's too soon to know, for sure, but I think they're off to a pretty good start."

"Maybe."

Rachael heard an uproar of laughter from across the room and looked over to the balloon arch near the entrance. Romero and two of the other soccer players arrived. He was wearing his hair cropped in a buzz, a near hairless look. His face looked tense and he didn't smile at anyone.

"I wonder why he cut his hair."

"I'm not so sure he did." Travis coughed into his hand trying to conceal his laugh. "The back part is still long- just the stuff on top is kind of…missing. Maybe it's premature balding."

"Since yesterday?" Rachael squinted her eyes.

Romero moved into the large ballroom and crossed the floor making a straight line across the dance floor, headed toward their table.

"Looks like there might be trouble." Travis took her by the hand and led her back to the table. Once there, he pulled out her chair, waited for her to be seated, and slid it in.

Romero stood close to where Shannah was seated. He yelled at her in his thick accent. "You did this to my hair!"

"I don't know what you're talking about, Romero." She stated. "I don't know what happened to your hair."

Wade slid his chair out from beneath the table and stood up.

"And I don't appreciate the tone you're taking with her."

Now Travis stood up. He walked around the table where Tristan joined him.

"See, the way we were raised, you don't insult ladies and you don't go around pushing yourself on them. Shannah had nothing to do with you washing your hair with depilatory hair removal cream, but we did. So if you'd like, we'd be more than happy to step outside with you and sort this mess out. If not, then you best be moving on." Travis winked at him.

Romero had no choice but to walk away. The rest of the table burst out laughing.

"Depilatory cream!" Shannah hollered. "Holy crap."

Travis, Tristan, and Wade all sat back down, sliding their chairs under the table.

"I can't believe how well the stuff actually works. Now he won't have to spend so much time on his long, lustrous hair." Wade mocked.

"Guess not. You girls should use that stuff on your legs."

"I tried once." Maysie admitted. "It kind of stinks."

All the guys made a face. Obviously chemical stink was a turn off.

"How did you do it?" Rachael asked.

"We didn't, but let's just say we're related to who did."

"Michael and Levi?" Maysie whispered.

Travis just nodded his head, not admitting as much out loud.

"I couldn't let them take the rap for it. The soccer team would find them and beat their butts. No one's going to mess with the three of us."

"How did they do it?" Shannah asked.

"They replaced the shampoo in the showers with it. Then I went around and warned the other soccer players who think he's a cocky jerk. No one else shampoos and blow dries their hair after practice anyhow."

"You better be careful, Rachael. If you tick Michael off you're liable to end up a baldy!" Maysie warned.

"We'll make that boy a redneck just yet." Shannah looked proud.

They saw the principal walking over to their table. He looked angry. Everyone went silent.

"Mr. Baxter," he greeted Travis. "And friends. Is everything all right over here?"

"Yes, sir. Everything's fine." Travis smiled.

"Good to hear. I heard about Romero Vazquez's poor behavior toward Shannah. It's unfortunate, but sometimes these things just have a way of sorting themselves out."

"Yes, sir, they do." Travis nodded.

"Have a good evening and enjoy the dance."

The principal walked away stepping over to the drink table to fix himself a soda.

Wade mumbled something to Travis.

"He played ball with our dads in high school." Travis answered.

Wade excused himself to pull Shannah out onto the dance floor.

"But I don't dance!" She protested.

"Do now." He said pulling her in tighter.

Maysie and Tristan went out to join them. Travis picked up Rachael's hand and kissed it gently.

"Is the Principal turning a blind eye because he knows your father?"

"Pretty much. He knows Romero's a jerk."

"What about Gabe?"

"Many guys joined in and made a wager. It doesn't make Gabe a great guy, but he's still my friend."

Rachael could see Heather across the dance floor. She was dancing with some other guy. She seemed to know this guy very well, especially for a girl with a boyfriend.

"I think they deserve each other, Heather and Gabe."

"Be nice." Travis sipped his drink and set it back down. "Where's Gabe anyway?"

"Who knows?" Travis glanced over to the farthest corner, at the back of the room. "He's over there with Selena."

Rachael looked over and saw he was with Selena.

"What are they doing?"

"Making each other jealous. They fight, they break up. They fight, they break up. He threatens to beat someone up. They get back together. That kind of bull..."

"I'm glad we only ever broke up once."

"Me, too. I barely survived it. It's not the kind of thing you should do. My attitude is don't say or do something you can't take back. You're stuck with me, girl." He leaned over and gently pressed his lips to hers.

"I like being stuck with you." She grabbed his hand and pulled him to his feet. "Let's dance. This is our last homecoming."

"Sure is."

They weren't on the dance floor longer than thirty seconds when the Principal came up to announce the Homecoming King and Queen. He asked everyone to line up.

"This year's Homecoming Queen is Shannah Carlson." The crowd cheered. Shannah had friends in every grade and from very diverse backgrounds. She was well-loved and respected across campus, it was obvious why. She bridged the expanse between city and country, rich and poor, popular and nerdy. Rachael and Maysie rushed over to hug her, careful not to bump her crown.

"You're right, no tiara for you! You get the real deal, a crown!" Maysie praised.

"This year's Homecoming King is Travis Baxter." The Assistant Principal stepped in front of Travis and placed the large plastic gold crown on his head.

The DJ played a slow song and they danced. Halfway through, Wade walked over and cut-in claiming that Shannah was his Redneck Princess. Travis came over and bowed to Rachael leading her out onto the floor for one final dance. Other couples joined them...and the music played on and on.

Around eleven o'clock they decided to call it a night and headed toward their awaiting limo. Rachael and Travis were the first to climb in. The others followed them. The car ride home was quiet, everyone not ready for the night to end. The limo pulled up to Travis and Maysie's house. The driver climbed out, assisting each of the ladies and then drove away.

"We're not going home?" Rachael asked.

"Not yet. Do you want to go home?" Travis asked.

"Nope."

They led the girls inside where Mrs. Baxter had set up an elaborate dessert buffet in the kitchen. Shannah immediately went over and fixed herself a plate of chocolate covered strawberries along with some marshmallows. Wade helped himself and they went into the TV room to make themselves at home.

Tristan went on a walk out to the barn to check on the horses. With them Maysie took a bottle of sparkling apple cider and two plastic champagne flutes. There were a couple of other bottles sitting on the counter. Rachael bent over to read the label.

"Don't worry, it's nonalcoholic. Mama always buys it for special occasions." Travis teased.

"I wasn't worried. I hardly thought your mother would be plying us with a bunch of liquor."

"Come on. Let's play darts." Travis pulled her along to the game room. Rachael wasn't exactly dressed for darts, but she figured why not. After spanking her at darts, Travis challenged her to a game of ping pong. She was a little bit rusty. Her first two shots whizzed over his head across the room.

"Bring it down a bit, slugger."

"It's been a while." She laughed. She picked up her paddle again and readied herself by taking off the chunky, heavy black beaded bracelet and matching large onyx ring. "Okay. Now I'm ready."

"Like a little jewelry is going to make a difference. You're still getting beat."

"You think so?" She challenged. They played ping pong until one o'clock in the morning when it was time to go home. Travis set down the paddles and walked around the table to hug her.

"Come on, I'll run you home."

They walked through the house. No one else was around.

"Where are they?"

"They're big kids. They can drive. I'd say they're on their own."

He led her outside where she saw Tristan and Wade's trucks were missing. He walked over to the driver's side and opened the door for her. He put his hands around her waist to lift her up, but didn't. He swept her hair to the side and trailed kisses across the top of her shoulders and back again. He worked his way around to her neck and exposed ear. He kissed her there and then back down her neck.

"Turn around." He whispered. "I want to kiss you goodnight, properly."

Rachael pivoted to face him. He traced gentle kisses across her jaw to her lips kissing her softly. He teased her mouth with his tongue and she was lost in his kiss. A short while later he brought her hair back down over her shoulders and righted her lipstick, wiping it away where he'd smudged it.

"Now, I'll take you home," He paused, a glint in his eyes. He slammed the door closed behind her and pushed her gently up against it. "But I don't want to." He bent his head and kissed her once more. She felt it in the pit of her stomach, a deep need that mere kissing couldn't quench. His hands traced her sides, working their way lower still. Her heart raced in her ears. Her body fit perfectly with his.

She reached down and held his wrists, stopping his hands before they strayed too far.

"Travis…" She whispered in the moonlit driveway.

"I know. Let's get you home."

Chapter Eighteen

The house phone startled her awake. The answering machine picked up. Her father's cheerful voice, a little after six o'clock on a Wednesday brought her upright in bed. Rachael scrambled out of bed to race up the hall to the kitchen to grab the phone before he hung up. She stubbed her toe on the door jam, hobbling past it.

She'd nearly made it to the kitchen when she heard Michael say, "Hello".

Rachael slowed her pace to a limp and went into the family room to join him.

"I will." Michael pressed the button on the phone for speaker phone. "Dad wants to tell us both something."

"Hey, kids. I've got good news. I've qualified for early release. I should be out in the next month."

Rachael and Michael erupted in screaming. They jumped up and down, hugging each other.

"Out in time for Easter." Their father continued.

"I can't believe it!" Michael yelled. "How does this happen?"

"I've served 85% of my sentence, it gets pretty technical, but since I'm in for nonviolent crimes I qualify for early release. Of course, there'll be probation, but I'm just glad to be coming home."

"We're so glad you'll be coming home, too." Rachael added.

"I have to go, but I told your mother yesterday. You guys were already in bed, so I wanted to catch you before school this morning."

"Bye, Dad!"

"See you in a few short weeks."

Rachael and Michael sprinted down the hall. Both dressed for school and went out to climb into her car. Halfway to school, Michael turned to her and started chatting nervously.

"Do you think this means we have to move back? I don't want to move back. I'm excited about Dad coming home, really I am. But I have so many friends here. I like our school."

"I don't know what it means." Rachael considered Michael's situation. It was different than hers. He was a freshman. He had four more years to go. She was nearly finished.

"Maybe he and Mom will move back, and let me stay with Aunt Margaret."

"I'm not sure. I wish I had all the answers for you, but I don't. Right now let's just focus on the positive, Dad is finally coming home! And earlier than we imagined possible. It was coming this summer anyway. Maybe we should've considered the possibility of a move back before now."

"I don't want to go back!" Michael wiped a stray tear from his cheek.

"Don't cry." She patted his thigh. "You might not have to. Right now we don't know anything, right? You have to have faith that everything will work out. It always does. We've survived it all so far."

He nodded his head but spoke not another word.

At school they parked in the student lot on the west side of campus. Rachael saw Riley standing on the sidewalk waiting for Michael to walk her to class. He got out and went over to hold her hand. They turned and walked away.

Travis sat in his truck listening to music. He cut his truck engine off when she climbed out of her Mustang.

"What's wrong with him?" Travis asked.

"Dad's getting out of jail right before Easter."

"That's a bad thing?"

"He's afraid of a move."

"It could happen, but maybe not. Your father may have his own reasons for not wanting to move your family back there."

"I know, but Michael is worried, and I can't blame him. Moving once and starting over is hard enough."

Travis grabbed her and embraced her tightly. "It's been a long, hard ride. It's time y'all got down out of that saddle and found some normalcy again. This too shall pass." He kissed the top of her head. "Trust in God."

"I know."

Rachael walked up the sidewalk and toward Mr. Richardson's class. Travis told her goodbye at the door. He stuck his hands in his pockets and walked away.

Mr. Richardson sat behind his desk, his nasty stained-up coffee cup in hand. He sipped it, reading the paper. Rachael looked toward the front row. There were three empty seats.

Samantha, Alex, and another girl named Melissa, who Rachael didn't know at all, were all absent.

The morning dragged by and when the bell rang everyone jumped to pack up. Rachael stood and put away her English vocab book. She'd fallen asleep the night before reading in bed and needed to finish the last two pages. Homeroom allowed her that opportunity.

Thank goodness.

She pulled her bag over her shoulder and started for the door. The Principal entered the classroom. He was wearing a full suit and had the School Resource Officer with him. Rachael glanced around. There were only a handful of students still in the room. All of them had the deer in headlights look and froze in place.

"Mr. Richardson. Could you come with me, please?"

Mr. Richardson stood up and slid his chair in. He looked around, then down at the ground.

"Please bring your things." The Principal added.

Mr. Richardson put his laptop and other papers into his bag and walked toward the door. They exited the room. The students looked around, exchanging glances. On her way through the door, a young substitute swept past Rachael. Out in the hallway Rachael watched as the Principal and Resource Officer led Mr. Richardson away. His hands were cuffed behind his back.

Stunned, Rachael rushed to her next class. She ran into Maysie and Shannah outside in the courtyard, where students frantically discussed the incident.

Maysie lowered her voice and whispered,

"Come with me."

Rachael and Shannah followed her into the locker room. It was empty this time of morning with most of the Physical Education classes scheduled for after lunch.

"Turns out you were right about Mr. Richardson. He is a creep."

"Does it involve Alex? I couldn't help but notice she was absent from school."

Shannah stood listening to their conversation. Rachael hadn't discussed any of this with her, and she appeared dumbfounded by what was going on.

"It does. She texted me this morning. Turns out Mr. Richardson has been giving girls extra credit after school, in his office, especially if they were in a pass slash fail situation." Maysie explained.

"Gross." Rachael added.

"It's more than gross. Dude's a pedophile." Shannah scolded.

"Of course." Maysie agreed. "Alex is okay, but she had a C in his class. I guess he asked her to stop by his office, and he made some sort of offer. She refused. I told her she needed to report it. That was last week. So she did."

"What about Melissa and Samantha? Remember that day I saw Samantha coming from his classroom?"

"That was months ago, but you were right about her. She was one of his victims. It's really bad." Maysie paused. Another girl walked into the locker room to use the restroom. No one spoke until she walked back out. "I don't know about this Melissa girl."

"They'll take care of him in prison." Shannah huffed. "That breaks even their code of conduct."

"For sure." Rachael answered. "We better get to class. I hope Alex is okay."

"She hasn't texted me since this morning. All she said is he was going down."

"She must've known it was coming."

The three scurried off in different directions for their classes. A few hours later they arrived to the lunch room and there was still no sign of Alex or Fred either. Wherever she was, he must be with her.

The minutes slowly ticked by and they became more and more worried. After school they met up in the locker room once more to change for dance practice. Everyone dressed in silence. By now word of the school scandal had spread to the entire team. Alex and her whereabouts occupied their every thought. Elena was there, one locker over from Rachael. She didn't say a word.

After initially seeing her as competition, she and Alex had become the best of friends. She'd ended up dating Bobby all year and was scheduled to return home in a few short months. Rachael considered her own move from West Palm and how life altering that had seemed at the time. That was nothing in comparison to what Elena would experience. Could she and Bobby's relationship really last separated by an ocean?

Everyone respected each other's need for quiet. No one asked questions because no one had answers. It was a bleak afternoon filled with doubt and uncertainty. One by one the team filed out of the locker room toward the rehearsal room. Basketball season was underway and their halftime routines were rehearsed indoors. No grass or mud, nor heat nor bugs, plagued them like during football season and while Rachael normally relished her afternoons spent dancing, today was different.

Shannah and Maysie walked beside her, carrying their stuff. Alex's absence brought to mind, for Rachael, the absence of two other dancers- Honey and Misty. The last she knew about them was that Honey's mother had yanked her out of school and sent her away to boarding school. Misty had gone into some drug treatment center. They'd all but vanished, beginning with them dropping off the team and then just going away altogether.

"I feel really badly about it."

"About what?" Shannah asked.

"The whole Honey and Misty thing. They quit the squad and then now they're just gone. Look how worried we are about Alex. None of us has even concerned ourselves with the other two." Rachael lamented.

"We tried to help Honey. Remember? And that didn't end well." Maysie reminded them.

"She's right." Shannah added.

"Yeah- but she's in boarding school now. Her parents did intercede on her behalf, and I have to believe that was in part due to Maysie reaching out to her mother. After they ditched Misty at my house and ran for the hills, Mrs. Baxter called and ratted Honey out. Because of that, Honey's life will be different."

"In a good way." Maysie nodded.

Rachael contemplated Misty. "I mean, look at us. None of us has had any concern at all over Misty. She's been in rehab for the better part of a school year."

"That's because she is a B." Shannah corrected. "Don't beat yourself up over Misty. She's where she needs to be."

"I know, but doesn't even she deserve our kindness?" Rachael questioned.

"I can't believe after all she's done to you, you want to be her friend?" Shannah asked.

"Not her friend, but to show her some…empathy."

"Maybe she's right." Maysie commented. "Maybe it's time for a little forgiveness and healing."

"You couldn't pay me to go." Shannah protested. "Unless, of course, I was armed."

"Come on. I'm not saying we'd become best friends with her, trust me. I don't want her around Travis- as in ever. I'm just suggesting we take her a balloon and flowers."

"I'm in." Maysie answered sweetly.

"I'm in, although I think it's possibly the worst idea either of you has ever had." Shannah added.

The girls stood outside the dance room. Two other dancers were missing and there was a note posted on the dance room door.

Practice is canceled for the week. See you back here after Spring Break.

The girls turned and headed to the parking lot. Travis pulled out of his spot and stopped when he saw them walking his way. Michael and Levi waited at the picnic tables. They ran over.

"No practice?"

"Nope. Some strange stuff is going on." Shannah answered them.

Travis walked over.

"Can you run them home?" Rachael asked in Travis' general direction.

"Will do. Where are y'all going?"

"We have something to take care of."

"I'm not sure I like the sounds of that." Travis clenched his jaw.

"She's making us reach out to Misty. I'm going on record now to say I think it's dumb with a capital D. Dumb." Shannah commented. She held her hands up. "My only reason for going is back-up. They'll need muscle, and that's me."

Travis didn't ask anything further and led the boys away.

Rachael and Maysie ignored Shannah's griping and climbed in the car. Shannah hopped in the backseat.

The rehab facility where Misty spent the last several months was an hour away. They turned the radio up to their favorite country station 103.5 FM and sang along. At the long driveway, they pulled in and parked in the near empty parking lot.

They walked in through the sliding glass doors. Rachael hadn't been sure what to expect, but this wasn't it. The floors were wood and there was a large seating area out front filled with oversized furniture and a flat screen television. The windows were large and offered exquisite views of the forty acre expanse that made up the grounds outside. Residents walked freely about, talking and visiting with their guests.

"This is nice." Maysie offered pleasantly.

"For a looney bin." Shannah observed.

"It's not a looney bin. She's not crazy, she's in rehab. This is a private facility."

"Private or not, don't be fooled. That girl's crazy."

Rachael nudged them both toward the check-in desk. A pleasant girl in her early thirties greeted them and asked them to sign in. She explained that she was the house mom. She gave them directions to Misty's room down near the end of the hall.

Rachael's heart pulsed in her ears. She felt as if she'd come to confront her enemy…while extending an olive branch and waving the proverbial white flag.

Was it possible to do all of these things?

Outside Misty's door, they knocked lightly. She responded, "Come in."

They stepped into her room. She sat painting in the corner. She'd regained most of her weight, and her hair was long and pretty once again- hanging to about shoulder length. Her eyes sparkled, and she grinned at the sight of them.

She stood up and came over to hug Maysie, then Shannah, and finally Rachael.

"Thank you for coming. I haven't had many visitors." She walked over to her small dinette. The room was set up more like a small studio apartment than a bedroom. She had a single sized bed, a small kitchen, a sitting area, and a small dining table. "Please sit."

She fixed them each a glass of lemonade and set it down in front of them. She pulled a chair out for herself and joined them.

"You look terrific." Rachael began.

"Thank you. I've been here for a few months now. Rachael…thank you. You saved my life. My mom told me how you dialed 9-1-1 and helped me, when the others just…dumped me out at your house. In life there are people who you think are your friends. Then you go through something like this, and you learn they aren't."

Everyone was at a loss for words. Misty was changed somehow. Her brush with death, perhaps time spent alone, she'd grown.

"I was glad to do it." Rachael didn't elaborate.

Maysie reached over and held Misty's hand. "What are your plans?"

"I'll be out of here in two more months. I've got enough credits, that if I take a math class and one English class this summer, I can get my diploma. Then, who knows? I'd love to go to art school in the fall, stay close to home. I've realized I'll need my parents support to move beyond this. Without them I couldn't have made it this far. They're helping me." She paused, looking down. "I haven't always been a good or even a nice person. I hope that you can all forgive me. I'd planned on coming to see each of you when I got out of here." She sighed, "And ask for forgiveness for the horrible things I've said and done to each of you, especially you, Rachael. I don't expect us to be close friends, but I will never behave toward you like I did before."

"Thank you." Rachael answered.

"We all appreciate your apology." Shannah interjected. "I feel better us getting it all out in the open."

"I feel better knowing if I see you on the street you won't kill me." Misty teased.

"Of course not. We aren't those kind of girls, anymore." Maysie directed her attention to Shannah. "We better go."

Maysie stood and fished a jeweled book out of her bag. She handed it to Misty. It was beautiful with elaborate rhinestone and silver beading along the front and corners. "It's a Bible. I think it'll help you on your journey."

Misty grasped it and stood to hug her goodbye.

Outside the building, the girls walked to Maysie's car.

"What do you say now?" Maysie asked Shannah.

"Went well. I'll admit it, but I'm still on the fence about her. Either she's acting or she's changed."

Rachael and Maysie laughed, knowing Shannah was right. Misty's journey wasn't over, and they all hoped she'd be able to stay the course after she returned home. No one expected it to be easy, but for her sake they hoped it would all work out for the best.

On the way home, Maysie's phone chimed. She handed it to Rachael.

"Check that. I'm driving."

Rachael swiped the screen and read the text.

"It's from Alex. She's fine. She's been at the police station with her parents. She can't really discuss the details of the case other than to say he propositioned her and nothing happened. A few other girls weren't as lucky. The details of the case will come out in the next several weeks she's sure. She'll be back at school after Spring Break. It involves a few other dancers and Samantha. That's all she's allowed to say for now."

"Mr. Richardson's going to fry." Shannah surmised.

"Sounds like it. What a pig!" Maysie gritted her teeth. "I had him as a teacher. He never approached me."

"You didn't need extra credit, you're a straight A student." Rachael commented. "He sat me in the third row. My pants were too long for his tastes."

"Dude's a nasty old man." Shannah commented.

Maysie dropped Shannah first. After Shannah climbed out, Rachael asked Maysie to run her to their house.

"I need to talk to Travis."

At the Baxter's driveway, Rachael saw Travis making rounds on the old blue Ford tractor, pulling a batwing mower behind it. It was nearing dusk.

"Oh, no. He's got the old Ford out." Maysie grimaced. She parked the car.

"What does that mean?"

"He's worried, angry, or frustrated, or any combination thereof. Bye." She fled into the house.

Rachael walked out and climbed over the board fence. She walked across the pasture where he drove up to her and turned it off.

"Care for a ride on my big, blue tractor?" He joked.

"Maysie said you're either worried, angry, or frustrated. Which is it?"

"Worried." He held his hand down to her. She grabbed it. He hauled her up to the steel platform. He sat down and pulled her onto his lap. "I'll let you steer."

"I'd love to." He turned the key and released the brake.

Over the hum of the loud engine there was no room for conversation. He admitted he was worried, but what could it be?

He's gotten quiet since the night of the dance, where things got a little hotter than we'd anticipated.

Maybe he's holding back, maybe his mom and my dad were right...now he's stopped talking to any of us about it.

Chapter Nineteen

Rachael and Michael decorated the living room with streamers and balloons. Rachael made lasagna with the help of Aunt Margaret, while Michael sliced and diced everything needed for their salad. He even set the oven to three hundred seventy-five degrees for the garlic bread and managed to bake it for the seven minutes, pull it out, and not burn it.

Travis and Maysie worked together to set the dining room table with Aunt Margaret's china. Rachael could hear Maysie in there scolding Travis regarding the place settings and the proper order for salad forks, soup spoons, and the various knives- butter versus steak.

"I know who was paying attention and who wasn't in all those cotillion classes now." Rachael said, setting napkins rings and cloth napkins down on the table.

"You don't get much out of it if you're only there to talk to good looking girls. That is what you said, wasn't it?" Maysie grinned at Travis.

"That's only because I didn't know the right one was living over in Palm Beach at the time. I was a man lost, that was until I met you, baby." He winked at Rachael.

Michael came in with a pad of paper.

"That's a good one. I'm writing that down." He joked, pencil in hand jotting down notes.

"I was a horse without a rider, wandering aimlessly through the vast ranch of life. I was a boat without a captain, trolling the endless waters of a vast lake. I was a bull without a cow…" He looked over at Maysie and Rachael to see if he'd achieved the desired response.

Maysie was armed with a wooden serving spoon ready to strike him if he kept going.

"How about you were a rooster without a hen searching the chicken coops of life?" Michael teased.

"That won't work. Everyone knows there's a lot of chickens out there and they aren't exactly known for being choosey animals. Any rooster would do." Travis added.

"We're going to leave you two brainstorming. Maybe in the next hour you can come up with an analogy that is somewhat intelligent between the two of you." Maysie chided. "While you're at it, could you go hang the sign on the gate?"

"I think she's throwing us out man."

Travis walked toward the foyer and picked up the large, newsprint sign he'd helped Rachael draw the day before. Michael grabbed the duct tape and jogged to catch up with Travis.

"Thanks for inviting us to share this day with you." Maysie stirred the ranch dressing she'd just whipped up.

"You're family to us. Even my dad asked if you guys would be here."

"We're happy and blessed to be here."

"How are things with Tristan?"

"We've got plans." Maysie smiled.

"What sort of plans?"

"Engagement in the fall and marriage next summer. Mama and Daddy know it's coming. They're prepared."

"What did they say?"

"I turn nineteen in August. We get to officially start dating. A few short months later we'll be engaged."

"Well, it's not like you don't know each other. While you haven't been officially dating these last several months, he does spend a lot of time at your house, and your parents love him."

"Yep- and only two slip up kisses during that entire time. He said he's learning a thing or two about patience and obedience."

"I'd say only two slip ups is pretty good. I can't imagine how hard this must be for y'all."

"I don't know, I'm finding if you completely remove the physical side of things it can make things pretty clear. The path you want to take and how you're going to get there. That's my opinion, I'm not sure he'd agree with me. He's got a calendar up where he's marking down the days until my birthday."

"That's sweet." Rachael grinned over at her where she mixed sweet tea. "Maybe your parents will let you start dating sooner, as in after you graduate. It's not like you're not already eighteen."

"I asked and they said they'd think about it. They like him a lot and since he started going to church with us every Sunday, it's sort of sealed the deal."

Rachael considered Maysie's statement. She wasn't sure if it was a hint of some sort or not. She'd gone to church with them one time in the nearly three years she'd known them. It had been a great experience and she'd enjoyed it. *What has kept me from going back?*

Her father was due to arrive home around lunchtime. Aunt Margaret and her mother had gone to pick him up and bring him home. There was a time where she would've insisted on being there for the release, but now she knew better. She didn't want to remember it that way. Her father walking out of a barbed wire ringed enclosure, passing check points, and such. No, she'd rather remember the day he walked back through the door, into the house, and into their lives as a celebration- a family party. That's exactly what they had planned.

It'd only be their immediate family and of course, Travis and Maysie. The sound of Michael yelling "They're here!" and dogs barking brought Rachael out of her daydreaming and back to reality.

She and Maysie turned on some cheery music and all of the lights. They'd opened the curtains and blinds, allowing as much light in as possible. Feeling closed in was something her father reiterated in many of the conversations with her mother. She didn't want him to feel that way ever again.

Michael threw the door open, panting from his sprint down the driveway.

"They're here!" He exclaimed.

"We heard you."

Travis walked into the house and smiled. "I saw him from the road. He looks good."

"Let's hide." Michael whispered. "Then, we'll jump out like old times."

No one could argue with that suggestion. Rachael, Michael, Maysie, and Travis crouched behind the dining room table, around the corner of the front wall and waited. They heard the car door open and close, along with a flutter of conversation.

"I don't know where the kids are." Mrs. Harte said as she opened the door.

Mr. Harte stepped into the foyer and everyone jumped up yelling, "Surprise!"

Michael was the first to run over and nearly tackle his father in an embrace. He hadn't seen him since their visit on Rachael's birthday. It'd been tough on Michael, but their father didn't want them to see him there and have those memories. Michael pushed back happy tears, talking nonstop about teaching his dad to hunt over the summer.

Rachael waited patiently for her turn. Her worries over Michael's inability to call and reach out to their father over the last few years were swept away. Any distance between them gone. When Michael stepped around their father to hug his mother and Aunt Margaret, Mr. Harte came over to embrace Rachael. He held her for a long time, not speaking.

"Welcome home, Dad." Her lips quivered. "We've missed you."

"I've missed you guys too." He lifted his head, glancing at Travis and Maysie.

He hugged Maysie and then shook Travis' hand.

"Thank you, Travis, for being the man in their lives while I've been away. You've been more than a boyfriend to my daughter. You've also been the big brother to Michael- providing him with support and guidance. Thank you." Mr. Harte pulled Travis in for a hug as well. Tears ran down his face.

"I was glad to do it."

"Let's eat! I hear Rachael made a homemade lasagna." Mr. Harte led the way into the dining room.

"I made the salad!" Michael cheered.

"I bet it'll taste fantastic."

Everyone went in and took a seat. Mr. Harte said grace. Lunch conversation flowed. Aunt Margaret was ecstatic to have a house full of guests.

"And while I'll miss y'all when you move out, we'll always have these memories."

Michael jerked his head up, as if he'd been struck.

"Yes, kids." Their father smiled. "Let's finish up lunch and help Aunt Margaret get these dishes cleared away. Your mother and I've something to show you."

The look of fear and dread vanished from Michael's face. "So it's nearby?" He asked.

"Very close. Over the last few weeks, since your mother learned about my return home, she has been secretly out looking for a home for us. This is our home now. I wouldn't dream of moving back to West Palm Beach. There's nothing for me there now. Everything I love is right here in this room." Their father stood from the table and slid his chair back in.

He grabbed an arm full of plates and carried them into the kitchen. Michael scurried to help. Rachael had never seen him so eager to clear a table, put away leftovers, and fill a dishwasher. He nearly knocked her out of the way.

"I've got this Rachael. Go get ready." He commanded. She smiled over at Travis.

They walked to the family room together and took a seat with Aunt Margaret.

"Did you know about this?" She asked Travis.

"Nothing."

Aunt Margaret didn't lift her head from her needlepoint.

"Aunt Margaret?"

"I know, but I'm not giving any secrets away. I know all sorts of things." She winked at them both.

Rachael excused herself and ran down the hall. She sent Ellery a text announcing her dad was home!

She already had on make-up, so all that was left was to do her hair. She opted for twin braids down either side of her face and a ball cap.

"That's a cute look." Travis stood in the doorway to the bathroom. Rachael had on a pair of camo cargo shorts and a matching forest green tank. "I might have to take you fire hunting tonight."

"Fire hunting?" She remembered back to Shannah's mention of fire hunting at the dance sleepover in the fall.

"Yep. With head lights. Fire hunting."

"Isn't that illegal?"

"Not if you're going after nuisance coyotes or hogs. It's a date. Wade's in town visiting Shannah."

"She didn't even tell me!" Rachael exclaimed.

"They've been dating since the dance. Even Maysie doesn't know."

"Why is she being all secretive?"

"You should ask her, but according to him they're pretty serious. They're making plans."

"She's going to Florida State?"

Travis nodded his head.

"Traitor!" Rachael couldn't believe her ears. Shannah had always been a diehard Gator fan.

"The things a woman will do for love." Travis teased.

"Love! She's not in love. She never told Gabe or any guy she loved him."

"Well, she told Wade. Like I said, they've got plans."

"You're just loving the fact that you knew first." She tossed the hand towel off of the counter at him.

"Nope. I'm just enjoying the fact that I can now say 'I told you so'."

"I love you, Travis Baxter, in spite of your cocky ways."

"That's good, because I'm not going anywhere. You could hog tie me and drive off in the middle of nowhere to throw me out, and I'd still trail you up."

"What does that mean?"

"I'd find my way home. You are home to me, Rachael." He bent and kissed her nose.

"Hey! None of that!" Her father griped from the hallway. "Are you even allowed back here?" He asked only half-serious.

"I have been, but if you want to change that I understand."

"Consider it changed. You're restricted to the front of the house only young man, until after y'all are married." Her father paused and smiled. "Some time in the far off future."

"Yes, sir." Travis retreated to the front of the house. "It won't happen again, Mr. Harte."

Rachael waited until he disappeared.

"Dad, Aunt Margaret has allowed him back here. Don't you think that was a bit harsh?"

"Humor your old dad. Besides, he knows I'm playing with him, but not about the front of the house part. Things are more intense between the two of you. A little stricter guidelines are in order."

Rachael decided to let it go. After her father's conversation with Travis about keeping it "put away", Rachael didn't want to push it any further. Her father was home and his rules would be his rules. As long as she lived under his roof, and wasn't married, she'd have no choice but to follow them. Maysie's earlier sentiments rang through her head like a clanging gong.

If you completely remove the physical side of things it can make things pretty clear.

Their relationship had never been a physical or overly intimate one. Sure they'd had one minor slip-up, but for the most part they'd been very well behaved. *I hope Dad knows that.*

"You ready?" He popped his head back into the bathroom.

"Yes, and Dad," She turned to face him. "I'm not having sex or anything physical other than kissing with Travis. I just wanted you to know."

"I know. I'm sorry for teasing him, but I do want him to stay at the front of the house from now on. I'm on board with Operation Avoid Nookie with Travis Baxter."

Mom!

"Good to know. Good to know." Rachael uttered hoping to change the subject. "Let's go see this surprise."

She walked down the hallway, her arm wrapped around her father's waist, walking side by side.

"Let's load up." Her father called. "We'll need to take two vehicles. Would you mind riding with Travis?"

"Nope."

"Remember our conversation." Her father took his two fingers making the *I'm watching you* gesture with his hand at Travis, then laughed.

"I haven't forgotten." Rachael smirked.

Travis helped Rachael up into the cab of his truck. After they closed the door and started it up she turned to him. "I'm so sorry about my dad! I don't know what's up with him."

"He's being a dad, that's all. He's just having a little fun at my expense."

"I think he's half serious."

"He is, but that's okay. He just came back into your life. There'll be lots of adjustments, you hussy. Quit comin' on to me in public. I'll have to beat you off with a stick." He laughed.

She swatted his leg. "I'm glad you think it's funny."

"Cut him some slack. He's just come home and he wants to pull you closer. You're his little girl. You'll be going off to school in a few short months and my parents have told me… nothing will ever be the same again. Give him this time. Get close to him again. You'll hear no protest from me. I need his blessing and his buy in."

"To what?"

"Wade and Tristan aren't the only ones with a plan."

"What plan?"

"Ain't telling."

They drove down a dirt road, with tall Bahia grass on either side.

"JJ's road?"

"I'm just following your dad. I have no idea where we're headed."

They pulled up to JJ's driveway and turned in. She remembered the long driveway with the pale yellow Victorian from her first few weeks in town years before. The house still looked the same. Huge, sweeping front porch and red tin roof. Swirling trim work and detailing painted in stark blossom white.

They parked out front and JJ came out to greet them in usual JJ attire. Cut offs, no shirt, barefoot, with snuff in his lip. She eyed his protruding belly and five o'clock shadow that was visible at one o'clock on a Saturday afternoon.

Yep- some things never change.

Rachael climbed out and went to give him a hug.

"Good mornin', Miss Rachael." JJ squeezed her back. Next he shook her father's hand. "Well, are you ready to go look at it?"

JJ walked over and fired up the Honcho. He backed out and idled down the road. Everyone else piled into their cars and followed him. At the gate he paused to check both ways and pulled out, driving south. When he gunned it and the Honcho's top driving speed surpassed forty miles per hour, it backfired.

A few miles down the winding dirt road, JJ slowed his speed and pulled into a gate entrance. He climbed out and opened it for everyone to drive through.

They drove down the large oak tree lined drive toward a line of trees ahead on the horizon. A few more small turns and a small clapboard house came clearly into view. It was two story with a small front porch, black shutters, and a red door. It looked freshly painted. While it wasn't large and appeared to have been built in the nineteen fifties, it was in great condition.

JJ pulled up out front and parked the Honcho under the shade of a tree so his dogs wouldn't get too hot.

"Well this is it." He produced the key to the front door. He unlocked the door and everyone stepped inside.

The small living room had wood beam ceilings and pecky cypress paneling on the walls. The floors were original heart pine. Rachael walked into the kitchen and found that it too was smaller than she'd like, but it had all the modern appliances and was painted a pale yellow. The cabinets were new, as were both the sink and countertops. It had recently been renovated.

"Why don't you kids go upstairs and choose a room." Their father pointed to the staircase.

Michael ran over and hugged him tightly. "Thanks for not making us move." He whispered.

"Like I said, this is home now. For all of us."

Michael shot past Rachael on the staircase and upstairs. They located three bedrooms at the top of the stairs. There was a bedroom that was tiny, maybe ten by eight. Rachael eyed it skeptically.

She walked out into the hallway and located Michael. He stood in a large bedroom measuring fifteen by fifteen. It had huge bay windows overlooking what Rachael recognized as the bull pasture for the Baxter ranch. Rachael saw the excitement in his eyes.

"You like your room?" She asked.

"I'll take the smaller room. You're a girl, you have more stuff."

"No, I'll take it. This will make the perfect bedroom slash game lounge, as long as you promise to play me in tennis on your system some time."

"It's a deal!" He ran out into the hallway. "Let's check Mom and Dad's room."

The third bedroom was smaller than Michael's, but had the only walk-in closet and its own private bathroom. Her mother wouldn't mind trading a little bedroom space for her own walk-in.

Rachael looked around for Travis. Maysie walked in.

"I like it." She grinned.

"Me too. Where's Travis?"

"He said he's restricted to the downstairs." She nodded her head. "Yep, now he's seeing what I've been going through. The double standard has come home to roost."

"That's one way of looking at it."

Rachael and Maysie walked back into her room.

"I need a smaller bed." She joked.

"Or less furniture."

"We'll come up with something."

Rachael and Maysie headed back downstairs. Travis stood outside talking to JJ.

Rachael greeted her dad in the kitchen.

"I love it, Dad."

"Good. Travis will help us put up a barn for Grace and she can graze in the bull pasture. We've got ten acres here. It's just a lease, but once we get back on our feet completely JJ said we can purchase it. He's given me a fair price and he'll honor it even if it takes me five years to be able to afford it."

Rachael hugged her mother and father, then walked out to the backyard to climb an old live oak. Maysie followed her out, along with Aunt Margaret.

"I used to be quite the climber." Aunt Margaret eyed the tree.

Rachael watched as she climbed it, limb by limb, getting nearer and nearer to the top. She sat perched up there looking around. Rachael looked at Maysie and decided to join Aunt Margaret up in the tree. Maysie followed her.

Michael came out of the house and said, "Hey, I can do that!"

He joined them, followed by Travis. Aunt Margaret climbed down first and asked everyone to smile while she snapped a picture.

"Wait for us!"

Shannah and Wade popped their heads out the backdoor. They sprinted over to the tree and scaled its lower limbs selecting one just for themselves. Tristan came out of the house behind them and climbed up boots and all. Maysie grabbed his hand, pulling him up to sit beside her on a branch.

"Okay. One more time!" Aunt Margaret announced. "On three."

Chapter Twenty

The roar of a diesel engine woke Rachael up a little after six o'clock in the morning. She rolled over and wondered what would bring Travis over this early- especially the morning after Maysie's guy-girl, post-graduation midsummer campout. Rachael hadn't stayed the night. Things between them were getting more *intense...and* she knew spending the night with Travis anywhere could prove challenging.

She did a mental check. *Fishing? No. Working? No.*

This was her day off. Rachael wanted to just roll over and go back to sleep. This was her last full week before she started college. She'd already cut her hours back at the Western Store to Saturdays only two weeks ago. Yesterday was her last shift until she would return home for the holidays after semester finals.

She reluctantly crawled out of bed and started downstairs. She wanted to answer the front door before he knocked and woke up the entire family. Then, she remembered the salad with entirely too much onion on it from last night. On second thought, she paused and detoured to the bathroom and brushed her teeth... twice.

Next, she tiptoed downstairs to the front door, the old boards creaking underfoot. When she opened it, Travis sat on the bench of her small front porch wearing swim trunks, a red t-shirt, and matching ball cap. Wisps of dark hair peeked out from under the edges of the cap where his hair had gotten long during the warm summer months. The swimsuit exposed his tan, muscular thighs that were rarely visible in his jeans and boots. In the driveway, his airboat sat hooked up to his truck.

"What's up?" Rachael tried not to stare. He was so fine his presence still made her heart skip every time she was around him. A constant nervous little pitter patter that intensified with every meeting. Only two nights ago their kiss had become almost unbearable. She knew they were nearing a point in their relationship where things could take a turn, and she wasn't sure even she could turn back.

"It's the three year anniversary of the day I first took you air boating."

"It's early."

"Not that early. The first time it was only just after five o'clock. This time I let you sleep in." He smiled. "Grab a hat and flip flops."

"Okay. Let me leave my parents a note."

Rachael disappeared back inside the house. She put on her new hot pink ruffled bikini, tank top, and flip flops. She sprayed her arms, chest, and legs with sunscreen and returned the ball cap to her nightstand, swapping it out for her cowgirl hat instead.

She tiptoed to the kitchen and scribbled a note.

"Need a chaperone?" Michael asked from the doorway.

"Nope. It's our anniversary of sorts. The first time we went air boating."

"I'll write that down." Michael shook his head.

"What?"

"You two are too much." He smiled and slunk back down the hall.

Rachael finished writing the note and heated up a microwaveable sausage biscuit for both her and Travis. She fixed herself a thermos of coffee and a bottle of water. He probably had a cooler full of stuff, but she thought she better grab some breakfast just in case.

Travis still waited outside. He appeared startled when she stepped out onto the porch. He walked around his truck, with purposeful strides, and opened the door for her to jump in. His hands on her waist caught her off guard. He wasn't usually this romantic so early in the morning. He bent around to lightly kiss her cheek, before lifting her up.

"So why are we doing this again?" She knew the reason he'd supplied her with, but she suspected something more was going on here.

"I wanted to take you back to the place, where in my mind, our friendship began."

"Our friendship? I'd have thought that was the first day at the creek."

"No, on that day I thought you were a trespasser, a pretty one, but a trespasser."

"So you wanted to have me arrested."

"Not particularly, imprison you maybe." He squeezed her hand from where he sat behind the steering wheel. "So college is only a week away."

"I can hardly believe it myself. We're officially Gators now."

"Sure are. College students- adults. Off on our own."

Where is he going with this?

"I'm not sure about the dorm thing, but my parents insisted I live on-campus for the first year."

"I know." He sounded displeased. "I'll have an apartment. I've already picked it out. I'll show you the floor plan online later this week. Close to campus and convenient. I'm hoping you'll visit."

"We've already discussed it all before and nothing is going to change." Rachael sounded annoyed. "You agreed to it. Dorm for me, apartment for you. Marriage down the road."

"That hasn't changed, but I just don't see why we couldn't get married a little sooner. The seven year plan is still four years from completion date. I think we need to revisit that. Remember when you said you'd consider getting married after the Associate's Degree?"

Rachael slid over to her side of the truck and blew out an exasperated breath.

"Hear me out Rachael, please."

"Go on." She sat her arms crossed across her chest. He patted the seat next to him, silently begging her to move back over. When she didn't, he started talking anyway.

"If you're telling me you want to go off to school and date other people, have that kind of college experience, I will respect that."

"I've never said that!" Rachael exclaimed.

"I know. What I'm trying to say is I'm not boxing you in here. If your reason for not wanting to get married before graduating college was that, I'd be hurt but I'd get it. Girls feel that way. You wouldn't be the first." He tried to sound like he was really open to her dating other people when she knew he wasn't.

Travis clenched the steering wheel with both hands. He stared straight ahead at the road, unblinking.

"Well, that's not what I want, Travis. Is this just your way of letting me know that's what you want?"

"No. And this conversation isn't going the way I planned at all."

"Me neither."

"Let's start over. Can we please?" He begged.

"Fine."

"I want to marry you, Rachael. You and only you. I know we are young to be getting married, and you've always been opposed to getting married straight out of high school or any time before graduating college. But I think it's best."

"Are you afraid I'm going to run off to school and fall for some other guy, because I won't."

"No, that's not it."

"Are you afraid I'm going to go wild off at school and start with some partying, reckless behavior? Go crazy and all that?"

"No." He shook his head.

"So this is all about sex- again."

"Not entirely."

When she looked over, she could see he was staring out the windshield at the sun rising above the clouds.

"Would you rather I lie?" He pulled the truck over and put his forehead on the steering wheel.

"Of course not. I don't understand why it's such a big deal. I find you attractive and all, but I can wait four more years," she paused, "I think."

"You're not a guy. I don't think I can and I don't want to be in a position where I'm forced to lie to your parents."

"Are you saying you'd break up with me to get it elsewhere?"

"Where did you get that from?" He pulled back onto the road.

"I'm sorry about that last comment." Rachael knew her face was seething by this point.

"No, I'd never go elsewhere. I want you and only you, forever Rachael."

Rachael sat and considered her own motivation for putting off marriage. She wanted to finish college. She wanted her degree. There was no guarantee if they got married there wouldn't be kids right away. Who knew?

"This is where you have to trust God. We won't have kids right away and if we did, he has a plan for us, but no matter what I promise you'll finish college." Travis turned his truck and backed into the boat ramp parking area and cut the engine. "Talk to me. I know you hate me right now."

"I don't hate you." She opened her door and climbed out.

Travis flew out of the truck. Rachael stormed toward the dock. In a few short strides he caught up to her. He gently caught her by the wrist.

"Where are you going?"

She stopped and looked him in the eyes. "If my parents say yes, then yes."

"Are you serious?"

"Yes."

Travis reached in his pocket and produced a ring box.

She sighed. "Don't you think you should ask my father first?"

"Already have and he said yes, your mother too."

"Okay." Rachael reached around to tuck a piece of flyaway hair behind her ear.

Travis opened the ring box and a beautiful solitaire set in a simple gold setting with a wide band sparkled in the morning light. He got down on one knee.

"I can't, Travis. Please get up."

"But you just said yes. I don't understand."

Rachael turned and stalked out onto the dock, her back to him. She glanced out at the river. The water was slick and peaceful, as the river's name suggested. It was all exactly how she imagined it would be, the ring, the guy, the location even... with one exception.

I'm eighteen.

Rachael felt a burning deep in her chest. She wanted to say yes. She'd said yes initially, *but what about college?* Travis' questions brought up a few things she'd never considered. She didn't want to date anyone else, but there was so much more to college than that.

The light footsteps of flip flops on the planks of the boards of the dock alerted her to Travis approaching from behind. He didn't speak. He just stood there, hands on his hips.

"I don't want to date anyone else, but there are so many other things I'd like to do." She couldn't face him.

"And you can't do these things married?"

Rachael turned around to look him in the eyes. "You don't think it's just a little taboo to get married so young? I mean, really?"

"I don't care if it's taboo or not. I love you and what does it matter what other people think." He stuck his hands in his pockets. "Come on. I'll run you home."

"So what? Now we're going to let it ruin the entire day?"

"What do you want from me?" He yelled. "I don't know what you want from me." He sat down on the bench and ripped off his cap throwing it across the dock. He bent forward and put his hands in his hair.

"I want to marry you, I do. Just not this way...forced into it." As soon as she spoke the words she regretted them.

"Forced? Is that really how you feel?"

"No. I didn't mean to use that word." Rachael rushed over and placed her hands on his shoulders kneeling in front of him. "I want to rush a sorority, I want to go out dancing with friends in clubs and stay out late, eat breakfast at three o'clock in the morning. All the things the college experience is about."

"You can still do those things. I wasn't saying you couldn't. We are going off to school together, I could join a fraternity. I'm not some old man. I want to do those things, too."

Rachael sat down on the bench beside him, but he still wouldn't make eye contact with her.

"We can do all those things together and more." He paused, then lifted his head to look her in the eyes. "Are you scared of marriage?" He asked in a hushed whisper.

"No!" Rachael stood and strode from the dock.

Travis watched her walk away, making no move to follow her. Rachael walked to the edge of the riverbank. She saw two otters playing further down the bank where they rolled this way and that. One raced down to the water and slid in. The other one quickly followed behind it. They disappeared below the surface.

Why couldn't I have been an otter?

Travis stood and returned to his truck. He backed the trailer down the boat ramp and slid his boat into the water. He drove over and parked his truck in the parking lot.

"You coming?" He returned, holding his hand out to her.

Rachael turned and walked toward the waiting boat. He assisted her in. They rode in silence for a long time. The slight breeze coming out of the west carried on it the smell of saw and needle grass. Cattails bloomed and water hyacinth, but she could think of nothing else than this morning's horrible conversation and how badly she was handling it. She just couldn't figure out how to fix it.

Travis continued working his way up the river. He opened himself a soda and handed one to her as well. She accepted it politely but uttered nothing.

They were an hour from the dock when he finally cut the boat off and sat smiling at her.

"What are you grinning at?"

"We can sit here all day not talking if you'd like, or you can answer my question honestly."

Rachael looked left and then right. The river was wide at this point and the large ten foot gator lounging on the neighboring bank told her swimming away wasn't an option.

"That's not fair. What am I, your prisoner?"

"Pretty much. The way I see it you have two choices. You can open up to me about what you're holding back about or we can just pitch a tent over there tonight next to that gator. Either way is fine. I've got all week."

Rachael walked over and sat beside Travis.

"Fine. So, I'm afraid of marriage. I don't want to end up like my parents."

"What's so wrong with your parents? They're happily married."

"How happy can you be when one of you was in prison for part of it?"

"For the record, I'm not planning on doing any stints in prison. And all marriages have ups and downs."

"That's good to know, but my dad wasn't planning on it either."

"Good point, but the positive thing here is that their marriage has survived prison. A strong marriage based in a solid foundation can survive anything."

Rachael nodded. "I'm not some backwoods hillbilly who wants to get married young. It's not in my plan." Rachael admitted.

"Am I the backwoods hillbilly?" He laughed.

"Maybe."

"Well, for your information, you weren't in my plan either. You moved here." He reached over and picked her up and set her on his lap. "I fell in love with you." He placed a light kiss on her check. "And my plans changed. Now I have a new plan, a very simple one."

Travis swept her hair away from her neck and ran soft kisses down her neck to her shoulder. He held his lips to her shoulder and gently brushed kisses across the top of it.

"Maybe I should've let Michael come along for the day." Rachael teased. The events of a few evenings before played through her mind.

"Might have been a good idea." He cleared his voice. "Like I was saying, my plan is simple. I'm going to marry you, Rachael Harte, and make you mine forever." He kissed his way back up her neck to the side of her earlobe where he whispered "And ever." He kissed her cheek. "And ever." He kissed her nose. "And ever." He kissed her lips, gently at first and then more ardently.

When Rachael lifted her head she looked in his eyes and saw the truth of what he was saying. The way she felt right now she knew he was right. At this rate, if she were being completely honest with herself, they'd be fortunate if they made it to their wedding day.

"Yes. I'll marry you." Rachael was quick to amend her statement. "Give me a freshman year of dorm and college life. We'll get married a soon as school lets out for the summer. Not a moment sooner."

"Great." Travis produced the ring once more and slid the solitaire onto her left finger. "Then, we'll share my apartment and finish school together. And I promise, we will finish."

"I'm afraid. I don't want there to be hard times like Mom and Dad have endured. I used to fear never finding the right person and ending up alone. Or even worse- marrying the wrong person and ending up divorced. But even when you marry the right person there are no guarantees. That's what scares me the most."

"There's one guarantee- I love you and I always will."

"Maybe we should just elope. That way I could stay at your apartment whenever I want to from day one. Why wait until next summer?"

"While you'd get no complaints from me with that option, I think your parents might freak. They agreed to a June wedding, no sooner. I think they figure if we get one year of college under our belts, we'll be more likely to finish."

"I always wanted a June wedding."

"Then June it is, but for the record…you can visit my apartment anytime between now and the wedding day. We're engaged now."

"Yes, we are." Rachael admired her ring where it sparkled in the bright sunlight. "Don't tell me you renegotiated our purity pledge?"

"No, but now that we're engaged it's not a bad idea."

"Travis! You wouldn't!" She smacked his thigh.

"No, I've learned my lesson there." He did some mental math. "Ten months and counting."

"Ten months and counting." She kissed him and then jumped up in the driver's seat.

"You think you can operate this?" He laughed.

"I'm sure I can."

Acknowledgments

To my husband and boys, I love you all so very much! You bring joy to me in so many ways, and I can't imagine our life together any differently.

A huge thanks to my big sis, Veronica, who always stepped in to defend or support me.

My little brother, Lem, for your outrageous personality and sense of humor!

For my sister-in-law, Mya, for being my sister in all things redneck!

For Momma and Daddy: Where do I begin? You took a child filled with tenacity and spunk- that's putting it nicely (smile)- and molded her into a lady. Thank you for being there to pick me up and set things right when I got off on the wrong path. You've inspired me to be the parent I am, always looking to serve my children's interests and do the best I can by them.

To Madeleine and Hannah, my nieces and friends, you served as my sounding board on this series! Thank you for taking the time to listen.

About the Author

JENNY HAMMERLE is a sixth-generation Floridian and grew up on a working cattle ranch. She's been bucked off more than a few times and lived to write about it. The *Redneck Debutante® Series* revolves around rural Florida and ranch life. "My favorite place to be is at the hunt camp, sitting around the camp fire and listening to, or in some cases telling funny stories! I also love to work cows in the cow pens- branding, tagging, marking, legging, and parting out calves to keep or sell!"

Jenny is the mother of two wonderful little boys and lives in Florida. On any given day, you can find her building fence on one of her family's ranches or working on her latest novel at home.

The *Redneck Debutante® Series* is a series about girls who are a mix of country and city, balancing two very different worlds. From cotillion to cowgirl, this is the story of one Redneck Debutante's life!

www.jennyhammerle.com
Twitter @jennyhammerle

The *Redneck Debutante® Series:*
Redneck Debutante, book 1
Cowgirl Down, book 2
Cowgirl Strong, book 3

Made in the USA
Charleston, SC
08 November 2015